A STRANGER'S GAMBLE

LORDS OF CHANCE BOOK THREE

TARAH SCOTT

SCARSDALE PUBLISHING

Ingram ISBN: 978-1-953100-34-4

Amazon ISBN: 9798482353295

Cover Design: Dreams2media

Editor: Penny Brandon

First Trade Paperback Printing by Scarsdale Publishing: September 2021

10 9 8 7 6 5 4 3 2

CHAPTER 1

ADAM SCOTT LOOKED FROM THE NEWSPAPER HE WAS READING TO the glass of brandy that sat on the table to his right. This was his fourth brandy at his club. The liquor, along with the warmth of the fire burning in the hearth had relaxed him to the point that he considered going to Lena's to see if he could persuade her to spend the rest of the evening with him in bed. They'd spent a good part of the afternoon in bed, but he felt ten years younger than his thirty years and believed he could make a night of lovemaking.

He lifted the brandy to his lips and caught sight of two long-time friends. Alistair and Nick walked with purpose across the carpeted floor, and he realized they were headed toward him. Their grim expressions told him they had news he wasn't interested in hearing.

When they reached him, he finished his brandy in one gulp, then said, "You two look as if you have just come from a funeral."

Something flickered in Alistair's eyes.

Adam sighed. "What happened?"

"Your father," Nick said.

Adam tensed.

"He is at Lady Fleming's."

Adam relaxed. "He often gambles at Lady Fleming's." He never worried when his father gambled at Lena's gaming hall. She always made sure his losses never got out of hand.

Nicholas shook his head. "He's been there since early this afternoon."

Adam cut a glance to the clock above the mantle. Half past ten. He'd left Lena's bed at six. Surely, she sent his father packing when she arrived at the gambling hall?

"Rumor has it, he has sustained heavy losses," Nicholas said.

Adam closed the paper, tossed it onto the table, and stood. He pushed past the two men, headed for the door. They followed him outside to the walkway.

"Have you a carriage?" Alistair asked.

Adam shook his head. "Nae."

Alistair pointed to where his carriage sat. "Come, we'll take you."

Adam wanted to refuse but didn't see a cab nearby. He nodded, and they hurried to the carriage. Adam entered first, then Nicholas.

"Lady Fleming's," Alistair instructed his driver, then pulled the door shut as he vaulted inside. He dropped onto the seat alongside Nick as the vehicle lurched into motion.

What a bloody fool he was to think his father, the Marquess of Monthemer, might be able to refrain from further ruination. A mental image rose of Adam turning the key in the lock on his father's bedchambers with his father inside, then throwing away the key. The only thing stopping him from living out the fantasy was the knowledge that his father would jump from the third story window in an effort to find a game of cards. Adam had never known a man so sick with the gambling fever.

They reached Lady Fleming's half an hour later, and Adam told Nicholas and Alistair to await him in the carriage.

"We're coming with you, Adam, and that's the end of it," Alistair said.

He had no heart to argue and allowed the two men to follow him inside. Adam turned left into the largest cardroom in the building. Half a dozen men sat at the large table. Cigar smoke hung in the air and the smell of liquor permeated the room. Three women dressed in tight gowns hovered nearby. To Adam's relief, his father was not among the men at the table.

He spun and hurried from the room, Nick and Alistair close behind. Adam headed up the stairs to Lena's private office. A large man came into view beyond the railing on the second floor. Lord Mornton.

The earl started down the stairs as they neared the second floor. "If you are looking for your father, he left not half an hour ago."

Adam halted one stair below the man. "He was here, then?"

The older man nodded. "Aye, he was here. I tried to talk him into leaving but…he had been drinking."

"How much did he lose?"

Mornton hesitated.

"That bad?" Adam asked.

"He lost nearly everything."

"What does that mean?" Adam asked in a soft voice.

"The townhouse here in Town. The land in Aberdeen. All but the entailed estate."

Alistair cursed, and Nick drew a sharp breath.

"Such losses are unheard of," Alistair said. "It is illegal."

"Signed and witnessed by a solicitor," the earl said.

Without another word, Adam brushed past him and hurried up the last half dozen steps to the hallway. Two doors down he turned into the open door of Lena's office. She looked up from a document lying on the desk in front of her and met his gaze, unwavering. No remorse, no guilt. But he read in her eyes the knowledge that his worst fears had been realized and that she'd been the instrument of his downfall.

"How bad is it?" he asked in a too-calm voice he barely recognized as his own.

"You know how your father is when he gambles."

Adam gave a single slow nod. "You took your usual cut." It wasn't a question, and she didn't reply. "How much?" he asked.

"Ten thousand pounds and the townhouse here in Town," she replied without hesitation.

Adam felt as if a team of horses had rammed into his chest. "Who is the fortunate man who will be living in my home?"

She hesitated, and his blood went cold.

"You."

"At your father's insistence—"

"Pray, do not blame others for your greed," he cut in.

Her expression cooled—something he'd witnessed a thousand times. "The marquess would simply have lost his fortune in another gambling hall," she said. "If not tonight, another night."

"And why should someone else benefit from the ruination of my father and me, the man you claim to love?"

"It is not personal," she said.

He gave a mirthless laugh. "How well I know."

Adam turned, and Nick and Alistair stood aside as he strode from the room.

CHAPTER 2

Olivia could scarce believe it, but her husband had just confirmed the rumor that their close friend Adam Scott, the new Marquess of Monthemer was destitute. She shifted her gaze from her friend Lady Charlotte Cassilis, who sat on the divan opposite her in the parlor, to their husbands, standing at the parlor hearth where a low fire burned.

"I knew his father gambled away his estate outside of Edinburgh before shooting himself last year, but what of his property in Aberdeen?" Olivia asked her husband.

"The old marquess lost all but the entailed estate in Inverness," Nicholas replied.

Her heart tugged. "How does a man lose so much in a card game?"

Charlotte shook her head. "How could Lady Fleming allow Adam's father to gamble away everything in *her* gambling hall? She was to marry Adam."

"Charlotte, I have asked you not to engage in gossip," Alistair said.

"So, you have," she replied without rancor.

"I'm impressed Adam was able to keep the details of his financial difficulties quiet this long," Nicholas said.

"Why did you not tell us, Nick?" Olivia demanded. "We have had him for dinner at least three times this last six months and seen him at parties, and I had no idea."

Nicholas lifted a brow. "I should think that obvious, my dear."

"Because men do not discuss financial matters with women," Charlotte said with a roll of her eyes.

Olivia looked at Charlotte. "He must marry."

Nick narrowed his eyes. "Olivia—"

"Oh! I know the perfect girl," she exclaimed.

Charlotte's brow creased, then her eyes lit. "You don't mean…"

Olivia nodded. "Yes."

Charlotte clapped. "How absolutely perfect."

"It is not our place to interfere," Alistair said.

"Alistair is right," Nick said. "Besides, Adam may not wish to marry."

Olivia slanted her husband a sideling glance. "Do not act as if marriage is a man's doom."

"Come, love. You know full well that I consider marriage to be the sweetest of prisons." He took two steps, grasped her hand, and brushed his mouth against her fingers. Despite five years of marriage and two children, she shivered. The man need only look at her with that fire in his eyes and she melted.

But she had power over him, as well. Olivia tilted her head and looked at him from beneath her lashes. "Do you not want the marquess to experience the same sweet prison you do?"

"She's got you there," Alistair said.

Charlotte arched a brow and pinned him with a stare. "Do you disagree with Nicholas, sir?"

"Not in the least." He leaned a shoulder against the mantle.

"Oh, but our husbands are charmers, are they not?" Olivia

asked. "But we shan't be distracted." She raked her gaze down her husband's long frame. "No matter how pleasing they are to look upon."

Or how much they please us.

Nicholas settled beside her on the sofa. "Love, fate brought me to you. Perhaps, one day, Adam will be as fortunate. Alistair is right, we simply cannot interfere."

"He is not consorting with Lady Fleming, again, is he?" Charlotte asked.

Her husband studied her. "Just how much do you know of Lady Fleming?"

"Everyone knows of his connection to Lady Fleming," she replied. "And she is the only woman to run a gaming hall in all of Edinburgh."

"For God's sake, Charlotte," her husband said in a stern tone.

"Please, Alistair." Charlotte rolled her eyes. "The affair between Adam—the Earl of Monthemer—and Lady Fleming is —was—one of the most notorious love affairs in Edinburgh, probably all of Scotland, notwithstanding the Royals. News of their association used to be in the gossip sheets at least once a week. Rumor has it, when the old marquess lost his estate to Lady Fleming, it was she who broke off her and Adam's association, but I don't believe that for a moment."

Olivia snorted. "Of course not. She is only trying to save face. Adam must have broken off with *her*. He would never marry the woman responsible for his father's death. A good woman will set Adam to rights."

Nick held up a hand, palm out. "Adam has made it clear he prefers ruin rather than marriage."

"Marriage to the wrong woman," Olivia said.

Nick sighed. "He did not tell you that."

"It really is a pity you did not tell Charlotte and me sooner of his financial difficulty," she said.

Nick compressed his lips. "I believe I already said that financial difficulties are not something a man discusses with a lady."

"Had we known earlier, we could have taken action," Charlotte said.

"There is no action for us to take, Charlotte," Alistair said in warning.

"Hush. Olivia and I know just the right woman for him."

"An heiress, I assume?" Nick said.

Olivia gave her husband a brilliant smile. She knew he would go along with the plan once he understood. "Of course. She is sweet natured and intelligent."

Alistair coughed. "It's the intelligent part that gets a man into trouble every time."

"I will speak with Sophie's father," Olivia said.

"Sophie? Sophie Shaw?" Nick whistled. "Her father owns Dalquhern Dyeworks—Liam Shaw. He is, indeed, wealthy."

"And angling for a good match for his daughter," Charlotte said.

"Like any good mama," Alistair murmured.

Charlotte narrowed her eyes. "Like any good *parent*. You are forever saying that you only have our children's interest at heart. Mr. Shaw only has Sophie's best interest at heart. He would be lucky to have a man of character like Adam for a son-in-law."

"What if they don't fall in love?" Nicholas asked. "You would not want to cheat Adam—or Miss Shaw—out of love, now would you?"

"Oh, pish," Charlotte said. "What's not to love? Sophie is high-spirited—"

Nick chuckled. "There's the catch."

"Her father had the marriage annulled once the man died a year ago. She was only sixteen when they eloped to Italy without his permission," Alistair said.

"He was twenty years older than her," Charlotte said. "You know how older men prey on young women."

"Did not her first husband die under strange circumstances?" Alistair asked.

Charlotte arched a brow. "Now who's listening to gossip?"

"Alistair is right," Nick said. "Wasn't she accused of poisoning him?"

"She was never 'accused' of poisoning her husband," Charlotte said in a tart voice. The men exchanged a glance, but Charlotte continued. "Sophie is a superb rider and, of course, she's beautiful."

"That's something," Alistair said, his voice full of good-natured amusement.

Olivia faced her husband. "Nick, you must speak with Mr. Shaw. He is much more likely to agree to the plan if it comes from you."

He grabbed a log from those stacked to the right of the hearth and tossed it on the low fire. "I cannot imagine what would induce me to speak with him."

"Never mind, Olivia," Charlotte said. "We will enlist the aid of Lady Meyers. She's close with Mr. Shaw."

"Heaven help us," Nick muttered. "Not Lady Meyers." Charlotte opened her mouth but closed it when he raised a hand. "Lady Meyers has made an art of the profession of 'busybody.' Adam will not appreciate her meddling."

"Then it's settled," Olivia said. "Nick, you will speak with Mr. Shaw about Adam. Tell him…tell him that the two shall meet at Lady Seafield's ball. The soiree is the event of the season."

"Olivia—"

She rose. "Come, Charlotte. We have some planning to do. Oh, and, Nicholas, I will be seeing Lady Meyers three says hence." She linked her arm through Charlotte's and led her from the parlor.

CHAPTER 3

Sophie set aside her book and left her sitting room. She turned the corner in the hallway and stopped short at the sight of Janie and Sarah, two maids in her father's household, each with an ear pressed against her father's study door.

"What if he's old and fat?" Sarah whispered.

"Or haggle-toothed?" Janie giggled.

Sophie tiptoed the few paces to the maids and whispered, "Move over."

The girls whirled, eyes wide.

"Excuse us, miss." Janie dropped a quick curtsey, grabbed Sarah by the ear, and pulled her down the hallway.

Sophie frowned at their disappearing backs. Odd. Usually, the three of them eavesdropped together. She faced the door and pressed her ear to the wood. She had excellent hearing and easily distinguished her father's voice.

"She is my only daughter, my lord," he said. "And an heiress in the bargain."

"He is a man of honor as well as a marquess," a cool male voice answered.

A marquess? Her mind catapulted back four months, when

her father urged her to consider Lord Declan's suit. At only twenty-eight, Viscount Declan turned the ten thousand pounds of debt he'd inherited upon his father's death into nearly twenty thousand pounds of debt, all within a year. When her father discovered the truth, he sent the viscount packing. Her father had told her she was too young to remain a widow. Still, she hadn't thought much of his matchmaking. Perhaps that had been a mistake?

Sophie grasped the brass doorknob and, with a slow, careful twist, eased the door open and peered through the crack. A small fire crackled in the hearth, just enough to dispel the early autumn chill from the room. Her father paced the red floral Brussels carpet. The silver clock displayed on the marble-topped mantle chimed five times.

Sophie glimpsed a polished boot before a tall, well-dressed man in his thirties with dark hair and a strong jaw stepped into view near the hearth. He strode to the fire and leaned against the mantle, a glass of sherry in hand.

Lord Nicholas Blair.

Lord Blair tapped his fingernail on the rim of his glass. "The Marquess of Monthemer."

Her father halted and locked gazes with him. "Tell me, Lord Blair, what assurances have I that the marquess will not gamble away Sophie's dowry as his father did his fortune?"

Anger swept through Sophie. A man whose family had fallen into ruin because of gambling? That was worse than Lord Declan. How could her father consider marrying her to a penniless nobleman?

Lord Blair tossed back the rest of his sherry and set the empty glass on the mantle. "The discovery of the old marquess's impoverished estate shocked us all. His penchant for gambling ran far deeper than anyone suspected. Unlike most noblemen in his situation, Adam did the honorable thing and paid his father's debts after his death. That is what has left him without any fortune. I give you my word, the man is an honorable fellow."

Her father heaved a sigh. "Sophie is a strong-willed lass."

He walked to the right, out of her view, and the clink of glasses told her he was filling a glass with liquor from the sideboard. He returned into sight, two glasses of sherry in hand and handed one to the earl.

Shorter and with a slight paunch, her father looked old alongside Lord Blair's height and muscle. She'd inherited her father's curly auburn hair but, thank heavens, not his bulbous nose. According to her father, she'd inherited her dear, departed mother's delicate build, heart-shaped face, and brown eyes lined with sooty lashes.

"I fear Sophie may not agree to the match," he said.

Sophie exhaled a silent breath of relief. He knew her well enough to know she wouldn't go quietly to the gallows. One marriage had been quite enough. She flushed. She'd eloped with Matthew of her own accord, so couldn't fault her father for that marriage. He now only wanted her to be happy, as he and her mother had been.

Like many girls of sixteen, she had mistaken an older man's age for quiet wisdom and strength. Matthew hadn't been a bad man, but he'd been an abominable husband. Brooding men of nearly forty years of age quickly lost their attraction. He needed to be the center of attention at all times, and he was terrible with money, which was far worse than his need for attention.

When he'd fallen ill, she had been his nursemaid the last eighteen months of their marriage and his life. He finally had enough of being ill and locked himself in his room and drank himself to death. He'd considered himself a poet in the right of Byron—many young women like herself had agreed—and, like all poets, his death was deemed a tragedy. Of course, a scandal followed, for no real poet died without scandal.

Matthew had died over a year ago, yet the gossip persisted. The idea that she poisoned her husband at all, much less because he'd had an affair—Matthew had precious little time for her, much less another woman—was laughable. But the gossip persisted, and she'd finally heeded the devil that whispered in her ear that she should give the gossipmongers what they wanted. When people had even remotely hinted that she'd had anything to do with her husband's death, she'd just smiled and shrugged. That had fueled the gossip and earned her the nickname *Belladonna,* after the nightshade family. No one said the residents of Invergarry were particularly imaginative.

She started to pull the door closed, then froze when her father said, "But it is time she wed. I will send the lass straight to her Aunt Madeline in Edinburgh without delay. She will see that Sophie is ready to meet the marquess at Lady Seafield's ball."

Sophie blinked.

It is time she wed?

Had the decision been made? Why not? Her choice of husbands had been terrible—or so her father would reason. He wouldn't be wrong on that account. But did that give him the right to choose a husband for her?

Her father stared into the fire. "I fear Sophie's marriage to that ne'er do well has wounded her."

Wounded her? Her heart softened. What made her father think she was wounded? Women had a right not to want to marry. Why should she give up her freedom a second time?

"Shall was toast the future Marchioness of Monthemer?" Lord Blair asked.

Her father nodded and lifted his glass. "The Marchioness Monthemer."

He and Lord Blair clinked glasses, then drank.

Sophie resisted the urge to burst into the room and vow she would marry no one, marquess or not. Instead, she eased the door closed. With measured steps, she headed down the hall then up the stairs to her room where she sat on the bed, hands on her lap. She imagined a doddering man in at least his late sixties who wanted a pretty young wife to remind him he was still a virile man. She'd seen such unions often enough to know the old men made prisoners of their young wives, who they feared—and with good reason—would take lovers.

How hard could it be to avoid an ancient marquess? She would attend parties in the oyster cellars, receive ball invitations, and go riding in the country. She longed for the general hustle and bustle of the city. Matthew had claimed he hated the big city, but Sophie had deduced that he didn't want to compete with the more sophisticated men in places like Edinburgh. Byron's lost cousin, they called him, and some still insisted that he'd died too young. She wouldn't mind getting away from the talk of her poisoning her husband. Worse than the gossip, were the men who thought they would bed a wealthy widow in hopes of charming her—or perhaps forcing her—into marriage. These days, she couldn't attend even a simple soiree without a gentleman—no, they weren't gentlemen—trying to seduce her.

Sophie thought back to the last time she'd been in Edinburgh. Her father used to take her and her mother every year in the autumn. She'd been twelve and had spent many of the days with her best friend Imogen Rose. When Sophie's mother died, they hadn't gone again to Edinburgh, and Imogen's new stepfather had shipped her off to France to attend school. Imogen had written three times, then the letters stopped. Sophie had been hurt at first but, as she grew up, she realized people simply went on with their lives.

A murmur of voices in the front drive below her window drew her attention. She rose and crossed to the bay window, then sank onto the seat. Below, Lord Blair spoke with her father beside the earls' crest-emblazoned carriage. Her father had taught her that a wise person always made a deal that put him—or her—in a better position than the one in which they currently resided. A husband was definitely a step down from her current situation.

She eyed the splendid bays harnessed to the carriage. She would insist that her father allow her to take her fine dappled mare Ophelia to Edinburgh. She smiled at the thought of cantering across the countryside surrounding the city. She would have a grand time in Town—*then* inform her father she wanted no part of his scheme.

Worry niggled. What if he insisted she marry the marquess? Widows usually enjoyed more freedom than an unmarried miss. She and Matthew had been almost completely dependent upon her father. Then, when Matthew died, her father had gotten their marriage annulled. He had said the annulment was to free her from Matthew's cloying family, but they were little more than an occasional nuisance. Sophie had the suspicion her father had gotten the annulment because he felt guilty that he hadn't been able to prevent the marriage. If Matthew had turned out to be a better husband, her father would no doubt have accepted that she was happy. But she hadn't been happy. Father would have taken care of her no matter what, but his overindulgence to Matthew's demands meant she had never truly left her father's protection. Did that mean he had the right to dictate who she married?

The two men shook hands, then Lord Blair vaulted into the carriage and pulled the door shut. A flash of sunlight caught the polished brass trim of the carriage as it lurched forward and started down the drive. She watched as the coach grew smaller. Why was Lord Blair matchmaking? He was a friend of her father's, but not a close friend. She wasn't aware they had conducted business together. Had this Marquess of Monthemer engaged Lord Blair to facilitate a marriage for him? Usually, attorneys facilitated marriage contracts. The carriage disappeared around a stand of trees.

"Is it true, Miss Sophie?"

Sophie shifted to face her lady's companion and good friend Beatrice. She hovered near the door.

"Beatrice, I swear, I have told you a thousand times not to do that." The woman made as much noise as a cat stalking prey.

"Are you to be married?" Worry lines etched deeper than usual between Beatrice's brows.

Sophie grimaced. "Good Lord, news travels faster in this house than does a wildfire." She waved a hand. "'Tis nothing to fret about. I will…"

An idea—a wild idea—struck. She and Beatrice shared the same build, height, and hair color. Sophie had met her Aunt Maddie as a toddler, so the woman didn't actually know her.

Sophie grinned. "Bea, you are coming with me to Edinburgh."

Beatrice's scowl deepened.

"Sophie?" Her father's voice rang in the hall. "Come to the study, lass. At once."

The plan would work. All she had to do was fool an old woman who had never met her and talk their faithful driver into keeping quiet. The latter would prove easy. The old driver was already an accomplice to other schemes.

CHAPTER 4

AFTER BREAKFAST A WEEK LATER, SOPHIE STOOD AT THE BOTTOM
of the front doorsteps, wrapped in an ermine-trimmed pelisse
as the footmen strapped the last of her three trunks onto the
back of the coach-and-six. The maids had packed twice the
dozen dresses Sophie had laid out for the trip. Having a calico
printer as a father ensured a never-ending supply of fashionable prints to wear. She would have to work hard to attend
enough parties and events to be able to wear them all.

A thrill rushed through her. *Edinburgh.* She would stay with
the aunt she hadn't seen since she was three. Aunt Maddie lived
in Italy until four years ago when she returned to Scotland.
Sophie's father never said it, but she suspected her aunt blamed
him for Sophie's mother's death. That was silly, of course.
People died of pneumonia all the time. She could just as easily
have died in Edinburgh as she had in Invergarry.

At any rate, it seemed Aunt Maddie had forgiven Sophie's
father enough to agree to her staying until she met the
marquess. Discomfort swirled in her stomach. She would have
preferred to stay at an inn and not deal with the woman who
had never bothered to visit her and her father.

Sophie breathed deep of the early autumn air and willed her shoulders to relax. She planned to enjoy herself on this trip, marquesses and aunts be damned. The footman nimbly leapt from the carriage with the last trunk finally secure. She eyed the vehicle. Three days in a carriage did not appeal to her. Thankfully, the day after tomorrow, she would break free of the confines of the vehicle and ride like the wind on her mare Ophelia for the final few miles into Edinburgh.

The scrape of her father's boots on the steps sounded behind her, and she turned as he reached her. She had told him that she had no interest in marrying a marquess. He had *put his foot down* and said she was going to Edinburgh—and that was that.

"Your Aunt will take good care of you," he said.

"Of course, Father."

"I won't be able to join you until the ball. We have a problem with the latest vat of Turkey Red."

Sophie nodded. "No need to worry. I shall be fine."

He grasped her shoulders and she looked up into his face. "This is for the best, Sophie. He's a good man. Not many noblemen would have paid their dead father's debts, especially to the tune of leaving themselves penniless."

"You have never met the man," she replied.

"That will be rectified when I arrive in Edinburgh. I have made arrangements at the two inns where you will stay the two nights. You are not to travel after dark."

"There is no need to worry, Father. You know I am a crack shot." She lifted her reticule, where she kept a muff pistol. She didn't mention that she'd stowed her favorite revolver in the valise Beatrice was bringing down.

Her father locked gazes with her. "Mr. Williams has strict instructions from me not to let you bully him into driving past sunset."

Sophie's heart softened. "I won't bully him, I promise."

When her cousin had been waylaid by highwaymen six years ago, Sophie had begged to learn to shoot. To her surprise, her father had acquiesced without argument. Though he had remained staunch that she would no longer be allowed to ride on a road after dark.

"I will see you in Edinburgh." He kissed her forehead, then headed back inside to his study where his men from the dye works waited.

Sophie sighed. He obsessed over his dye works. She understood his passion. She felt the same with her horses. She shifted her gaze to her prized mare tied to the back of the carriage. Nothing compared to the wind in her hair and the feel of a horse moving beneath her as she galloped across the heather.

Beatrice emerged from the house, a cloth-covered basket looped over one arm and the valise in the other.

Sophie grinned at the bag. "Thank you, Bea."

Beatrice scowled and lifted the basket. "I heated stones for the journey, miss."

"You think of everything," Sophie said. "You did think of everything?" She glanced meaningfully at the canvas bag.

"Aye," Beatrice said. "But no good can come of your shenanigans, miss."

Sophie winked. "What good is life without shenanigans?"

She had everything she needed in that bag, but she couldn't take advantage of the items until the day after tomorrow. On that point, Mr. Carney was adamant. On the third day of their trip, when they were an hour from Edinburgh, she would ride like the wind on Ophelia.

The footman opened the door. Sophie descended the stairs to the coach with Beatrice at her side. Sophie paused and looked back at her childhood home. The stately stone manor with its black slate roof lay nestled amidst gardens on the edge of town. She felt certain nowhere on earth was more beautiful. She would have a nice adventure, then return home to the heather covered hills she and Ophelia loved to travel together.

Sophie faced the carriage and allowed the footman to hand her up into the carriage. Beatrice followed, then busied herself with the warming stones and the fleece-lined lap blankets. The carriage tilted slightly as the footman hopped onto his seat beside the driver, then the crack of Mr. Carney's whip sounded, and the carriage jolted into motion.

Sophie peered through the plate glass window and let the sun warm her face. Thick, white puffy clouds dotted the bright blue sky. As they turned out onto the open road, excitement hummed in her belly. The last of the thatched roofs of the village disappeared behind them.

CHAPTER 5

Adam stretched his arms and gave a loud, luxurious yawn. From the lumpiness of the bed, he knew he lay in his lodgings at Alston House—but how he'd gotten there was a mystery. He'd spent an enjoyable evening at Luckie's Oyster Cellar, dandling a bonny wench on his knee while bellowing drinking songs at the top of his voice. Fueled by an endless supply of cheap porter and even cheaper whisky, the last thing he recalled was slipping under the table in a delightful stupor.

He rubbed the sleep from his eyes. This wasn't the first time he'd stumbled back to his lodgings too drunk to remember a step of the journey back, even though he hadn't done nearly as much of that of late. A bankrupt estate had a somewhat sobering effect on a man. He sat up slowly and rubbed his chin, noting the scratchiness of his whiskers. It was time for a shave.

"You're awake earlier than I expected," a deep voice commented from near the door.

Adam started and glanced over his shoulder to see his friend, Lord Nicholas, his back against the door, arms folded across his chest and his polished boots crossed at the ankles.

"I apologize for my late arrival last night, Adam. You forgot to tell me where to meet you." Humor gleamed in Nick's eye. "However, you were easy enough to find. I merely had to walk down Cowgate to hear the singing. How does the song go… A lusty young smith at his vice stood—"

"I know the words," Adam cut in. He rolled onto his back. "You should've joined me for a drink."

"I did." Nick laughed. "Have you no recollection of last night, at all?"

"Cheap whisky interferes with such pesky things as memories," Adam remarked with a dry smile. "I trust you didn't find drinking it too much of a chore?"

"Nae, lugging you up two flights of stairs, however, was tasking. You are damned heavy. Get dressed. We have important business to discuss at the Poker Club."

Adam climbed out of bed, stretched his arms over his head, then grabbed his shirt from the foot of the bed. "Poker Club? Have you no burning desire to stay here in my sinfully extravagant lodgings?"

He glanced about the small depressing room, furnished with just the lumpy bed and a table—with no chairs. A broken mirror hung sideways on one wall, and a torn print depicting a cow standing near a stone cottage adorned the other. The single small window with its extensive view of the rooftops below provided the only light. He'd quit buying candles. They only vanished into the pockets of Alston House's other tenants. Many a time, he'd caught Mrs. Latimer from the room above picking the lock of his door.

"I have news," Nicholas said, interrupting Adam's introspection. "Be quick, man. I'm in the mood for Luther's goose pie."

"Luther does serve a particularly tasty goose pie." Adam crossed to the table where sat an empty water basin. "Damnation, I need shaving water." He fastened the last button on his shirt.

Nicholas reached for the brass bell hanging by the door. "I'll summon the maid—"

"No, not the bell." Adam pointed at the ceiling. "Mrs. Latimer is weary of the bell. She claims I ring it far too vigorously and far too often." He picked up a sheet of paper from the table. "Your obnoxious ringing of the bell disturbs my rest. Only the most ungodly of creatures would ring the bell as you do…so on, and so forth."

Adam tossed the letter back on the table, reached into the saddlebag resting on the floor, and withdrew his finely crafted pistol. He crossed to the window and threw it wide open. The bright light made him wince as he leaned out, pointed the pistol skyward, and pulled the trigger. The loud crack shattered the morning silence. Something thudded in the room above, followed by loud swearing and the pounding of feet on the floor.

Nick lifted a brow.

Adam shrugged. "Mrs. Latimer complained of bells. She said nothing about pistols."

Nicholas's upper lip quivered in the vain attempt to prevent a smile.

Feet pounded on the stairs—from both above and below— and seconds later, someone banged on the door.

"Open the door, will you?" Adam asked as he shoved the pistol back in his saddlebag.

Nicholas unlatched the door. A maid bobbed nervously on the threshold as a bitter shrew of a woman loomed angrily behind her.

"The pistol shot?" the maid asked.

"'Tis naught but a simple signal for shaving water, and I thank you very much," Adam replied. As she darted away, he locked gazes with his neighbor from above. "Good morning, Mrs. Latimer. I only seek to accommodate your requests of the bell. I presume you find the pistol more palatable?"

"I'll throttle you in your sleep," the woman growled. "I will see you tossed out on the streets. We are too fine a folk for the likes of you here." She turned more quickly than he would have thought a woman of her size could and hurried away.

Nick kicked the door shut.

"Such an unpleasant soul. I fear for the man who finds comfort in her embrace." Adam grimaced. "Is such a thing possible?"

Nicholas lifted one shoulder in a nonchalant shrug. "Finding comfort in a good woman's embrace will remove you from this place."

Adam shot him a frown. "What the devil are you talking about?"

"Marriage," Nick replied.

"I called things off with Lena long ago, as you well know."

Adam tried to ignore the tightening of his gut at having spoken the name of the woman who was responsible for him losing his family fortune—not to mention his soul. Then there was his father's death. Nae. Lena was to blame for a great deal, but he couldn't blame her for his father shooting his brains out. The old marquess had chosen that cowardly path all of his own volition.

"You are better off without her," Nicholas said. "I am talking about a respectable woman—"

"Good God, don't say it." Adam grimaced again. "I may have sold what remained of my family estate, but I will not sell my soul. I have *some* pride left." Or so he told himself. "Is marriage the business you wish to discuss?"

"What do you care?" Nicholas asked. "I'm going to feed you."

Adam was saved from having to reply when the maid returned with the shaving water.

Nicholas made no attempt to hide his amusement. "I shall await you downstairs," he said, then left with the maid.

Adam poured water—tepid water—into the basin, squinted into the grimy glass of the mirror, then began to scrape his chin with a razor. His dark hair nearly brushed his shoulders. He would have to have it trimmed. After a few expert swipes, he inspected his square jaw bare of stubble. Good enough. He wiped his face, then surveyed his appearance as he tied his cravat. He was far too well dressed for a penniless marquess. He grabbed his coat from the bed and swung it on as he walked to the door. It was time to set Nicholas straight—after lunch, of course. Adam jogged down the common stair and nearly bowled over Mrs. Latimer on the bottom step.

"Where might you be going?" The woman eyed him up and down.

He gave a low bow. "Mrs. Latimer, I have no candles for you to scavenge from my room, so there's no need to pick the lock. Have a pleasant afternoon."

She shouted after him, but he deliberately slammed the door to drown out her words. Nick waited on the street, and they set off in the crisp morning air. They soon turned down a narrow-cobbled lane where the large, ambling tavern The Poker Club sat in the middle of the block.

The proprietor, a jolly man with apple cheeks and bright blue eyes, met them at the door and ushered them to a private room that smelled of spice and cigar smoke.

Nicholas ordered pigeon pie, ham, half a dozen vegetables, and sweetmeats. "And wine right away," he added.

Adam felt certain the lavish meal was intended to remind him of the niceties he had lost as a result of paying his father's debts. The proprietor bowed, clearly pleased with the order, and left them to settle into tufted leather chairs that faced the crackling fire.

The door barely clicked closed behind the man when Nicholas said, "I am a man of my word, Adam and, while I will facilitate the sale of what remains of your estate, I must beg a favor."

Adam stared into the fire. "So long as the favor does not involve a wealthy heiress."

"Her wealth is not why I'm here, and the fact she has money is merely a happy coincidence to your circumstances."

Adam scarcely heard him. His attention had snagged on "your circumstances".

His circumstances.

His father had all but destroyed everything they owned with his addiction to drink, gambling, and loose women. It had taken Adam some time to let go of the raw anger his father's actions had unleashed. Not that he couldn't forgive his father his foibles. Quite the contrary. In truth, Adam saw in his father an older version of himself. No, the anger had stemmed from the fact that he'd frittered away too much of his youth. Perhaps if he'd began to invest in his horses ten years ago instead of five, he might not have been forced to sell all he owned. Except Merlyn. The Friesian was his future.

"Adam?" Nick's voice pierced his thoughts.

Adam took a deep breath and looked his friend in the eye. "I narrowly escaped one cold-hearted, title-hungry woman. Why should I want another?"

For the money that might save the estate in Inverness, the only home he had left, the place he planned to raise his horses and forget the world?

The door opened and a maid entered, a tray with a decanter and two glasses in hand. She set the tray on the table, filled each glass with wine, then bobbed a curtsey and left.

Nicholas sipped his wine. "Do you know Liam Shaw?"

Adam frowned. "The owner of Dalquhern Dyeworks?"

Nick nodded.

"I know of him."

"He is interested in marrying his daughter to a good family."

"He is interested in a title, you mean." Adam gulped half his glass of wine.

"Do not judge the man before meeting him," Nick said. "He loves his daughter. He will not marry her to just anyone."

Adam lifted a brow. "He has standards, eh?"

"In fact, he does." A small smile touched Nicholas's mouth. "When you have a daughter, you will understand."

"Perhaps, but—"

"But nothing, Adam. Meet the woman. She is quite lovely." Nick paused, then sighed. "You will have a difficult time raising your Friesians without capital. Do you really want to see Brewhold crumble?"

Adam finished his wine, then refilled his glass. "Perhaps it is better that way. I can return to university and learn a useful profession. I always thought I would make a fine solicitor."

Nicholas snorted. "No, you wouldn't. You would hate the long hours poring over paperwork, the business deals, and the noblemen who would like nothing better than to have a marquess as their solicitor—and don't think they would ever let you forget that they are *now* above you. Nae, you need to be outdoors with your horses. Imagine having enough money to set Brewhold straight, horses and all."

"You make it sound so easy." Adam lifted the wine glass to his lips, but the wine suddenly smelled sour, and he set the glass back on the table.

"She will attend Lady Seafield's ball. Surely, you can at least meet her."

Adam sighed. "I will meet her. But be warned, whatever mad scheme you have planned is doomed to fail. What is her name?" Adam suddenly wondered if lunch were worth the trouble of this discussion.

"Sophie Shaw." Nick grinned. "You will never guess who her relatives are."

Adam thought for a moment. "Not the Forsyth's on Lacy Street?"

"One and the same." Nicholas gave a single nod. "Number ninety-one."

"Not Madeline Forsyth?" The spry, fifty-five-year-old woman was the life of Edinburgh's oyster cellars.

"I seem to recall you telling me that if she were twenty years younger, you would have pursued her." Nicholas said. "Maddie is Miss Shaw's aunt."

Adam grunted. "I agree to attend Lady Seafield's ball and dance with the lass her two dances. But do not get your hopes up."

Nick's expression sobered. "Give the matter serious thought, Adam. Not every woman is like Lena."

AFTER LUNCH, NICHOLAS LEFT WITH A PROMISE TO RETURN THE night of the ball, and Adam headed for the stables that housed his last possession. He'd sunk his last penny into stabling the superbly high-spirited Frisian stallion of unequaled speed and beauty. The animal represented his future. He had a winner and, with it, he would take not only the races at Musselburgh, but he would breed other fine racehorses, as well.

He'd chosen the best stables in Edinburgh, a small establishment near the end of Cowgate. He arrived to find the stable master exercising his stallion in the yard.

"He's a beauty, my lord." Jack halted, bridle in hand, and dipped his head in greeting. "I have yet to see a finer animal."

"He is unmatched." Adam ran a hand along the horse's muscled neck. "I would like to ride him. Would you fetch me a saddle, please?"

Jack beamed. "Aye, sir." He hurried away.

Adam grabbed a brush hanging from the fence then began brushing the horse's back. A shadow fell across the ground beside Adam. He looked up. A tall, fair-haired man took the last two steps to where Adam stood and stopped. Adam returned his attention to his horse and openly ignored the man.

"Fine horse," Kenrich Balfour said.

"What do you want, Balfour?"

"I thought perhaps we could discuss business."

"I have no intention of selling Merlyn." Adam continued to brush the animal's back.

"That wasn't quite what I had in mind, but we both know you need the money to finish paying your father's debts."

"You are mistaken," Adam said. "I have paid all debts."

"Indeed? I suppose I should say congratulations. Few men would be so honorable. You do still need money to run your estate. I am willing to double my price."

Adam looked up in surprise. "Five thousand pounds?"

Balfour smiled in obvious satisfaction. "Five thousand pounds. I can have the money in your account today."

Adam gave a low laugh. "You must feel confident he will produce a winner."

"Just as you do."

Adam ran his hand along the horse's back. "I told you, he's not for sale."

"You cannot make a single shilling on him for two more years," Balfour said. "Even then, studding him out will not make you enough money to run your estate. You will not survive long enough to race him—or any of his progeny."

"How long I survive is none of your concern," Adam replied with more calm than he felt. People like Kenrich Balfour were predators who attacked with a ruthless accuracy that usually brought down their prey—which made Adam want to drive his fist into the man's nose. Merlyn tossed his head, as if in agreement.

If not for the bargain he'd made with Lord Wilmingly,

Adam very well might plant a facer on Balfour's jaw. But the five thousand pounds he would receive upon learning where Balfour had hidden the gold he'd stolen from the Crown while in the navy, would sustain Adam's estate for two years, though he wouldn't be able to purchase anymore horses. Should the gold turn out to be worth more than fifty thousand pounds—and Adam knew that was likely the case—he would receive ten percent of the find.

"I suggest you go home, Balfour," he said. "I tire of your company."

As expected, the man's expression tensed, then he relaxed. "I would not wait too long."

Adam understood a threat when he heard one. Balfour wanted Merlyn. He wasn't the first man to become obsessed with a fine piece of horseflesh, and Merlyn was one of the finest. But a man's desire to own a horse wasn't enough of a reason to account for the fury Adam felt certain lurked beneath Kenrich Balfour's relaxed façade. What Adam believed accounted for Balfour's attitude were the rumors that Balfour was connected to a smuggling operation owned and run by his uncle. A fine extension to his piracy. Adam wasn't one to engage in gossip, but this was one bit of *on dit* he counted on having more truth than lies.

"I will keep that in mind." Adam returned his attention to the horse.

Balfour turned and Adam cursed. He'd overplayed his hand. He racked his brain for a way to bring the man's interest back to him but came up empty. Anything too direct would put Balfour on notice.

The man halted and faced him. "Are you willing to make a wager?"

Adam kept his expression neutral. "I'm not a gambling man."

"Even when the gain is great?"

Adam gave a mirthless laugh. "What would you know of great gain?"

"Enough to know that you could finance your love of horses for the rest of your life."

Adam paused his hand for the barest of moments, then continued brushing Merlyn. The animal swished his tail.

"I find it interesting that a man of your…*reputation* paid his father's debts," Balfour said.

This was the one snag in his plan. How did a man who paid his dead father's debts prove he was a pirate?

"I'm in no mood to indulge your curiosity," Adam said.

"But I ask that you do." Balfour stepped up to Merlyn and ran a flattened palm down the animal's back. The horse nickered in satisfaction. "Why not tell the creditors to go to the devil? You would have had enough money to survive for at least five years."

Adam hesitated. "Because I knew it would anger him, even beyond the grave."

Balfour's brows shot up. Then he smiled. "Fathers can be… difficult. My father was difficult"—a distant look entered his eyes—"until I reached sixteen." His expression cleared and he smiled. "But that is a story for another time. I propose a bargain…a wager. I need a man like you."

"*A man like me?*" Adam repeated.

"Indeed. A man with experience making money."

"Stealing money, you mean," Adam said.

Balfour slowly nodded. "That, too. However, we now need to make our money appear legitimate."

"You mean invest your ill-gotten gains?" Adam asked.

"I understand your desire to have the last say with your father," Balfour said. "But it's a shame that desire took your last shilling. I am surprised you do not have a…reserve."

"If you are referring to the rumor that I turned pirate and stole from our king, those rumors are untrue."

Balfour flashed a smile. "Of course they are, just as the rumors about my piracy are untrue. Shouldn't two men who society has decided aren't worthy work together?"

"I thought you said you had a wager."

"Merlyn against the five thousand pounds I offered—"

"I will not sell Merlyn," Adam cut in.

Balfour shook his head. "Not sell. A wager. This is about gold guineas headed to England."

"And you want to rob it." Adam barely managed to keep the shock out of his voice.

"Then we must melt the gold," Balfour said.

Wilmingly hadn't said anything about a shipment of gold coins. Then again, he wouldn't. Like most noblemen, he thought himself superior to those beneath him, so it probably never occurred to him that a man like Balfour would make such a bold move. It would serve the Crown right if Balfour robbed them. A thought struck. What if that had been Wilmingly's plan all along? What if he was smarter than Adam was giving him credit for? Adam mentally grimaced. Was he as arrogant as Wilmingly in underestimating Balfour?

"I wager we can take the gold with a dozen men," Balfour said.

Adam frowned. "Take a frigate with a dozen men? Impossible."

"I plan to take the gold without firing a single shot, at least not at the ship."

Jack emerged from the stables, carrying a saddle. He stopped, stared for a heartbeat, then turned and hurried back inside.

"What do you mean 'at least not at the ship'?" Adam demanded of Balfour.

"When the ship docks in London and is unloaded for transportation, we will take the gold on route to King George."

Adam looked up from brushing Merlyn. "Rob the transport? That is suicide. At least two dozen soldiers will be guarding the gold."

"Hardly," Balfour replied. "The ship's hold isn't laden with gold. This is but one chest. George believes he has kept secret the transport."

"Who's to say someone else does not know?" Adam asked.

"Who's to say anyone does know?" Balfour countered.

Twenty minutes later, Adam left the busy streets of Edinburgh behind for the open countryside. The exceptionally warm autumn day made him want to ride all the way to Inverness. He left the road and cut through a deserted orchard. When he reached the stretch of grassland beyond, he gave the horse his head. The horse's massive hooves pounded out the most beautiful rhythm Adam had ever heard. He let the animal run until the land turned more densely forested, and Stirling Castle, high on its hill, appeared little more than a speck. Adam slowed. The horse tossed his head, as if to say, "It's about time," and Adam swayed in tempo with the brute's gait.

A rider came into view beyond the open countryside on the road. The rider, a lad, hunched low over the horse's neck as they flew down the road. Adam watched in appreciation. The lad could ride, but it was the horse that captured Adam's attention—a chestnut mare with beautiful lines and a smooth gait.

A carriage rattled and Adam looked down the road about half a mile behind the rider where a magnificent coach-and-six traveled at a sedate speed. The lad on the mare pulled rein at the top of the rise and waited until the carriage reached him minutes later. Adam could discern no crest emblazoned on the side and nothing to hint at the identity of the passengers within. The six horses were fine creatures, but still, the lad's mare outshone them all. As the coach rolled past, the rider took off again, and in minutes, they vanished along the road toward Edinburgh.

If they stayed in Edinburgh long enough, he might be able to hunt down the mare's owner. The horse could be just the mare to breed with Merlyn. A gust of wind blew his hair, carrying with it the scent of rain. He glanced heavenward. A line of dark clouds were sweeping down from the north. He had better turn back if he didn't want to get caught in the rain. Adam cut across the heather and galloped toward the city.

The sky had darkened when Adam handed his horse's reins to a boy in the stables. Adam rubbed the back of his neck and stretched his legs. The exercise had stimulated his appetite. A dog barked in the distance as he headed toward his favorite tavern on Lacy Street. As he neared the church, the creak of harness reached his ears an instant before the coach-and-six he'd seen on the road turned the corner of the church.

"Well, damn," he murmured.

Half a dozen seconds later, the mare he'd seen also came into view. Adam stepped out of the road as the coach passed. Boys' shouts went up behind Adam. He glanced over his shoulder to see three lads chasing one another down the street toward him. He chuckled, then faced forward as the rider and mare neared him. Adam started to lift a hand to hail the rider. The boys reached where he stood, and one of the lads pushed the other into the street. He tripped and fell in the mare's path.

The mare screamed and reared, pawing the air. Adam dove for the fallen boy. The mare's rider yanked the animal's reins to the right, away from the boy. The horse's hooves hit the ground two feet from where the boy had fallen as Adam rolled with the lad in the opposite direction. The boy pushed away and jumped to his feet. Without a backward glance, he raced off after his companions, who had taken off down the street.

"Blasted fool," the mare's rider shouted after them.

Adam agreed. With a groan, he rose. The rider turned his mare toward Adam as a gust of wind whipped Adam's hair. The rider's hat flew from his head. Adam froze when a wealth of brown curls spilled down onto the rider's shoulders. A woman. The rider was…a woman.

She gave a gasping sort of laugh and shifted as if to dismount. Adam scooped up the hat from the ground and looked up into a pair of laughing brown eyes. She held a finger to her lips, begging his silence. His gaze caught on her full mouth and his cock twitched. The little piece of baggage was a hoyden. He extended the hat toward her. She grasped it and tugged, but he held fast.

"What is your name?" he asked before checking the impulse.

Dimples appeared on cheeks flushed pink from the chill air. "I am no one, sir."

His mind snapped to attention. No one? She spoke far too cultured to be *no one*. He released the hat, and she quickly clamped it on her head, stuffing as many curls as she could beneath the rim, then kicked the mare's flank and trotted down the street. She sat straight in the saddle. She would, of course. The woman was clearly born to ride. He slid his gaze downward along her slender breeches-clad legs.

The coach-and-six rattled to a halt before a row of affluent townhomes down the street. A mist began to fall as Adam strode toward the carriage. Perhaps the driver might tell him who the lass was. He reached the carriage, then halted when he caught sight of the numbers on the large brass doorplate where the carriage had stopped. Number ninety-one.

The footman hopped from his seat and opened the carriage door. A long, slender arm appeared, and the footman helped a woman from the carriage. She wore a fine ermine-trimmed pelisse over a light blue gown. The lady paused and glanced around. She drew her brows into a scowl and thinned her lips in displeasure.

He drew back in dismay.

Surely, she couldn't be? Sophie. Madeline Forsyth's niece.

CHAPTER 6

Sophie kept her attention on the carriage parked in front of her aunt's house up ahead. A black iron handrail led up the three steps from the street to the front door of the townhouse. Dare she stop while the gentleman watched her? He was watching. She could feel his gaze on her. He had been too interested in learning her identity, and she feared he would try to talk to her, thus give away the fact she was a woman. Sophie prayed Beatrice would keep her nerve and not say anything the man might hear.

Sophie hadn't planned on Beatrice pretending to be her anywhere but in Sophie's bedchambers by the low light of the hearth. This is what she got for not getting back into the carriage before they reached Town. Not to mention, she hadn't given any thought to the servants seeing her arrive in breeches —or a handsome gentleman discovering that she was a woman.

Sophie passed the coach then drew her horse up in front of the other horses. Maybe the gentleman would turn off before he reached them. The door of the house opened, and a footman stepped outside.

She couldn't have asked for more perfect timing. As the coachman handed Beatrice out of the carriage, Sophie called to the footman at the door, "Have you a stable?"

He sniffed and lifted his nose in the air. "To the rear."

Sophie called to Beatrice, "I will send your maid to your room soon, miss."

Beatrice frowned, then gasped. Sophie tensed, then gave thanks when Beatrice didn't call out. Sophie faced forward and urged Ophelia on.

"Haddies from Newhaven," a nearby fish-woman cried.

Hooves clattered on the cobblestones around her. In the distance, a church bell rang. Sophie halted at the corner and waited for a carriage to pass so she could turn left toward the alley behind her aunt's house. A nervous tremor rippled through her stomach. Her aunt hadn't seen her since Sophie was three.

"I trust you suffered no lasting harm, lass—er, lad?"

Sophie started at the deep male voice and jerked her head in the direction of the man who had rescued her hat from the street. He stood on the corner. Her gaze caught on stunning hazel eyes flecked with green and gold. His dark hair, longer than the usual cut, nearly brushed his broad shoulders.

"I am hale and hearty, sir." She smiled. "Thank you for keeping my secret."

He executed a bow with an elegant grace that spoke of much practice. His brown coat and dark blue waistcoat were finely made and topped off with a rakishly tied cravat. A gentleman.

"It is my pleasure, I assure you. Miss Sophie Shaw will never hear a word from my lips."

Her pulse jumped. "You know Miss Shaw?"

The carriage passed and Sophie urged her mount to take the left turn, then kept a sedate pace as the man kept pace with them on the sidewalk.

"I have not had the pleasure of Miss Shaw's acquaintance," he said. "But I have been informed of her arrival."

Sophie tensed. "By whom, sir? Are you acquainted with the Marquess of Monthemer?"

Surprise quickly gave way to a cool expression. "I am acquainted with the man."

"He sent you to spy on m—my mistress to report back if she is worthy of marriage?"

"Your mistress?" he said. "The marquess is a rogue and not particularly interested in the match."

So, the marquess didn't wish to lower himself to marry a woman not of noble birth? Hadn't he ever heard that beggars couldn't be choosers?

"Miss Shaw has no wish to marry the marquess," she said.

His brows rose in surprise…or was that amusement?

She reached the alley and turned left onto the gravel road. The rear of the townhouses sat to the left, and to the right, small stables were interspersed among smaller homes, likely occupied by servants. To her surprise, the man followed. The devil gripped Sophie and she didn't bother to resist.

"Miss Shaw is a somber woman," she said.

"From the looks of her, I quite agree," he replied.

She blinked. He'd seen her? Of course, out front when Beatrice had exited the carriage—and he'd mistaken Beatrice for herself. Oh, this was simply too delicious.

"She is a paragon of discontent. I have yet to see her smile." Sophie looked down at him. "How do you know the marquess?"

A strange smile played at the corner of his mouth. "I am his man of affairs."

They reached the rear entrance to the house marked Number ninety-one, and Sophie pulled Ophelia to a halt.

Allow me to introduce myself," the man said. "I am Adam… Adam MacAlister."

"I'm Beatrice Frasier. Pleased to meet you, sir."

"Likewise, *Miss* Frasier." He emphasized the word Miss and glanced meaningfully at her tight breeches, then winked. "Well, I must be off." He took two backward steps. "Good evening, Miss Frasier."

"The same to you, Mr. MacAlister." She angled her head in farewell.

Her attention caught on the way his coat stretched taut across broad shoulders—and the tendrils of hair that brushed those shoulders. He turned onto the road and out of her view, and she jarred at the realization that she'd been staring.

Fifteen minutes later, valise in hand, Sophie thanked the maid who showed her to Miss Shaw's room and slipped inside a bright room. Beatrice jumped up from the chair where she sat in front of a window. To the right, sat a large four-poster bed with a peach-colored counterpane. The four trunks sat near the armoire to the left near the hearth where a fire burned.

"*Finally.*" Beatrice wrung her hands. "Where have you been? Your aunt has sent a message that you are to attend to her in the drawing room once you have refreshed yourself. Oh, dear, but this is a mess you've gotten us into." She took a breath, clearly with the intent to carry on her tirade.

"Calm yourself, Beatrice. As you can see, I changed into my dress. The breeches are well hidden in my valise." She lifted the valise to show her.

In her desire to ride Ophelia, another thing Sophie had given no thought to was how a young male footman would gain entrance to Sophie Shaw's chambers. However, she wasn't about to admit that to Beatrice. Luckily, Mr. Carney arrived, and Sophie had quickly changed inside the carriage. She would plan better in the future.

"A woman of your station should not wander the streets of Edinburgh alone," Beatrice said.

"My station?" Sophie snorted. "I am no lady, silly. No one cares what a calico-printer's daughter does."

"Your *father* would. He will have my head on a platter if he catches a hint of this escapade."

Sophie took the breeches and shirt from the valise.

"Please, I beg you, burn those hideous clothes," Beatrice wailed.

Burn them? She needed them.

"Cease fretting, Bea." Sophie crossed to the armoire, folded the clothes, then tucked them into the far corner of the chest, along with the valise.

She faced Beatrice. "Now, close the drapes. We must prepare for my aunt to visit me. I have a headache, you know."

Beatrice frowned. "You never have a headache."

Sophie grinned. "I will be having a lot of them while I am in Edinburgh. Now, do as I say. Close the drapes."

Beatrice obeyed while Sophie searched her trunks until she found a nightgown, cap and robe. Beatrice helped her wash her face and arms, then combed her hair and splashed a little rose water on her locks. Even Sophie had to admit she could still smell the hint of horse on her hair. When Sophie finally slipped into the nightgown, cap and robe, she ordered Beatrice to turn off the lamp.

Beatrice complied, and Sophie crawled into bed and pulled the covers up to her shoulders. When Beatrice pulled the drapes, firelight bathed the room in a low glow that pleased Sophie. Her aunt wouldn't be able to get a good look at her.

"Now, call for a maid," Sophie said. "Tell her to inform my aunt I have a headache. If she decides to visit me—"

A sharp rap sounded on the door, and a woman said, "Sophie, it's your Aunt Maddie."

Sophie looked at Beatrice whose eyes had gone wide.

"*Hide*," Sophie whispered.

"Hide?"

"No argument." Sophie shooed her away.

Beatrice hesitated, then hurried to the small antechamber on the far side of the room and went inside.

Sophie burrowed deeper into the bedding and pulled the covers up to her chin. "Come in," she called in a small voice.

The door creaked slightly, and a sliver of light fell across the carpet to the left of the bed. "Sophie."

"Here," Sophie said.

Her aunt entered, closed the door behind her, then walked to the bed. She frowned down at Sophie. "What is wrong, child?"

"I am sick."

"Sick?" She sat on the mattress, and Sophie looked into dark keen eyes that she feared took in far too much. "Have you a cold?" Maddie asked.

Sophie gave what she hoped was a wan smile. "Too many hours in a carriage, I fear."

Her aunt nodded. "Oh, yes, too many hours in a carriage will drive a body beyond endurance."

Sophie checked the impulse to agree too vigorously and simply gave a single nod.

"Riding in a coach too long often irritates my gout," her aunt said.

"You have gout?" Sophie asked.

She nodded. "A good rain can force me to a chair in front of the fire with my foot propped on a stool."

"That's terrible," Sophie said with feeling. "How do you feel now?"

Aunt Maddie chuckled. "Never you mind, my dear."

"What does the doctor say?" Sophie surprised herself at the unexpected concern that flooded her.

"He prescribed Dr. Anderson's Pills."

"Have you been taking them?" The older woman's brows shot up, and Sophie realized she'd caught her aunt in a fib. "I will fetch them for you tomorrow," Sophie said.

Surprise shone in Maddie's eyes, and she laughed. "I can see you will keep me on my toes. But you needn't worry about that tonight. I will have a tray sent up for you and Miss Frasier. You rest. You have a busy day ahead of you tomorrow."

"I do?" Sophie realized she's displayed a little too much enthusiasm. She winced and rubbed her left temple.

Her aunt patted her arm. "I have sent for the seamstress. She arrives tomorrow to work on your gown for the ball. But we will worry about that tomorrow."

Sophie groaned inwardly. Suffering through fittings wasn't what she had in mind for tomorrow. "I have a dozen gowns I can wear to the ball," she said.

"You must arrive in the latest fashion, if you are to impress a marquess."

"I do not want the marquess any more than he wants me," she blurted.

"Nonsense, why wouldn't he want you?"

She recalled Adam MacAlister telling her the marquess was not in favor of the marriage. Sophie also recalled Mr. MacAlister's wink and flushed.

"Sophie?" her aunt prompted. "Oh dear, I have worn you out." To Sophie's surprise, Maddie pressed a kiss to her forehead, then stood. "You rest. Tomorrow, you will feel much better." She looked around the room. "Where is Miss Frasier?"

"I sent her to bed," Sophie replied. Her aunt frowned. "She was exhausted from taking care of me."

Maddie nodded. "My room is three doors down should you need anything."

"Thank you, ma'am."

Maddie gave Sophie one last smile, then left. When the door clicked shut behind her, Sophie threw the covers back and jumped from bed as Beatrice emerged from the small room.

Sophie waved her over. "We have plans to make, Bea."

CHAPTER 7

THE FOLLOWING MORNING, ADAM LAY IN BED, STARING AT THE ceiling. A man would be a fool to shackle himself to a creature such as Miss Sophie Shaw. If he were to consider marrying a rich heiress, Miss Shaw wasn't his only choice. Impoverished marquesses were in high demand. He couldn't throw a stone without hitting a determined mama poised to throw her daughter at him. God help him. Was he really considering marrying strictly for money? Why not? The decision to marry for love had left him penniless.

He would never forget Lena's words the day after his father's death. *"Given recent circumstances, I believe it is better if we sever our relationship."*

Given recent circumstances.

Recent circumstances being that, as the new owner of his father's Edinburgh townhouse and her newfound riches—the twenty percent of his father's losses she had collected as owner of the gambling hall—she was now a woman of means. She had no intention of continuing a relationship with a man of no means, even if he was a marquess.

He barked a laugh. He'd already told her they were

through, but she preferred to act as if she had tossed him aside. Adam threw back the covers and jumped from bed. To hell with feeling sorry for himself. His father may have gambled away Adam's inheritance, but the old man had still managed to save him from the hell of marrying Lena. Adam had loved her, but she would have slowly killed him. He hadn't been able to admit her true nature, so blind was he with passion.

Memory rose of their lovemaking the afternoon his father seated himself in her card room and laid down his first bet. By the time Lena arrived at her gaming hall that evening, the old marquess had suffered heavy losses and was nigh drunk. Did she put a stop to the game? Nae. Rumors circulated about how she called for the solicitor she kept installed in the gaming hall, and he witnessed the signing of the old marquess's marker.

The personal items and furnishing in Brewhold were all he had left. To a man with money that might mean something, but without the money to maintain the estate, the house would fall into disrepair all too quickly. Even if he scrounged together enough money to maintain the estate for ten years, that would only make him ten years older with fewer options to support himself. Still, ten years of peace, ten years to forget, was hard to resist. Adam shook his head. He might survive ten years, but he wouldn't raise any horses.

THE MORNING BUSTLE HAD JUST BEGUN WHEN HE REACHED LACY Street an hour later. He hadn't really thought of a plan beyond befriending the coachman to learn more of Miss Beatrice Frasier. She was his best chance of learning something about Miss Shaw. He had eleven days until the ball. Eleven days to decide whether or not he could sell himself like a common whore.

He strode down the street, headed for the townhouse

stables when a woman called out, "Lord Monthemer, is that you? Oh my, but it *is* you."

Adam didn't recognize the voice, but he recognized the tone of a determined mama who now had him in her sights. He grimaced and quickened his step, as if not having heard her.

"Sir," she called.

The quick click of heels on the walkway told him she was hurrying after him. Bloody hell. A woman willing to chase a man down the street was a dangerous woman, indeed.

"Sir." The woman was so close he swore he could feel her breath on the back of his neck.

Adam halted and turned. Then wished he hadn't. He remembered all too well the woman, Mrs. Walker. She had a daughter, a sweet young girl who belonged anywhere but the jungle of a ballroom. Mrs. Walker, however, was determined to get a title for her daughter at all costs and cared not one whit that her country daughter was shunned by the females of society and hunted by desperate males who would rut between her legs, then spend her money.

"Mrs. Walker." He bowed.

She halted in front of him, heaving so loudly he feared the large woman would collapse. "I-I am s-so pleased to see you, sir."

"It is always a pleasure to see you, madam. I am late for an appointment, however."

"Oh-oh, of course. I am hosting a party. I am not certain where to send your invitation."

"I am afraid I am not staying in Town," he replied.

Panic shone in her eyes. "But the party is tonight. Surely, you will be here tonight? Lucy is so looking forward to seeing you." She leaned a little closer and said in a conspiratorial tone, "My husband has an important matter to discuss with you."

Adam gave her a cool smile. "He will have to forgive me, but my business cannot wait."

He gave another small bow and started to turn. She grasped his sleeve. Adam stiffened.

Her eyes widened and she released him. "Oh, but you must forgive me, my lord. It is just..." Tears welled in her eyes.

Adam checked the anger that rushed to the surface. The woman was a master manipulator.

"You see—" she broke off. "Well, my husband will be very angry with me for telling you—"

"Then perhaps you should not tell me," he cut in.

"I know it is not the done thing," she said, and Adam ignored the two women who stared as they passed. "But my husband—good man that he is," she continued, "does not understand the heart of a young girl. You see, Lucy, well, she has formed a, ah, that is, she has formed an affection for you."

"Mrs. Walker, your daughter is barely out of the school room, seventeen, if I recall. Any attachment she might have formed for me"—and he felt certain she hadn't—"will dissolve when the next handsome young man asks her to dance."

He wished the right man would ask her to dance, but knew it mattered not. Mrs. Walker cared more for her climb up society's ladder than she did her daughter's happiness.

"I wish you well." Without another word, he turned and walked down the street. If the infernal woman followed him, this time, he would run.

Minutes later, Adam turned on the cobblestoned lane and caught sight of a slender figure emerging from the rear gate of townhouse Number ninety-one. Beatrice, he realized. She carried a basket, and this time, she wore a worn brown velvet spencer and a peach-colored morning dress that clung sensuously to her curves. She had pinned her brown curls under a simple bonnet. She hurried down the street and disappeared around the far corner. He quickened his pace and followed.

He caught sight of her up ahead conversing with a woman

hawking oranges out of a wheelbarrow. He arrived as Beatrice dropped a penny in the woman's outstretched hand.

"Thank ye kindly, miss." The street hawker grinned. "Pick your six."

Beatrice looked up at his approach. Surprise flickered in her eyes. "Mr. MacAlister, how...interesting to see you here this morning." She returned her attention to the street hawker and chose her fruit. A slight twitch of her lip betrayed her pleasure at his presence.

By God, was she toying with him? As the street vendor trundled away, he stepped closer to Beatrice. "Call me Adam."

She wrinkled her nose into a smile. "Only if you call me s-uh—" She clapped her hand over her mouth and hiccupped. Her brown eyes sparkled over her fingers as she continued with a slightly strangled laugh. "Why, I beg your pardon. Call me, Beatrice."

He angled his head in acknowledgement. "I'd be delighted. You're out early this morning."

"Hold out your arm," she ordered.

"Hold out my arm?" It was an odd request, though he did as she asked.

She deftly looped the basket handle over his arm. "I need someone to carry this for me."

His gaze caught on her lips, lips that could bring a man to his knees. "Perhaps there's a price for my help," he murmured.

"Indeed, there is," she said in a businesslike manner. "Few can afford the honor of my company. But for you, sir, I shall bestow the gift of my company freely. My aunt—my mistress's aunt—is in sore need of Dr. Anderson's Pills. Do you know the way to the apothecary?"

"I do." He affected a low bow. "This way, Beatrice." They set off down the street at a leisurely pace, him carrying the basket. "That was a fine animal I saw you riding yesterday. I'm surprised your mistress allowed you to ride."

Beatrice laughed. "She was exceedingly displeased, but the mare needed exercise."

"Is your mistress that difficult?" he asked.

"Is she? Why yes, I suppose she is. I had to sneak out today before she awoke. She'll be furious to find me gone."

He frowned. "Why? How else does she expect you to run your errands?"

She shrugged. "As I said, she is not easy to deal with. Plus, she is fretting over the upcoming ball."

"I thought you said she did not wish to marry the marquess."

Beatrice nodded. "Which is why she is fretting."

A group of sooty men barreled around the corner of a candle shop. Adam grabbed Beatrice's arm and pulled her aside just in time to keep the men from knocking her over.

Beatrice looked up into his face, and Adam stared into kind brown eyes that made him wish he were a simpler man. When he'd fallen in love with Lena, he'd been glad to be a rich earl. He hadn't fooled himself. If not for his money, she wouldn't have looked at him twice. Now, he wished for nothing more than a quiet life and perhaps a beautiful woman to smile at him as did Beatrice. Adam jarred and realized he was staring. Hell, she was staring back.

He released her and she exclaimed, "Oh, dear, we have lost two of the oranges."

One lay on the walk near him, the other rolled slowly toward the edge of the curb. She lunged with the clear intent of catching the orange before it rolled into the street. Adam seized her arm and yanked her back as the orange dropped off the curb and into the street just in time to be squashed by the front wheel of a passing carriage.

Beatrice yanked her head up, a deep frown on her face. "Why did you do that? Now I have lost an orange."

He released her and scooped up the nearby orange, then

dropped it back into the basket. "I do not think an orange is worth your life. Are you always so impetuous, riding horses while dressed in breeches and trying to fight a carriage for an orange?"

"I promise you, sir, my ride in breeches was well planned."

Adam blinked. Then laughed—hard. "Someday, I may ask you to explain." He offered his arm. "Shall we?"

She eyed him for an instant, as if uncertain he might bite, and he was surprised to find he half wanted to. Beatrice slipped her hand into the crook of his arm, and they resumed their walk. Adam allowed her to chatter on about the vendors hawking their wares and the fine carriages that rolled past.

"Why is your mistress opposed to marrying the marquess?" he asked in a casual tone. "Most women cannot resist a title."

"What woman wants a man who only marries her for her money?" Beatrice replied with enough force that Adam looked sharply at her.

"She would be a marchioness," he said, feeling oddly affronted.

She angled her head and looked up at him. "You said the marquess was no more pleased to marry her than she was him. Why?"

"Perhaps he does not want a woman who only wants him for his title."

"Oh, what does a man care for such things?" she replied with an airy wave of her hand. "They do as they please, no matter who they marry."

He lifted his brows. "You are jaded for one so young."

She snorted. "I am pragmatic. The marquess may marry anyone he likes and continue to live life very much as he always has, particularly if he decides to send Miss Shaw back to the country. It happens all the time. So, you see, she has much more to lose than he does."

A pedestrian shouted at a carriage that came a little too

close as the man leapt up onto the curb. Adam turned his attention forward as they neared the corner. They paused and waited for a rider to pass, then crossed the street.

Once on the other side, Adam said, "I take it you share your mistress's feelings on the matter?"

"I can't say I would like being chosen for my money—if I had any."

He couldn't help wondering if she thought he believed she had money and that was why he was pursuing her. He *wasn't* pursuing her, but she might think he was.

"The whole situation rather makes a woman feel like a cow on the auction block," she said.

He knew exactly what she meant. Was it possible Miss Shaw wasn't as bad as he thought but was simply not happy with her father marrying her to a man she didn't know?

He recalled the grim downturn of her mouth. Was it too much to ask to find a woman to marry who didn't hate life… and perhaps men? He could tolerate her living her own life—once she had provided children—but a woman who found no joy in life would kill him just as Lena would have. Of course, if he was forced to live his life scraping out only enough money to keep Brewhold from falling into ruin, what kind of life was that?

They reached the apothecary, a tall, antique house with dovecote-like gables at the end of Market Street. The purchase of the pills took no time at all, and within minutes, they started back toward home, the pills tucked in the basket he carried.

They walked two blocks in silence, and Adam began to wonder if something was amiss. "Is something amiss, Beatrice?"

"Not amiss, exactly," she replied slowly. "I cannot help but wonder why you were outside my au—my mistress's house this morning."

"Good fortune, I suppose. Just as when I saw you on the street yesterday."

"Once, I could believe to be happenstance. Twice…" She looked up at him. "You were waiting for me, were you not?"

He silently cursed. She'd caught him off guard. The girl was intelligent.

"I hoped to see you," he said. "Do you mind?"

She smiled, and his breath caught. "You are a handsome man. Why would I complain?"

He laughed. "I am relieved to hear that."

They turned down Cowgate. As another street vendor passed selling hot mutton pies, he offered to buy her one, but when he returned from his purchase, he discovered she'd continued down the street to Luckie's tavern.

"Beatrice?" He strode toward her.

She didn't respond.

"Beatrice?" He raised his voice.

She jumped when he stopped beside her. "Look, Adam." She pointed to the iron sign hanging above the door. "It's Luckie's tavern. I hear they hold the most wonderful oyster parties for the most fashionable in Edinburgh."

He handed her a pie. "They do."

He should know. He'd spent almost every night there the past week. He much preferred the entertainment of the oyster cellars to the stuffy affairs hosted by the majority of the gentry.

"I would so love to attend one," she said in a wistful tone. "I hear they dance until dawn."

He laughed. "Nae, not until dawn, but into the wee hours, most assuredly."

She turned wide eyes on him. "Have you attended one?"

"Once or twice," he replied.

"Then I shall go," she whispered.

He frowned. "I beg your pardon?"

She nodded, her attention still on the building. "Tonight, I think."

With her dark hair and eyes, and sultry voice, she would attract more than one kind of man. "A lady shouldn't wander around unchaperoned," he said.

"Then 'tis fortunate I am not a lady." She took a large bite of her mutton pie and rolled her eyes in pleasure. "Delicious. I have lived my life without the restrictions pressed upon ladies of rank. Frankly, I don't know how they bear it."

Beatrice studied the tavern and bit her bottom lip as if already planning her escapade. She took another bite of the pie, and he was startled to realize he wondered what those full lips tasted like.

She tilted her head and looked at him from beneath her lashes. "I won't be in danger if you accompany me."

He blinked. "Beatrice, you may not be of the gentry, but you are still a young woman and—"

"I suppose I can find someone else to accompany me."

Adam narrowed his eyes. "It's like that, is it?"

"I would much rather go with you, but if you do not wish to be seen with me—"

"Enough, minx." He lifted his hand, palms out, in surrender. "I will take you."

Her smile made another appearance, and he could deny her nothing.

"Truly?" she asked.

He grasped her free hand. "I shall collect you this evening—if, that is, your mistress will allow it."

She shook her head. "Oh, she will not stop me. Nothing will. I will climb out the window, if necessary."

An image of slender legs encased in tight breeches sliding out her window flitted across his mind. "No doubt you would," he murmured.

CHAPTER 8

AUNT MADDIE'S THREAT TO CANCEL HER PLANS FOR THE DAY IF Sophie didn't sit for the fittings Maddie had arranged elicited quick agreement from Sophie. Maddie left with instructions to order anything Sophie liked for lunch—and supper—for Maddie would not return home until late. True to her promise, Sophie endured the fittings, though perhaps with less grace than her aunt would have liked, had she been there. Sophie ate a light supper in anticipation of her night at the oyster cellars and now stood in front of the mirror in her room dressed in her plainest evening gown, a lavender muslin with white satin ribbon.

"If your father finds out you have gone out at night *with* a gentleman—to a tavern—he will flay us both alive, miss." Beatrice stood from her perch on the foot of Sophie's bed.

Sophie shrugged. Her father was miles away. "He will never know."

She squinted into the mirror and adjusted her curls. Night had fallen. She had to hurry. In keeping with her charade as a lady's companion, she would wear Beatrice's worn brown spencer again—this time, *with* her permission.

Sophie gave her hair a final pat. "Have you the key to the back door, Bea?"

Beatrice hesitated, then pulled a large brass key from her pocket.

"I could kiss you." Sophie took the key and tucked it into her reticule.

Beatrice knit her brow with worry. "If you must go, I should go with you, miss."

Sophie bit back an exclamation. Beatrice standing in the corner of a dark tavern huffing in shock was unthinkable.

"That is impossible. A lady's companion doesn't have a companion, now does she? Do not fret. Mr. MacAlister is my escort."

"You still have your reputation to fret over. You are matched with a marquess, and he will not want a scandalous bride—"

"Bride?" Sophie shuddered. "There is naught to fear on that score, I assure you. Once Father discovers the man is no more interested in me than I am him, it's back home for us." She twirled, flaring her dress around her ankles. "Really, you worry far too much. I will return at a decent hour with no one the wiser." She flashed her most winning smile.

"If your father finds out, he will lock you in your room and dismiss me."

Sophie rolled her eyes. "Hush, Beatrice. Now, off you go. It is best you don't see me sneak away."

The girl flared her nostrils and, for a gut-wrenching moment, Sophie feared Beatrice would refuse. At last, she turned and walked from the room. No sooner had the door clicked shut, when Sophie tossed her reticule on a nearby chair and shrugged into the spencer. Beatrice was right. Should Sophie's father ever find out she sneaked out, he would lock her in her room. A sliver of guilt surfaced, and she paused in picking up her reticule. He wouldn't truly turn out Beatrice.

Would he? Nae. She had been with them since Sophie was thirteen. Beatrice was part of the family.

How could Sophie resist the excitement of Town—especially in the company of the tall, handsome Adam MacAlister? Butterflies skittered across the insides of her stomach at the memory of his hard chest when he'd yanked her against him on the street. There was something raw about Mr. MacAlister. Perhaps this was the difference between the refined gentlemen she associated with and the common folk? A strange sense of guilt niggled. Her father wanted to make her a lady, but common folk like her didn't belong in *Polite Society.*

Sophie shook off the confusion, eased open the door and stuck her head out into the dimly lit hallway. As expected, empty. She crept from the room and down the servants' stairs. Heart thudding, she reached the kitchen door, turned the knob, and stepped outside. Stars twinkled in a cloudless sky, and a bright moon cast long shadows over the garden as she continued toward the back gate. No sooner had she clicked the latch behind her and stepped out onto the cobblestoned lane than a shadow peeled itself from the stable wall to her right. She drew a sharp breath.

"Easy, lass." Mr. MacAlister stepped so close she could feel his heat. "Did I frighten you?"

She heard the amusement in his voice. "You will not talk me out of this night, sir."

He gave a low laugh. "Perish the thought."

He winged an elbow. She slipped her hand into the crook of his arm, and they started down the alley.

When they reached the street, he said, "I feared your mistress would prevent you from coming."

Sophie shook her head. "Nothing would stop me from this night, least of all Miss Shaw."

"Is she really so harsh a mistress?" Adam asked.

Something in his tone caught her attention. His voice sounded measured, almost as if his interest was…personal?

Here was her chance to get word to the marquess how difficult a wife Miss Shaw could be. "Indeed, she is. She's flighty and suffers from headaches. At times, she reminds me of a panicked hen."

"Typical female," he said in a near whisper.

"I beg your pardon. Not all women are the same, sir."

"A woman such as you, perhaps?" he asked.

"Not just me. I know plenty of women who are hearty and quite sensible."

He laughed. "Indeed? I should like to meet these ladies."

The idea of him wanting to meet other women pricked her pride. "Enough of me and Miss Shaw." *And other ladies,* she mentally added. "What of your master? Does he give you as much freedom as you wish?"

"Ah, the marquess." They stepped from the alley onto the sidewalk. "His lordship will soon bow out from gentle society and employ no one in the forthcoming weeks. I have all the freedom in the world."

Sophie halted. "Bow out of society? But why?"

"Have you not heard? The marquess's father lost all his money in a card game."

"And he expects to buy himself a wife?" Sophie couldn't disguise her shock.

"A title is a commodity, my dear."

"I do not think it is a fair trade, at all."

"Is that so?" he asked in a silky voice.

She looked up and met his gaze square. "I suppose you believe a woman should hand her money over to a stranger?"

"It is her father's money, if I understand correctly," he said.

She tried to pull her hand from his arm, but he held firm. She wanted to punch him.

"*Her* dowry," she said.

"A dowry her father is paying for."

She blew out a frustrated breath. "Oh, but you are rude."

He regarded her. "I have angered you."

The words were clearly meant to convey surprise, but she didn't believe he was surprised one little bit.

"You *meant* to anger me."

He turned his attention forward and released a breath. "You are right. I am rude. Forgive me."

Sophie hesitated. He didn't sound sincere, not exactly, at any rate. He sounded…sad. Had she done something to upset *him*? He'd said that once his master retired to the county that Adam would no longer be employed. That had to be the source of his upset.

"What will you do? Have you found employment?" she asked.

He steered her around another couple on the sidewalk. "I have yet to decide."

The melancholic undertone in his voice tugged at her heart. "Perhaps you can convince his lordship to keep you on. What will the marquess do when he withdraws from society?"

His attention remained forward. "Spend his wife's money, of course."

"Spend his wife's money?" Her heart began to pound. She'd been right. The marquess was nothing more than a fortune hunter sanctioned by society. "So, he does intend to marry? Miss Shaw will not marry him."

"You are so certain?"

"You said the marquess was not in favor of the match."

He gave a mirthless laugh. "That does not mean he will not marry her."

"If he plans to marry—anyone—why retire to the country? Does he expect his wife to languish in the country?" she asked.

"Is Miss Shaw not from the country?" Adam asked.

"That does not mean she wishes to live there forever."

She did, in fact, plan on living at her home in the country forever, but that didn't mean she wanted a husband who would abandon her. She suspected this notion of living in the country was a ruse on the marquess's part to make her think he wanted a country life when, what he truly intended was to install *her* in the country so that he could go on just as he always had in the city.

"Is the marquess so cruel as to force his wife to live in the country?" she demanded.

"Cruel?" He said the word as if tasting it. "He has been called many things, but never cruel."

"He's been called many things? Such as?" She winced inwardly at the obvious curiosity in her voice.

He looked down at her. "Why? Has your mistress sent you to spy on him?"

A beam of moonlight caught his face and for a moment, she stared at the beauty of his face. Glittering eyes, a square jaw… full lips. Masculine perfection.

He lifted a brow.

She blinked. It took her a moment to recall his question. "Spy?" Hadn't she asked him a similar question? "Hardly," she said. "Miss Shaw scarcely spares the man a thought. She's obligated only to meet him at the ball and dance two dances. Beyond that, she doesn't care to think of him. Why should she? She will *not* marry him."

"Has she ever met him?" he asked.

"She does not have to meet him. He is a fortune hunter."

To her surprise, he laughed, deep and rich. The sound caused her stomach to do a somersault.

"Perhaps Miss Shaw has a brain after all," he said. She started to reply that Miss Shaw had more of a brain than did the marquess, but he gently squeezed her hand, and said, "But why are we speaking of them? Is not this night ours?"

She'd never heard a man speak with such a…smoky quality

to his voice. The weakness in her knees caught her off guard and she stumbled. He caught her to his side. She snapped her head up and met his gaze.

He frowned. "Are you well?"

She nodded, unable to speak. Laughter danced in his eyes. Embarrassment warmed her cheeks. He was laughing at her.

Sophie pushed away, and he released her. "A crack in the sidewalk," she said.

"What?"

"The sidewalk." She motioned to the sidewalk. "I stumbled on a crack."

He glanced at the walkway, then looked back at her. "How fortunate for me."

The man was a rogue! She turned her attention forward and they began walking again. A carriage drove past, its interior lit with twinkling lanterns that illuminated its singing occupants.

"Do you think they're headed to the oyster party?" she asked. Her voice sounded breathless and she hoped he attributed her tone to the excitement of attending the party. "I wonder who will be there."

"Who they are remains a mystery at Luckie's, lass," he said. "That is the beauty of the oyster cellars. Edinburgh's fashionable lay down their titles at the door." He grasped her hand. "Let's take a shortcut, shall we?"

Sophie nodded and tried to ignore the warmth of his long fingers gripping hers. He pulled her through a cobbled square and down several narrow, twisting lanes. Laughter and song echoed from the alleys as they passed. Within minutes, they emerged onto the street where Luckie's tavern lay directly ahead. As they arrived, three more carriages trundled down the street to join the line forming in front of the building. A small crowd of partygoers chatted in front of the tavern, men dressed in elegantly cut coats topped off with intricately tied cravats, and women wearing fine evening gowns of taffeta and shimmering silk. Lords and ladies, all of them.

Sophie couldn't hide the bounce of excitement in her step. "I cannot believe I am here."

"You are, indeed, here," he said with a wink.

He placed his hand against the small of her back and guided her through the crowd. Once or twice, she thought someone called his name, but his gaze remained straight ahead. They ducked inside the tavern.

Smoke hung heavy in the air as they continued deeper into the tavern's gloomy interior. Men and women sat around rough-hewn tables and drank from pewter mugs while muffled music emanated from somewhere below. Adam hurried her through the taproom where the music and the din of conversation grew louder. At the back, in front of a door, a young man with a full brown beard sat on a barrel. When Adam and Sophie stopped, the man held out his hand. Adam dropped a coin into the man's hand, and he waved them through.

"After you." Adam stood aside and motioned her to precede him. "Have a care. The steps are steep."

Sophie peered through the opening at a dimly lit flight of stairs that descended into the cellar. She gathered her skirts in one hand and began down the stairs, with Adam close behind.

Halfway down, she wrinkled her nose at the smell of oysters and damp earth. The music and drone of people talking and laughing grew louder. She stepped from the last stair onto the dirt floor and glanced around. Men and women chatted around a long table that ran down the center of the room. Brass candlesticks, platters of oysters, and mugs of porter lay scattered over its rough-hewn surface. Several musicians sat in the corner and played a lively tune.

Adam lightly touched her back, guiding her forward. She took her seat on a simple chair near the far end of the table, and Adam sat to her right. A woman dressed in a dark blue gown took the set next to her.

A woman with long blonde hair swept into a soft chignon darted over to join them. "Adam? Why, Adam, it *is* you," she said in a loud voice. "It's been far too long."

"Ah, Ann." Adam stood and swept a low bow. "It is a pleasure to see you again." He stepped aside. "Beatrice, this is Ann."

Sophie began to dip into a curtsey, but Adam smoothly captured her arm and lifted her up. "There is no rank here, my dear. Such is the beauty of the oyster cellars."

Ann's laughter sounded like the tinkling of silver bells. "Indeed, here we may be as rude as we wish. Have you tried the Whiskered Pandores, Beatrice?" Ann scooped up one of the oysters still in its shell from the table and offered it to Sophie. "Edinburgh's finest."

Sophie accepted the shell and tipped it to her mouth. The oyster slipped between her lips, and she bit into it. Salt and a taste of the sea burst across her tongue. She swallowed then looked up at Adam in surprise.

"It is delicious," she said.

He stared down at her with eyes that glittered in the candlelight.

"Is something wrong?" She nearly had to shout the words to be heard over the din, yet her voice still managed to sound breathy.

He shook his head. "Not a thing."

The musicians struck up a Scottish reel. Sophie glanced at the musicians, then turned to Adam. "Oh, we must dance."

"We must?" he repeated in mock seriousness.

Sophie narrowed her eyes. "Indeed."

He closed his hand over hers, warm and oddly comforting, and he tugged her to her feet and toward the dancefloor. They reached the other dancers, and Adam swung her into his arms and stepped into the music as if a highborn gentleman.

Sophie startled at the hard body pressed so intimately close to hers. She'd danced reels, but a gentleman always held a lady at a respectable distance. How many times had she told Beatrice that she was no lady?

Watch what you ask for, a voice whispered. *You might just get it.*

Air whipped across her face, and her dress flared when Adam turned them in a tight twirl that made her dizzy. She closed her eyes and threw her head back. When Adam brought the turn to a halt and backed her up several paces, she opened her eyes to find him watching her as he executed another quick turn.

He skillfully dodged another couple, then pressed his mouth to her ear. "Does this evening live up to your expectations?"

She shivered at the warmth of his mouth against the sensitive flesh of her ear and nodded. "Even more so than I expected."

And the night had only just begun.

He whirled her close again. This time, she clung to him, for it felt as if they were twirling so fast, she would fly out of his arms. He tightened his hold on her, and she became aware of her breasts pressed against his chest. Her heart thundered. Here, at the oyster cellars, it mattered not if they danced more than two dances together—or if a man held a woman scandalously close. Did that mean no one would be aware of the warmth that spread through her? The music ended, and Adam slid his arm around her waist and led her back to their seats. Oysters were laid out before them, along with porter. Sophie ate and drank until she thought she would burst.

When Adam finally escorted her back to their table after their *third* dance, he asked if she thought it might be time to return home. In the dim recesses of her mind, she knew she'd danced the night away, but she didn't care.

Sophie shook her head. "Nae. I have never had so grand a time. Why would I want to leave?"

He smiled, clearly pleased with her answer. They sat down and, for the third time that night, a man stopped beside Sophie and asked her to dance. As Adam had the previous two times, he met the man's gaze with the lift of one brow, sending him away without another word. A thrill raced through Sophie. She had ever had a man act so possessively toward her. This truly was the most thrilling night of her life.

A tall, dark and very elegant woman—a lady, Sophie felt certain—halted where they sat, and faced Adam, her back to Sophie as she bent to whisper something in his ear. Sophie froze in lifting her glass of porter to her mouth. There was no mistaking the woman's slight toward Sophie. Had Adam been wrong when he said the partygoers left their titles at the door? They may have left their titles at the door, but the ladies wore fine gowns that bespoke of their place in society.

Embarrassment washed over Sophie. Her modest dress must have given her away as someone of the lower class. Oh, how she wished she had worn her fine sky-blue muslin. That dress would have put the rude woman in her place. Guilt stabbed. Since when had she cared about society? And when had she forgotten that it mattered not what dress she wore. She would always be the daughter of a man in trade.

The woman straightened and sauntered away without so much as a glance in Sophie's direction. How did a common man like Adam know such a fine lady? The answer came before the thought had fully formed. He was a handsome man—the most dashing man at the party. Handsome men were always in demand, no matter their class.

"Beatrice."

Sophie started from her thoughts at hearing Adam's voice.

He leaned close and still had to almost shout to be heard. "Are you all right?"

Her cheeks warmed, and she prayed any flush that might have appeared on her cheeks he would mistake as a reaction to the warm room.

"I am fine," she said.

He hesitated, as if uncertain, then motioned to the maid for more oysters and refills on their porter. Sophie ate and drank more, though her taste for the party had suddenly soured. She didn't ask him to dance again, and neither did he ask her. Were his thoughts on the fine lady? Had they made an assignation for later, after he rid himself of Sophie? She suddenly wanted to go home but couldn't think of how to tell him without arousing suspicion.

Suspicion of what? She didn't care if he met the woman. He could meet with a dozen women. Sophie opened her mouth to tell him she was ready to leave when a cheerful female voice cut through the air.

"There you are." Ann plopped down into a chair next to Sophie and leaned back with a sigh. "I fear I shall collapse from exhaustion." She groaned. "I shall have to be carried home. Already my feet protest at the mere thought of standing."

"Then I shall carry you to your coach," Adam said.

The stab of jealousy that seemed to pierce clear to Sophie's soul surprised her.

Ann laughed. "I wouldn't dream of taking you from your Beatrice's side, my dear lad." She nodded at a group of men clustered at the end of the near-empty oyster table. "That lot over there are wagering which one of them can win my attention for the evening." She leaned closer to Sophie. "I believe the lad to the far right is smitten with you. He is a fine male specimen. Do you not agree?"

Sophie coughed.

Adam shot Ann a narrow-eyed glance, then stood. "The hour is far too late. We should be going."

"Then carry me to my carriage, and I will give you a ride."

Ann fanned her cheeks. "But you'll *have* to carry me, chair and all. I fear I cannot move."

"I shall see you safely to your coach, but Beatrice and I shall walk in the moonlight," Adam politely said.

"Walk?" Ann shuddered. "Have you no fear of Major Weir?"

Adam snorted. "I have nothing to fear of your ghost tales."

Ghosts? Sophie glanced around the room. "Major Weir?"

"I heard the racket myself, on a night such as this," Ann said, clearly warming to her tale. "Nigh on a month ago. Before Hogmanay. I left the party before my husband and in only the company of my maid. We had not yet walked a dozen paces from the door when a great howling filled the air. Rumor has it, footpads set upon Major Weir and stabbed him to death. He mourns for he left behind a wife who was to bear him their first child."

"Utter nonsense," Adam said.

"You don't believe me?" Ann asked, a challenge in her voice.

"That sounds thrilling," Sophie said in breathless wonder.

"I quite like you, Beatrice." Ann patted Sophie's hand. "Perhaps I will meet you at the theater? It's not London, but it's better than nothing. Now, I must be going." With a laugh, she sprang to her feet and skipped across the dance floor with no difficulty at all.

"Who is she?" Sophie asked. "She's such a delightful soul."

"Remember, here we leave rank behind," Adam said.

Sophie's heart sank. The partygoers might leave their titles at the door, but they still had them.

Adam grasped her arm and pulled her to her feet, then led her across the room. They had nearly reached the stairs when a woman halted directly in their path. The woman was everything Sophie wasn't. Tall and fair with a willowy figure to make the angels cry, and a grace she must have inherited from Aphrodite herself. Sophie suddenly felt like a twelve-year-old girl pretending to be a woman. Adam met the woman's gaze, and all the warmth in his expression vanished.

"Adam," she said in a husky voice Sophie was certain would drive men wild.

He grasped Sophie's hand and pulled her forward. She stumbled. Adam shot his arm around her waist and yanked her to his side. She snapped her head up. His gaze remained straight ahead, his mouth a thin line as he continued toward the stairs. Upon reaching them, he urged her ahead of him. Sophie took two steps, looked back at him, and caught sight of the woman, who shifted her gaze from Adam to Sophie. Adam stepped up onto the stair beneath Sophie and blocked her view. She looked down at him, but in the dim light she discerned only shadows. Another couple halted at the bottom of the stairs. Adam gently urged Sophie to continue upward.

They reached the upper level, and Adam pushed open the door and allowed her to precede him. Sophie stepped out into the cool night. The clear sky allowed the moon to shine brightly. A chill wind whipped the tendrils of her hair that had come free of its pins. Carriages waiting for their owners formed a line three blocks long. Patrons of the oyster cellar exited and headed toward their carriages. Adam placed Sophie's hand in the crook of his arm, and she allowed him to steer her around a small group, then began walking toward home.

Sophie looked out of the side of her eye at him. He still had his mouth pressed into a thin line. Curiosity burned hot. Who was the woman to have so quickly changed his mood from carefree to…what? Dark? Dare she ask him about the woman? Did she really want the answer? It was clear the woman meant something to him—or once did, at any rate—and things hadn't ended well. Sophie recalled the look on the woman's face when she'd stared at Adam. She had seemed…curious.

"Sophie? Sophie? Is that you?"

Sophie jarred at hearing a woman call her name.

"Sophie?"

Sophie tensed. She would know that high pitched nasally voice anywhere. Jane Goodman, an Englishwoman with a voracious taste for gossip. Sophie ducked her head and quickened her pace.

"What is amiss?" Adam demanded.

"Amiss?" Sophie winced inwardly. She would have thought him too much in his dark mood to notice her.

They turned the corner as she racked her brain for a response. Sophie slowed at sight of three women standing on the street corner.

"I don't recall a river here this morning," one said on a gasp as she pointed to the shadow cast by the church steeple across the street.

The women tottered back a step, giggling behind their hands.

"Can we wade across it?" one asked.

Sophie couldn't repress a laugh.

"You can wade across," Adam called out. "It's not too deep."

"You are certain?" the first woman asked.

"I am," he replied with deep gravity.

The women sat on the sidewalk, and Sophie and Adam stared as they took off their shoes and stockings. They scrambled back to their feet, hiked up their skirts, and began to pick their way across the street.

"The respectable dames clearly had a little too much to drink," Adam murmured.

"I hope they don't forget to put their shoes back on," Sophie said as the women continued down the sidewalk on the other side.

Adam remained silent, and Sophie found she could think of nothing else to say. She'd been convinced Adam had enjoyed her company during the party, but it was now clear she had been nothing but a distraction. Isn't that what he was? It wasn't as if she intended to see him again once she returned home. But that was different than using someone to forget a past love. Wasn't it?

"Perhaps I should take a hackney the rest of the way," Sophie said.

He looked down at her and frowned. Then his expression cleared. "I am ignoring you. Forgive me."

"There is nothing to forgive. We have had a lovely time, and you must be tired."

"Not at all," he replied. "Besides, it isn't safe for a lady alone, even in a hackney."

She laughed. "Lady? I'm no lady. I'm a lady's companion."

"Being a lady has a great deal more to do with a woman's morals and virtue than it does money, lass. You are a lady. I will escort you home. If you tire of my company, I will remain quiet."

She groaned. "Please, no. That is exactly what I wish to avoid. I suppose I shouldn't complain. I had a grand time tonight." She simply hadn't expected the night to end on such a low note.

They turned down Lacy Street, and Sophie halted under the meager light of the streetlamp. "Oh dear," she said.

Adam stopped and turned toward her. "What is wrong?"

"The river runs deep here, does it not?" She waved a hand in the direction of the street as a carriage slowly passed.

Adam frowned. "What?"

Sophie looked up at him. "I suppose I could take off my shoes like the other ladies did."

For a moment, Adam stared at her, then he arched his brows. "Shall I carry you across?"

Her pulsed leapt. She hadn't expected *that* response. Before she could reply, he swept her into his arms. Sophie gasped and threw her arms around his neck. Adam stepped from the sidewalk onto the street, then dodged a passing hackney. Sophie buried her head in his neck when he stumbled and seemed he would fall. The musky scent of masculine soap assailed her, and she had the strange desire to press her lips against the saltiness of his skin. What would he do if she kissed him?

"Fear not, my lady," he said. "I shall fight the monstrous current and set you safely down on the other side."

Sophie turned her head slightly with the intention of sneaking a peek at him, but he halted as he reached the far sidewalk and looked down at her. He stared, his features in shadow, and she tensed with anticipation when he lowered his head toward hers, but then he released her legs, and Sophie found herself standing on her own two feet. When Adam stepped away, she could have sworn a chill air whipped past.

"Are you well?" he asked.

She jumped at the sound of his voice. "Yes, very well, thank you."

Sophie faced home and began walking. Adam fell into step alongside her. The townhouse came into view up ahead, dark and silent. They continued past the front gate, around the street to the alley behind the house. This time, he escorted her through the back garden and all the way to the kitchen door.

Sophie fished the key from her reticule. She unlocked the door, then dropped the key back into her reticule and faced Adam. "Thank you for escorting me."

To her relief, he smiled. "It was my pleasure." He executed a small bow that reminded her too much of the gentlemen her father threw into her path. "Good evening, Miss Beatrice Frasier. I shall look forward to our next meeting." He backed up a step.

"When will that be?"

He halted, and her cheeks warmed. Had she been too forward?

"We shall see, I suppose," he replied.

"I have always wanted to see the wharfs."

"Beatrice..." His voice held warning.

"I know. It is not safe for a woman alone. I will be ready at seven tomorrow evening."

Before he could reply, she slipped inside and closed the door. She waited a long moment, heart pounding in anticipation of his knock on the door, but none came.

Sophie released a slow breath and headed up the servants' stairs to her room.

CHAPTER 9

Fury rammed through Adam. He hadn't seen Lena since the night after his father shot himself. The anger that had surfaced when he'd seen her tonight had caught him off guard. He'd been angrier seeing her at the oyster cellars than he had the night she told him his father had lost his fortune in her gambling hall. He needed to get as far away from Lady Lena Fleming as possible. He would never be able to forget her betrayal, but he would be able to busy himself, so he didn't think of her as often as he did.

Adam stepped from the alley out onto the walkway. He strode to the corner, stepped aside for a man and woman, then hurried across the street. It had been a mistake to take Beatrice to the oyster cellar. He blew out a frustrated breath. She would have gone with or without him. He wouldn't see her again. Oddly, the thought bothered him. Perhaps—

He cut off the thought. He was a fool. Even a lady's companion deserved more than he had to give. She would be hurt. He could see that in her eyes—but she would be far more hurt if she learned of his ruse.

He silently cursed. If he married Miss Shaw, Beatrice would

learn of his true identity. Adam turned left at the intersection and leapt up on the curb just in time to miss the carriage that turned the corner. One more reason not to marry Miss Shaw.

The tension in his shoulders eased slightly. Other than running into Lena, he had enjoyed himself. Beatrice was a delightful companion. She was more than that, if he was honest. She was a breath of fresh air. The fact she was beautiful didn't hurt.

Mrs. Latimer's boarding house came into view up ahead. A man stood in front of the gate. Adam slowed. Was that Nicholas? By thunder it was. There could be only one reason the earl would need to speak with him at this late hour. Adam considered turning and walking back the way he'd come, but Nick waved. Adam sighed and continued forward.

"Adam," Nick said, when Adam reached him.

"I am in no mood to talk marriage," Adam said.

"You will be when you hear this. Mr. Shaw's solicitor has sent the marriage contract."

Adam shot him a narrow-eyed glance and opened the gate leading to the house. Nick hurried to catch up as Adam strode up the walkway. The front door burst open, and two men hurried out. They brushed past Adam and Nick. Adam reached the door and, of course, Nicholas followed Adam up the stairs to his room.

Once inside, Nick said, "Once the contract is signed—"

"I do not care if the man is offering to buy me a stable full of horses. I have no wish to marry that dour woman."

Nick frowned. "What the devil are you talking about?" Adam started to reply, but Nick waved him off. "You will receive twenty thousand pounds upon signing the contract."

Adam blinked "You cannot be serious?"

The earl nodded. "That isn't all. On your wedding day, you receive another twenty thousand pounds."

Adam dropped onto the chair beside the table. "My God,

that is equivalent to five years income on the property outside of Edinburgh that my father lost."

"There is more," Nicholas said. "Upon the birth of your heir, you will receive another twenty thousand pounds, and ten thousand pounds for every other child girl or boy."

Adam stared. "Bloody hell, the man has more money than most of the peerage. How is that possible?"

Nick laughed. "It is not all that difficult when you consider that he is a very astute businessman, and he doesn't squander his money like most in the peerage. Of course, it doesn't hurt that he has no wife to spend his money."

Adam couldn't believe it. Forty thousand pounds. If he was frugal, he could run the estate for ten years and buy more horses. With every child born, he would receive even more. He'd always wanted children. Lena had said she would consider children, but he always knew that if she became pregnant, there was a good chance he would never know. When his father lost his wealth and killed himself, Adam's dream for family died with him. Now—

His mind screeched to a halt. He would have to sell his soul to obtain his dream. Was Miss Shaw really that bad? After all, he'd planned to marry Lena, a woman who traded him for his father's fortune. Miss Shaw certainly couldn't be any worse. Beatrice had said Miss Shaw was not in favor of the marriage. It seemed she had no more wish to be sold into marriage than did he. Could he spend his life with the woman who didn't want him? Perhaps he could get more information from Beatrice. Nae, he couldn't use her that way. It was a damn shamed Beatrice wasn't Miss Shaw.

"I can see the logic of the situation is finally becoming clear."

Nick's voice intruded on his thoughts.

Adam shook his head. "That is an obscene amount of money."

"You almost sound offended. Oh, I see," Nick said before Adam could reply. "You're angry that you are considering the proposition." His friend pinned Adam with a hard look. "I hate to be blunt, but few women could be worse than Lady Fleming."

"Perhaps. But there are plenty of women just as bad."

Nick laughed. "Not Miss Shaw. Come now, Adam, do you believe I would urge you into a union with anyone but a woman of the finest character?"

"I saw her."

Nick frowned. "What?"

"The day she arrived. I happened to be walking on Lacy Street as she descended her carriage. The frown on her face was clear as day and could have made even the angels run."

"I didn't know Miss Shaw was capable of frowning. She is a delightful young woman. A bit of a hoyden, but nothing you cannot handle. She is young, only twenty. But—"

"A hoyden? I believe you have mistaken Miss Shaw for her lady's companion, Miss Frasier."

"I grant you, I have only seen Miss Shaw and Miss Frasier once—no, twice—at parties. They look a great deal alike, but—" Nick raised his brows. "How do you know Beatrice?"

Adam snorted. "The little baggage was wearing breeches and riding a fine Friesian mare."

"Beatrice wearing breeches?" Nicholas shook his head. "She would never do such a thing. Sophie's father once commented that Beatrice acts more the lady than does his daughter. No, my friend, you have the two confused."

"Nick, I have spoken with the woman. I promise you, I am not mistaken. I—" Adam broke off and stared at his friend.

"What is it?" Nick demanded.

"Bloody hell," Adam muttered.

He *did* have the two women confused. He felt certain, however, Miss Sophie Shaw knew exactly who he was.

CHAPTER 10

Murky images floated before Sophie. She discerned broad shoulders and became aware of a warm palm sliding upward on her thigh. A familiar scent surrounded her.

Adam.

Desire tightened her belly. His body came down upon her and crushed her into the mattress in the delicious way that only a man's weight can. She slid her arms about his neck and wrapped her legs around his waist. Oh, it had been so long since she'd been close to a man. His warm breath bathed her neck, and she shivered. In the murky darkness of her room—

Were they in her room? Something felt unfamiliar.

He reached between them and slipped into her wet channel. His thumb brushed her sex—

Sophie cried out and snapped her eyes open. Morning sunlight streamed into her bedroom. She jammed her eyes shut against the sudden intrusion. She'd been dreaming of Adam. She hadn't dreamt of a man since Matthew, and her dreams of Matthew hadn't been so vivid or…sensual.

She drew in a deep breath, the juncture between her legs throbbing in rhythm with her pounding heart. Adam was to accompany her to the wharf that evening. Her face heated. How would she face him after that dream?

Her heart slowed, and Sophie opened her eyes. She didn't have to tell Adam she'd dreamt of him. She was a widow. It wasn't strange for a woman of the world to dream of a man. Was it? But the dream wasn't really the problem. The problem was, she found him desirable.

Sophie threw back the covers. So, he was desirable. She wasn't the schoolgirl she'd been when she met Matthew. She could find a man desirable and still keep him at bay. Adam was the perfect escort and she very much wanted to visit the wharf. In particular, she wanted to visit the wharf with him.

She forced her thoughts to what lay ahead for the day and grimaced. This afternoon, she had to attend a dull party. It would be her first social engagement, but she had no interest in attending parties. She wanted to see Edinburgh—all of Edinburgh.

A soft knock sounded on the door, then Beatrice entered, a tray with hot chocolate and biscuits in hand. "Good morning, miss." She set the tray on the bed beside Sophie.

Sophie drew in deep of the sweet scent of chocolate and biscuits.

"How are you feeling this morning, miss?" Beatrice asked.

Sophie pushed to a sitting position. "I feel excellent, Bea. I had a wonderful time last night." She took a small sip of the hot chocolate. "I half expected you to be here to scold me when I returned."

Beatrice picked up the pillow to Sophie's left, then gently eased her forward and placed the pillow behind her. "If I had waited in your room, that might have given away your secret."

"Ah," Sophie said with a sage nod. She sipped more of her chocolate.

"Your aunt will be out for the day."

"Out for the day. That means I need not attend the card party."

Beatrice shook her head. "Your aunt has instructed her driver to take us to the party. She was very specific this morning before she left."

"Aunt Maddie spoke with you this morning?"

"She did."

"Her driver, you say?" Sophie asked.

"Miss, I suggest you do not underestimate your aunt. If you try to get out of going to this party, she will discover the truth."

Sophie took a bite of the biscuit. "You are right, of course. It isn't worth the risk that she might prevent me from seeing Mr. MacAlister tonight."

"Tonight?" Beatrice blurted. "Surely, you are not seeing him *again*?"

Sophie laughed. "Of course I'm seeing him again. I will see him every night, if possible."

Beatrice's eyes widened. "You cannot spend so much time alone with a gentleman. They will have…expectations."

"He may have all the expectations he likes," Sophie said with an airy wave of her hand. He did have a few, she suspected. "I have no intention of succumbing to passion." Despite her dreams. "Though a kiss or two would be nice."

"That is always how it starts," Beatrice said. "A woman thinks a kiss or two would be nice. The next thing you know, her father is challenging the man to a dawn appointment."

Sophie took another bite of her biscuit and rolled her eyes. "There will be no dawn appointment. That is far too dramatic for my liking. I want to see Edinburgh, and Mr. MacAlister is the perfect guide."

"Surely, the marquess would love to be your guide?"

Sophie grimaced. "I have no desire to fend off the attention of a man who would like nothing better than to force me into marriage by getting me with child."

"Good heavens, what makes you think he would do that? I thought Mr. MacAlister said the marquess doesn't want to marry."

Sophie snorted. "The marquess is desperate for money. Such men cannot be trusted."

"You don't want children?" Beatrice asked.

Sophie wrinkled her nose. "Aunt Maddie never married and had children. Look at the gay life she lives." Beatrice opened her mouth to reply, and Sophie cut her off. "Never mind. I will attend the card party. Then, this evening, I will slip out and meet Mr. MacAlister."

THAT AFTERNOON AT PRECISELY TWELVE O'CLOCK, THEIR carriage halted in front of a large three-story townhouse.

Sophie peered out the window and sighed. "I would rather be with Mr. MacAlister."

Heaven help her. Was she actually developing a *tendre* for him? That could be dangerous.

"Perhaps the party will be amusing," Beatrice said.

The carriage swayed slightly as the driver leapt from his seat to the ground. An instant later, he opened the door and helped first Sophie, then Beatrice from the carriage.

"Thank you, Mr. Jones," Sophie said. "I believe we will be no more than two hours."

Beatrice shook her head. "Two hours? That will be just after lunch. Your aunt said Lady Ella planned games until teatime. Then we will have tea."

"I have no intention of wasting an afternoon playing games," Sophie said. "Two o'clock please, Mr. Jones."

He bowed. "As you wish, miss."

Sophie turned with Beatrice and started up the walkway toward the house. As they ascended the three steps to the door, the door opened, and a tall woman dressed in a gray dress greeted them.

"Miss Shaw, I presume?" the woman said.

Sophie nodded. "Aye, and this is my companion, Miss Frasier."

The woman angled her head in acknowledgement. "Lady Ella and her guests are in the Gold drawing room. Please follow me."

Sophie followed with Beatrice at her side. They entered the house and Sophie's attention caught on the ornate mahogany table to the left of the door, where sat two lamps and an ornate silver candelabra, polished to blinding brightness. They followed the woman down the hallway. Sophie glimpsed a room she guessed to be a study, with a large oak desk and shelves of books. Portraits hung on the walls, and she recognized Lady Ella's grandfather, the late earl. He had once attended a party Sophie's father hosted when her mother still lived.

They ascended one flight of stairs and continued down a long hallway then turned a corner. Doors to a room at the far end of the hallway stood open. The pianoforte Sophie glimpsed was enough to confirm that Lady Ella's family was quite wealthy. Maybe even wealthier than her father. Perhaps Lady Ella would be a good candidate for marriage to the marquess. Aunt Maddie had said the girl was an only child. Surely, she would like to be a marchioness?

They reached the drawing room where a dozen men and women milled about the room. An unusually tall, pretty blonde surrounded by four other women looked their way and her face lit. She said something to the women, who also looked in their direction, then she glided across the room toward them.

When she reached them, she said to Sophie, "You must be Miss Shaw."

Sophie gave a small curtsey. Beatrice followed suit.

The young woman laughed. "We'll have none of that. I am Ella." She extended a hand and Sophie grasped her hand, surprised when Lady Ella gave a firm handshake.

Sophie released her and angled her head toward Beatrice. "This is my friend Miss Frasier."

To Sophie's surprise, Lady Ella extended her hand toward Beatrice.

Beatrice accepted and they shook hands. "My lady."

"Ella," she corrected.

Beatrice looked at Sophie, eyes wide. Sophie bit back a laugh and gave a slight nod.

Beatrice looked back at the woman. "Ella."

Ella smiled. "There now. Come, let me introduce you to everyone."

She began with the four women she'd been talking to when Sophie and Beatrice had arrived. Slowly, they made their way through the room. By the time Ella had introduced them to everyone, Sophie had decided she liked the girl.

Ella next fed them meat pies, cakes and lemonade, which Sophie thoroughly enjoyed. She felt certain Beatrice also secretly enjoyed the food for she asked for seconds. They played two hands of whist—which was torture for Sophie. For others, as well, she suspected, as the room was too quiet.

She now sat with Beatrice on a small sofa near the French doors, which opened onto a lawn. Sophie glanced at the mantle clock. One fory-five. Thank heavens. Their driver would arrive within the quarter hour. He likely was already waiting for them.

Two women sat on the couch opposite them.

"I hear he has his eye on a very wealthy heiress," said the dark-haired woman. "I am certain she will capitulate, whoever she is, for Lord Monthemer is terribly handsome."

Sophie tensed.

"But there was that scandal with Lady Fleming," the other woman said.

"Scandal always follows attractive men," the first woman replied.

Sophie glanced at Beatrice, then leaned forward slightly. "Forgive me, but I couldn't help overhearing your conversation. I, too, heard that Lord Monthemer was on the hunt for a wife."

The women exchanged a look, then nodded. "He is penniless, so he needs an heiress."

"You have no idea who he has in mind?" Sophie asked.

Both women shook their heads and the fair-haired woman said, "I did hear he made an offer, but I have no idea who the lucky lady is."

Lucky lady, indeed, Sophie thought, but said, "What is this scandal with Lady Fleming."

"We ought not to tell tales," the dark-haired woman said.

"Well, it was a year ago," said the fair-haired woman. "And the incident is common knowledge." She leaned forward a little. "You see, Lord Monthemer was to marry Lady Fleming. However, Lady Fleming owned the gaming hall where Lord Monthemer's father lost their fortune."

Sophie blinked. "Lord Monthemer's betrothed owned a gaming hall, and…."

The two women nodded.

This was the man her father wanted her to marry? Did her father know of this scandal? He couldn't know.

"The old earl shot himself two days later," the dark-haired woman said.

Sophie drew a sharp breath. "That is…terrible."

She hadn't known any of this story. Was Lady Fleming a true lady? What lady owned a gaming hall? What kind of man wanted to marry a woman like that? His father lost his fortune, then shot himself. She knew such things happened but had never known anyone who had faced such a tragedy.

The clock on the mantle gently chimed, and Sophie realized the two o'clock hour had arrived. It was time she and Beatrice leave. Lady Ella approached as Sophie and Beatrice stood.

"Let us take a walk in the garden," Ella said as she neared them. "Perhaps the fresh air will invigorate us."

"That is kind of you," Sophie said. "However, our driver awaits us."

Ella frowned and glanced in the direction of the clock. "You have been here less than two hours." A twinkle appeared in her eyes. "That does not quite satisfy an afternoon visit."

Sophie blinked. Was the girl threatening to tell Sophie's aunt if Sophie left so early?

Lady Ella linked arms with Sophie. "Come, a walk will do us good."

The other guests rose, and Sophie sighed and allowed herself to be led from the room and through the open French doors. Autumn sun beat down upon them, and Sophie breathed deep of the crisp air. She looked over her shoulder at Beatrice and motioned for her to come up on Sophie's left. Beatrice shook her head and maintained a short distance behind.

Sophie faced forward and, an instant later, they reached bushes a head taller than her. "Is this a maze?" she asked in delight.

"Indeed, it is," Lady Ella replied.

"I have never been in a maze."

"Then you are in for a treat," her host said.

Half a dozen of the guests brushed past them and disappeared around the bend.

"They seem in a hurry," Sophie said.

Lady Ella laughed. "My guess is they have a wager who can reach the other side of the maze first."

Sophie looked at her. "Is the maze really that difficult?"

"That depends on who you ask. I grew up here, so I know the maze well. Though Father does have the pattern changed on occasion."

"Really? Why?"

"I think he does it to peeve my mother."

"Oh dear," Sophie said. "That doesn't sound good."

"I do not know," Ella replied with a small laugh. "I think they like to irk each other."

Sophie wasn't sure what to make of that, so said nothing.

"How are you finding Edinburgh?" Ella asked.

Sophie thought of last night, the oyster cellar and Adam MacAlister. "I am finding Edinburgh quite wonderful."

Lady Ella looked down at her. "Indeed? What have you done since you arrived?"

Sophie recognized the curiosity in her eyes and hid a smile. Lady Ella had a taste for mischief. They would get along famously. Of course, Sophie wouldn't mention her escapades with Mr. MacAlister.

Sophie grimaced. "To be honest, my aunt has had me busy with fittings and preparations for the social life she has planned for me."

"Such as this luncheon?" Lady Ella asked with no little amusement.

They turned the bend, and Sophie cried out in surprise at the sight of the intersection that led in three different directions. They stopped.

"Which way is out?" she asked.

"Don't you want to find out for yourself?"

Beatrice stopped beside Sophie.

Sophie looked at Ella and narrowed her eyes. "I believe you inherited your parents' love of irking people."

Ella laughed. "I am a slave to my family bloodline."

Sophie tossed her head. "Beatrice and I will find our way

out. Come, Beatrice," she said, and started down the path directly ahead.

Fifteen minutes later, Sophie had to own that they were hopelessly turned around.

"Surely we can retrace our steps?" Beatrice asked.

"We said that five minutes ago," Sophie said.

Laughter wafted to them from somewhere to the left.

"Hello!" Sophie called.

The laughter quickly grew fainter, and Sophie had the suspicion that Lady Ella had instructed the others not to aid her. Sophie peered through the bushes to the right and glimpsed another pathway on the other side of what had to be at least ten feet of foliage.

"They must be around here somewhere," a woman said.

Lady Ella.

So, she had finally come in search of her and Beatrice.

Sophie strained her ears in an effort to discern the direction of Ella's voice.

"I had no idea you wanted to meet her," Lady Ella said.

"Seems Lord Monthemer is full of surprises these days," a man said.

Sophie froze. Lord Monthemer? Here?

"I will go to the left, you take the right," the man said.

Sophie broke from her stupor. She recognized that voice. Lord Blair. So, his matchmaking didn't end with informing her father that Lord Monthemer wanted to marry her. But why—

Bootfalls on the gravel walkway approached. They came from up ahead.

"Should I find her first, I will let her know you are looking for her," Lady Ella said.

"I prefer that you don't, El," another man said.

Sophie barely stifled a gasp.

Adam MacAlister? Yes, she would know his voice anywhere. What was he doing here?

Ella laughed. "A little wickedness, Adam?"

"Now off with you, Ella," he said.

The crunch of gravel grew louder.

Oh Lord! Sophie spun to face Beatrice and yanked her close. "The Marquess of Monthemer is headed this way—along with Adam MacAlister." Sophie ignored Beatrice's frown. "You must pretend to be me. Do everything you can to discourage the marquess."

Beatrice's eyes widened. "I cannot—"

"Hush," Sophie said in a harsh whisper. "Mr. MacAlister is with him. He knows me as—well, *you*. I cannot be discovered."

Sophie's thoughts skidded to a halt. Oh dear, would Lord Blair recognize Beatrice? Sophie racked her brain. She had never met Lord Blair, had she? She had met his wife…. Oh, she had no time to think.

"Do as I say, Bea." Before Beatrice could reply, Sophie plunged into the foliage.

"Miss," Beatrice called.

Sophie fought her way through the thick bushes until she reached what she estimated to be about five of the ten feet width of the bushes, then halted, heart thundering in her ears.

"Oh, how do you do, sir—er, I mean, my lord," Beatrice said.

"Miss—"

"Shaw," Beatrice said in a shaky voice that Sophie feared would give poor Beatrice away."

"Miss Shaw?" Adam MacAlister spoke.

"Y-yes, sir—my lord."

Sophie's head spun. God help them, they were sure to get caught with Beatrice bumbling things so. How could she help Beatrice?

By not getting caught.

Beatrice might be nervous, but she would never betray Sophie by admitting she wasn't Miss Shaw. That meant, as long as they didn't discover Sophie's presence, Lord Monthemer would have to accept that Beatrice was Sophie Shaw. Well, that is, so long as Lord Blair didn't realize Beatrice wasn't her. Sophie and Beatrice did look a lot alike.

Carefully, Sophie eased through the bushes. A branch scraped her leg, and she barely missed another branch that slipped from her grasp and snapped back near her eye. She stifled a cry and finally stepped out onto the path on the other side. She looked down at her dress. One long tear bared her left calf. That must have happened when she plunged into the bushes. Other small tears had left small openings, but she was respectable enough to at least try to reach her carriage. But which way was out?

Sophie turned and nearly cried out with relief upon seeing the path open onto lawn. She hurried forward and, a moment later, caught sight of the house to the left, beyond the lawn and garden. She couldn't go through the house. Her torn dress would raise too many questions, and Beatrice and the marquess could show up at any time. She looked to the right and hurried toward the gate at the far end of the garden. That had to be the door for deliveries.

Ten minutes later, Sophie reached her carriage, which sat parked outside Lady Ella's house as expected. Sophie opened the carriage door. The driver twisted in his seat and his eyes widened. He leapt from his seat to the ground so quickly that Sophie halted in stepping into the carriage. He hurried to her side.

"What happened, miss?" He looked around for what she wagered were the people he feared had accosted her.

"I am fine, Mr. Jones."

"But, miss, you are *not* fine." His focus locked onto the tear at her calf, then he jerked his gaze up to her face. "Your aunt will be furious, miss."

"Never fear, Mr. Jones, I took a tumble into the bushes."

He frowned. "Are you sure? If—"

A door opened, and Sophie didn't wait to see who was exiting Lady Ella's house. "I am fine, Mr. Jones." She nearly jumped into the carriage and pulled the door shut.

She caught the murmur of voices and a horrible thought struck. What if the marquess insisted on escorting Beatrice to the carriage? Sophie strained to discern the voices but her heart beat so hard all she could hear was the blood pounding through her ears. She looked wildly around inside the carriage as if she could locate some nook in which to hide. She spotted the folded blanket sitting on the opposite cushion. She grabbed it and flung it open, then wrapped it around her shoulders and reached for the door facing the road. Hand on the lever, she jumped when the other door opened. Sophie jerked her head around as Beatrice stepped up into the carriage.

"Quickly, Mr. Jones," Beatrice said in a breathless voice.

Mr. Jones caught Sophie's gaze, then closed the door. Sophie dropped back onto her seat as Beatrice sat on the opposite side. The vehicle listed slightly as Mr. Jones climbed back into his perch then, an instant later, the carriage lurched into motion.

"What happened?" Sophie demanded.

Beatrice exhaled a loud breath. "That Lord Monthemer is a man to be reckoned with."

"What does that mean?"

"It means, I am certain he knows."

Sophie rolled her eyes. "Don't be ridiculous. He cannot know you are not me. Unless—Lady Ellis did not tell him?"

Beatrice shook her head and waved her hand dismissively. "Lady Ella was not there. Another man was there, Nicholas someone or another."

"Lord Blair," Sophie said. "Oh, he did not say you weren't me?"

Beatrice shook her head. "Nae. But that does not signify.

Lord Monthemer stared at me as if he were studying me under a microscope. He knows, I tell you."

Sophie collapsed back onto the cushion. "Oh, Bea, you goose. He was acting like that because he is trying to decide whether or not he should marry you." The carriage swayed and she leaned forward again. "Did you make yourself disagreeable?"

Beatrice stared. "Disagreeable? Why would I do that? All I could think about was getting away from him as quickly as possible."

"That is a shame," Sophie said. "Oh! How did you get away from him?"

"I told him I needed a moment in the ladies' retiring room."

Sophie's mouth fell open. "You mean, he is still waiting for you to return?"

Beatrice shrugged. "By now, he likely knows I left."

"That was terribly rude, Beatrice," Sophie murmured.

"Do you think so?"

"Indeed, I do." Sophie slapped her leg. "That is wonderful. No man will want to marry a woman who left him waiting with the excuse that she needed to visit the ladies' retiring room."

CHAPTER 11

To Sophie's relief, her aunt did not return home that evening. Still, she was taking no chances.

"Off with that dress," Sophie told Beatrice after she had dressed to leave with Adam.

Beatrice frowned. "Is something wrong with my dress, miss?"

"Not at all." Sophie spun her around and began unbuttoning the buttons.

Beatrice twisted, then whirled to face her. She backed up two paces. "You cannot mean—"

"You will sleep in my bed until I return tonight." Sophie nodded toward her bed.

"But why?" Beatrice wailed. "No one will know you are gone."

"Just in case my aunt decides to check on me when she returns home tonight. This is easy compared to what you had to do this afternoon. This time, all you must do is sleep?"

"Your aunt will not like being fooled," Beatrice insisted.

"She will never know."

Sophie managed to get Beatrice's dress unbuttoned despite her protestations. Sophie hung the dress in the armoire, then slipped the nightgown over Beatrice's head, tucked her hair into the cap and urged her into the bed.

"You need not worry about anything." Sophie pulled the covers up to Beatrice's chest, then blew out the candle on the side table and straightened. "Perfect. Not even my own father would know you aren't me."

She grabbed her cloak from the armoire, then picked up her reticule from the table and returned to the bed. "Rest well, Bea. I shall see you in a few hours."

"Miss—"

"Hush," Sophie said, then hurried to the door.

She slipped out into the hall, her thoughts on broad shoulders and dark brown eyes. She ducked into the servants' stairs and descended to the kitchen. Sophie reached the kitchen and stepped onto the floor. A light flared. She cried out and took a faltering step backward into the wall, her gaze glued to the man standing in the doorway leading to the hallway.

"Father," she breathed.

He glanced at her cloak. "Going somewhere, Sophie?"

Sophie forced herself not to glance at the back door where Adam surely waited. What would he do when he saw the light in the kitchen? Gone, no doubt.

"I—uh, yes, I was going for a walk," she replied. "What are you doing here?"

"For a walk?" he said in a quiet voice Sophie had never before heard coming from her father's mouth.

"Yes, you know how I love an evening walk," she said.

His eyes flicked downward again, then returned to her face. "I have never seen you wear such a heavy, drab wool fabric. Could that be Beatrice's dress?"

"Father—"

"Is what I hear true?" he cut in. "Were you out dancing all night with a *man?* And at a *tavern?*"

Sophie's head whirled. How had he found out? She recalled her name being called when she and Adam left the oyster cellars.

Jane Goodman.

The woman had clearly contacted her father.

Footsteps approached down the hallway, and her father stepped aside as Aunt Maddie entered.

She gave Sophie a quick glance, then a corner of her mouth twitched upward in amusement. "Like mother, like daughter."

"Madeline," her father growled.

"Oh, do be quiet, Liam." She faced him. "What did you expect, keeping her in the country all these years? It is a miracle she didn't run away from home long ago."

"We are going home, Sophie," he said. "Pack your things."

Sophie opened her mouth to refuse, then remembered that the very reason she had come to Edinburgh was to meet the marquess. She didn't want to meet the marquess. She did, however, want to meet Adam. But that was now ruined. Would she ever see him again? Her heart unexpectedly twisted at the thought.

"Stop your blustering," her aunt said. "You sent the girl here to meet a charming marquess."

"I do not care," he snapped. "I cannot have her going about at night with strange men."

"He is not strange," Sophie protested.

"Dear, you are not helping," Aunt Maddie said. "Liam, this is not going to end. Do you intend to lock her up in her room for the rest of her life?"

Her father opened his mouth to reply, then hesitated.

"Just as I thought." Aunt Maddie leaned toward him and said in a whisper clearly meant to be heard by Sophie, "When she marries the marquess, she will no longer be your problem."

"Madeline!" he burst out.

She waved a hand. "You know what I mean."

Her father looked at her, and Sophie feared that he did, indeed, know what her aunt meant. Sophie knew exactly what her aunt meant. It was time Sophie marry.

CHAPTER 12

WHEN A LIGHT FLARED TO LIFE IN MADELINE FORSYTH'S kitchen. Adam drew back the booted foot he rested on the second of the three steps leading to the kitchen and melted back into the shadows beyond the light. Beatrice—Sophie Shaw—wouldn't turn on the light. Was the unexpected person who'd turned on the light someone in Madeline's employ?

Damn it, he wanted to speak with Miss Shaw before letting her father know he wouldn't marry her if she were the last woman on earth. Lena's beautiful face flashed in memory. Well, perhaps the second last woman on earth. Women—all women —were faithless.

A large shadow passed in front of the window. The shadow passed again, then the room went dark. Adam waited. Miss Shawn didn't emerge from the house. He waited another ten minutes, then walked to the back gate. He stepped into the alley, then strode around the block to the street in front of the house. A light shone in the front parlor. Had Madeline Forsyth returned home early? The woman was known for staying out so late she put the youngsters to shame. Two—three—figures passed in front of the window. A man and two women.

What man was Madeline entertaining? Not just Madeline, he realized, but Miss Shaw as well. And who else would they be meeting with but Sophie's father? That had to be the answer. He would wager Mr. Shaw caught his daughter sneaking out of the house. She would have been wearing Beatrice's clothes. How Adam would have liked to see the look on her face when she was caught.

Why *couldn't* he see that?

Adam left the garden, then strode around the block and to the walkway leading to the door. He knocked. A moment later, the bolt turned, and the door opened.

A young footman peered up at him. "Can I help you, sir?"

"Lord Monthemer here to see Miss Madeline Forsyth," Adam replied.

The boy glanced over his shoulder, then faced Adam. "If you will wait a moment, sir."

Adam angled his head in acknowledgement, then waited while the boy closed the door. A moment later, the door opened, and Madeline Forsyth stood in the doorway.

"Lord Monthemer, what an unexpected surprise. Please, do come in." She stepped aside, and Adam entered. She closed the door and faced him. "To what do I owe the honor of this visit?"

Adam gave her his most charming smile. "Forgive the intrusion, Miss Forsyth. I was hoping we might talk."

Her brows shot up. "Talk?"

"I'm sure you're aware that Mr. Shaw and I have been in negotiations for marriage between his daughter Miss Shaw and myself."

A shadow fell across the hallway behind Madeline, then a man of medium height and portly build emerged from the parlor on the left.

"Indeed, we have," he said.

Madeline smiled. "My lord, may I present my brother-in-law, Mr. Shaw."

"My lord." The man executed a bow worthy of court.

Adam crossed to where Mr. Shaw stood and extended a hand. Mr. Shaw's brows rose, then he accepted. Adam liked the man's firm grip.

"Shall we sit down, my lord?" Shaw indicated the parlor.

"Only if you agree to call me Adam."

Respect appeared in the man's eyes. "If you will call me Liam."

"Of course," Adam replied.

He entered the parlor, Madeline close behind. "I will have tea brought," she said as she indicated the men should sit.

"I wonder if Adam might prefer a brandy," Shaw said.

"If Miss Forsyth does not mind," Adam said.

She laughed. "Not at all. In fact, I will pour."

Adam and Liam sat on opposite ends of the couch near the hearth. Madeline brought them each a brandy, then poured one for herself and took the chair to Liam's left.

"I assume you are here to discuss Sophie?" Shaw asked.

A man who got straight to the point. Adam liked that.

"I will admit I did not know you were here, Liam."

"I understand," Shaw said. "You thought you might get some information from my sister-in-law."

"That was the idea."

Shaw nodded. "One never can be too certain. All the money in the world isn't worth tying oneself to a shrew."

Adam angled his head. "Thank you for understanding."

"I will be direct," Shaw said. "Sophie is a good girl, but she is a handful."

Madeline hmphed.

"Have you something to add, Miss Forsyth?" Adam asked.

"Just that when a man is strong and intelligent, he is, well, forceful and someone who knows how to get things done. When a woman is strong and intelligent, she is a 'handful.'"

Shaw shook his head. "Madeline, you cannot deny that

Sophie can be difficult. For God's sake she— Well, youngsters can be difficult and young girls, in particular, are filled with flights of fancy."

"I seem to remember you trying to talk my sister into running off with you," Madeline said in a sweet voice.

He frowned. Adam fought to keep a straight face. When they discovered him at their front door, they had clearly sent Miss Shaw to her room—likely with the threat of death should she try to sneak out again.

"Lord Blair informed me that he told you of my offer," Liam said.

Adam sipped his brandy. "He did. Very generous."

Shaw narrowed his eyes. "Do not misunderstand. Sophie is young and impetuous, but she is a fine girl and will make a good wife. I am offering a good contract to ensure she makes a match worthy of her."

"She will be a marchioness," Adam said.

"Now, see here—"

Madeline waved a hand. "Oh, please, Liam, you cannot fault the man for seeing the marriage as a business deal when that is how you approached him."

Shaw's mouth thinned.

"Marriage involving this much money and a title usually are business," she said. "I have seen his lordship about town. He has a fine reputation—aside from that dalliance with Lady Fleming." She laughed. "But no one is perfect. He paid off his father's debts—which, as you know, Liam, isn't something the nobility likes to do, even when they're alive."

"Lord Blair told me. I agree, that speaks highly of his character," he said, as if Adam wasn't present.

Adam leaned back and sipped more of his brandy.

"Your biggest hurdle is convincing Sophie to marry him," Madeline declared.

"She is against the marriage?" Adam asked.

"She is against marriage, altogether," Shaw muttered. "Has some ridiculous idea that she can remain free as a bird to do whatever she likes."

That explained much.

"A woman does have the right to choose her husband," Adam said.

"The girl doesn't know what she wants," Liam replied.

Madeline locked eyes with Adam. "Do you wish to marry her?"

Adam silently cursed. Leave it to a woman to back a man into a corner.

"I am considering the possibility."

Was he really considering the possibility? Shaw was right, all the money in the world wasn't worth a man tying himself to the wrong woman. He thought of Lena and his narrow miss. Was Miss Shaw really the innocent she appeared? She had pretended to be Beatrice Frasier—and quite convincingly. He hadn't for a moment thought her to be anyone else but a lady's companion. She wanted freedom, did she? Perhaps he would marry her then send her on her merry way.

"You're considering the possibility?" Madeline asked. "That is a fair start. After all, you have yet to meet her. She is very beautiful."

"Indeed?" Adam said.

Madeline nodded. "Yes, and she is quite the horsewoman."

"She will have to give up riding when she marries," Shaw said.

Madeline frowned. "Why? A married woman cannot ride?"

"Of course, she can," he replied in an impatient voice. "But she will be too busy running the household and raising children to galivant about the country."

Children. That was right. Shaw was going to give an extra ten thousand pounds per child. Adam felt half like a stud stallion and wondered how Miss Shaw would feel about knowing her father put such a premium on her popping out babies.

"Lady Seafield's ball is in a week's time. You will meet her then and decide?" Madeline asked.

Shaw studied him. This meeting hadn't gone at all like Adam had envisioned. He'd thought he would catch Sophie off guard by showing up on her aunt's doorstep but had, instead, been cornered by the aunt and father.

CHAPTER 13

SOPHIE REACHED THE SECOND FLOOR WITH HER AUNT'S MAID close behind. Sophie would have halted and eavesdropped on Lord Monthemer and her aunt in the foyer below, but that wouldn't do with the maid at her side.

Back home, Sophie and the maids often eavesdropped on her father, but she could trust them not to repeat anything they heard. She didn't know her aunt's staff and understood too well the importance of not directly involving the staff in the family's affairs.

They reached Sophie's room, and Sophie bade the girl goodnight, then slipped inside. Beatrice bolted upright in bed and looked in Sophie's direction. Her nightcap sat askew on her head.

"Miss, you decided not to go." Beatrice threw back the covers and jumped to her feet. "Very wise of you."

Sophie shook her head impatiently as she unclasped her cloak then tossed it onto a nearby chair. "I was caught, Bea. My father is here."

Beatrice's eyes widened. "God save us. He will send me away this night."

Sophie rolled her eyes. "Oh, do cease the dramatics. He knows nothing of your involvement. He caught me trying to sneak out the kitchen. We have a bigger problem."

"What could be bigger than your father catching you?"

"Lord Monthemer is here."

"Here?" Beatrice frowned. "Was he supposed to visit your father tonight?"

"Indeed, not. The man was rude enough to show up unannounced."

"How strange," Beatrice murmured.

"I want to get a look at him." Sophie hurried to the couch that sat against the window overlooking the street. She knelt on the couch and pulled back the curtain. Sophie scanned the street, but found no carriage waiting out front. She looked at Beatrice. "Where is his carriage?"

Beatrice came to the window and looked out. "Did he have a carriage?"

"How could he not have a carriage?" Sophie asked. "Do you think he decided to walk here from his home?"

"Where is his home?"

Sophie scowled. "How should I know?"

"He may live very close."

Sophie looked back out the window. "I have never heard of a marquess walking anywhere."

"He has no money," Beatrice said. "That is why he's marrying you. Perhaps he has no carriage."

Sophie shook her head. "He is *not* marrying me. He only thinks he is. But you do have a point. He probably doesn't own a carriage." She let the drapes fall back into place and plopped down onto the couch. "Can you imagine a man thinking he can walk to a lady's house? Has he no pride?"

"I suppose, if he doesn't have a carriage, it can't be helped," Beatrice said.

Sophie flushed with embarrassment. "He could have taken a hackney."

Beatrice sat beside her. "He might have."

"Then where is it?"

"If he has no money, he can't very well ask the driver to stay."

Sophie's cheeks heated even hotter. "Please fix your cap, Bea. You look like a madwoman."

Beatrice felt on top of her head. "Oh," she said, clearly embarrassed before she straightened the cap.

"Oh, Bea, I'm sorry." Sophie grasped her friend's hands. "I'm angry with my father for spoiling my plans tonight and with the marquess for—well, for existing—and I am taking my frustrations out on you. It's not your fault."

"That's all right, miss. You have had a trying evening."

Sophie released Beatrice's hands and leaned against the couch back. "This is all my fault—except the part about the marquess thinking he's going to marry me. That is my father's fault. I won't marry."

"As I said before, Lord Monthemer does seem to be a decent sort," Beatrice said. "The man with him was very pleasant—not that his lordship wasn't pleasant, but he was a bit stern."

"How is that a 'decent sort'?" Sophie demanded.

"I have seen much worse, miss."

"That is not a glowing recommendation," Sophie muttered, then regarded Beatrice. "Was your last employer that bad?"

"My most previous employer wasn't too terribly bad, but the one before him was—or his son was, at any rate."

Sophie didn't have to ask what that meant. Servants—female servants—were too much at the mercy of their male masters.

Sophie patted Beatrice's hand. "You need never worry about such things again. You will stay with me forever."

"Not if your father discovers I have been helping you sneak out and disguise yourself as a man."

Sophie couldn't help a laugh. "He would not be pleased."

Beatrice paled.

"Easy there, Bea. I know my father well. He can be pigheaded about silly things."

"Like insisting you marry?"

Sophie narrowed her eyes. "Yes, like insisting I marry. But he would never send you away. He knows what you mean to me."

CHAPTER 14

THE DAY OF LADY SEAFIELD'S BALL ARRIVED, AND SOPHIE practically chomped at the bit to get out of the house. Even the prospect of being forced to dance with the loathsome Marquess of Monthemer wasn't enough to make her stay home. Her father had kept her a veritable prisoner. She had been allowed to leave the house only once and that had been in the company of her father, her aunt and Beatrice for church.

If the marquess did not marry her, they were to return home three days hence. Sophie had no intention of returning home without at least one more adventure. She had received no word from Adam. Not that she had really expected to. He couldn't know why she hadn't met him the night they were supposed to go to the wharf, and he was too much of a gentleman to simply appear at their door. Still, she had hoped he might send a note to at least ask if she was well. Her only hope of seeing him was if he was in attendance with his master at Lady Seafield's ball. The chances were slim, she knew. But one never knew.

After dinner, Sophie dressed in a violet-colored muslin dress with darker ribbon around the hem and sleeves. She had to admit the gown was beautiful. Beatrice wore a yellow muslin that complimented her creamy skin to perfection.

"Bea, I would not be the least bit surprised if you had to fight off the suitors," Sophie told her.

She hid a smile when Beatrice's cheeks pinked.

"Your father has insisted I come with you, miss. I will not be dancing."

"Oh, pish, you will dance every dance, just as my father has insisted I must."

"Two dances with the marquess," Beatrice said.

Sophie shot her a narrow-eyed look. "I will step on his toes and make myself generally disagreeable."

"He is handsome," Beatrice said.

"So you have said. At least a dozen times."

"You feared he was a snaggle-toothed old man. He is not. He is tall and very handsome."

"I do not care if he is a Greek god," Sophie retorted. "I will not marry him."

"Your father might make you marry someone else who is not so agreeable."

"Agreeable?" Sophie grimaced. "Nothing about the man is agreeable. I hear he's difficult, and you remember that gossip about him and Lady Fleming."

"That is terrible gossip," Beatrice said.

Sophie couldn't help but wonder what kind of woman would allow the father of the man she claimed to love lose his fortune like that? Sophie had told her father the story only to find out he knew and didn't believe the story painted Lord Monthemer in a negative light. That was men for you. They protected one another. Still, Sophie couldn't prevent a pang of sadness for the marquess. His whole life had been before him. Then, poof! He'd lost everything, his fortune, his father and the woman he loved. That did explain why he wanted to leave Society.

Sophie scooped up her gloves from the bed, then nodded at the other pair still lying on the quilt. "Put on your gloves, Bea. You know how Father hates being late."

They put on their gloves, and Sophie gave her hair a final look in the mirror. Beatrice had done a beautiful job of arranging Sophie's hair in a fashionable chignon with soft curls that framed her face. She had tried to do the same for Beatrice, but Bea would only allow a simple chignon at the back of her neck. Still, Sophie privately thought her friend looked more beautiful than she ever had and believed she truly might attract the attention of some young gentleman. They would only be in town another three days, but Beatrice deserved to be worshiped by a lovesick swain.

They went downstairs and found Sophie's father waiting at the front door for them.

"You look lovely, Sophie," he said. "Beatrice, you, as well."

"Thank you, sir," Beatrice said.

Her father locked eyes with Sophie. "You will dance two dances with the marquess, and you will, above all, behave."

"Of course, Father."

"Sophie," he said in a warning voice. "You will not dance with any other gentleman more than once. Lady Seafield has seen to it that your dance card is full."

"I will dance with the marquess, but that is all," Sophie said.

"Let me make myself clear," her father said. "Your antics here in Edinburgh have proven to me that you need to be settled once and for all. Therefore, if you find a way to ruin your chances with the marquess, when we return home, I will marry you to Robert Barrett."

Sophie frowned. "The pastor's son?"

He nodded.

"You might as well damn me to purgatory. The man is a mealy-mouthed, self-righteous—" She floundered, at a loss for words.

"Prig?" her father finished for her.

Sophie glared.

He gave a single nod. "I am pleased to see we understand one another."

Half an hour later, the carriage let them off in front of Lady Seafield's home. Vehicles jammed the street, and they walked behind two other couples. Sophie linked arms with Beatrice as they ascended the stairs with her father and aunt to the third floor. When they reached the ballroom, Sophie was surprised to realize she was nervous. Not because of the party, but because tonight was the moment of reconning. If not for her father, she would be able to completely avoid the marquess, or at least brush him off after the obligatory first dance—for she hadn't any intention of granting him a second dance. But that was not to be the case.

They were met by their host, and she and Beatrice were given dance cards.

"Oh, my lady, no," Beatrice told Lady Seafield. "I am only here as Miss Shaw's companion."

Lady Seafield laughed. "My dear, you are far too beautiful to stand on the sidelines."

"My lady, really—"

Lady Seafield waved a hand. "If I do not give you a dance card, fights are likely to break out for the privilege of dancing with you. I cannot have that."

Beatrice blinked.

"Oh look," her ladyship said. "Here comes your first partner now, Miss Frasier."

Beatrice's eyes widened, and she cast Sophie a pleading look. Sophie shrugged and didn't quite hide the smile she fought.

A young man no more than twenty years old stopped beside them. "My lady." He bowed to Lady Seafield, then faced Sophie and Beatrice and bowed again.

"Baron Kinley, may I present Miss Beatrice Frasier." Lady Seafield angled her head toward Beatrice.

Sophie was silently pleased when the young man's eyes lit with pleasure.

"Miss Frasier, a pleasure to meet you," he said.

Beatrice extended a hand—as Sophie knew Beatrice had been trained to do at Miss Childer's School for Young Ladies in Inverness.

The baron grasped her hand and bent over her fingers. Beatrice blushed, and Sophie realized she'd been thoughtless to have not seen before now that her friend was lonely.

The music ended and Sophie quickly helped Beatrice tie the small string attached to the dance card around her left wrist, then watched as the baron lead Beatrice to the dancefloor. The orchestra began a country dance, and Beatrice and the baron became lost in the sea of dark suits and flared silk and taffeta.

"She does not know how beautiful she is, does she?" Lady Seafield asked.

Sophie chuckled. "No, my lady. She has not the slightest idea."

"I would say the same of you."

Sophie tied the string on the dance card around her left wrist. "I have endured enough male attention to know I am beautiful."

Lady Seafield lifted a brow. "Endured?"

"Sometimes, that is the case." She leaned close. "But not always."

"Exactly," the older woman replied. "Ah, I believe I see your dance partner. He is late."

Despite knowing this partner was not Lord Monthemer, Sophie's heart began to beat fast, and she looked in the direction Lady Seafield stared. A man of about thirty years of age nodded to a man to his right, then his attention shifted onto Sophie. He was very handsome. Tall, fair haired with broad shoulders. A perfect companion for a dance or two. Nae, only one dance, as her father ordered. *Maybe.*

The gentleman reached them and bowed. "Lady Seafield. I beg your forgiveness in being late. Miss Henshaw took a fall and sprained her ankle, and I was obliged to help her to her carriage."

"How gallant of you," Lady Seafield said, but Sophie thought she detected a touch of sarcasm.

"Hardly, ma'am," he said. "It was my fault she tripped. Helping Miss Henshaw to her carriage was the least I could do."

"You will have to explain that to me in more depth—later. For now, if you wish to claim any part of your dance with Miss Shaw, you had better get onto the dancefloor." Lady Seafield faced her. "Miss Shaw, this is Mr. Gilroy."

He bowed. "A pleasure to meet you, Miss Shaw. Would you do me the honor of finishing the dance with me?"

"Of course."

He winged an arm, and Sophie nodded at Lady Seafield, then allowed him to lead her onto the dancefloor. Mr. Gilroy turned out to be an excellent dancer, and Sophie found herself quite out of breath and ready for something to drink when the song ended.

"If you will give me a moment, Miss Shaw, I will fetch us some lemonade," he said.

Sophie would have preferred champagne but nodded and thanked him. He quickly disappeared in the crowded ballroom, and she wondered who her next partner would be. She opened her dance card to see if Lady Seafield really had filled every dance as her father had said she would.

"Lord Monthemer may be handsome, but he's still a pirate," said a woman behind Sophie. The woman spoke in a voice just loud enough to be heard over the din so that Sophie instantly realized they intended that she hear.

"And penniless," replied another woman. "Can you imagine a penniless pirate?"

So, word had finally leaked out that she was Lord Monthemer's victim. She rolled her eyes. She knew society in Edinburgh loved to gossip, but she hadn't expected to be the center of gossip here as she was in Invergarry. Sophie faced the two women. They weren't quite as young as she'd thought. She would guess them to be at least three or four years older than herself.

"Ladies," she said.

They both blinked as if startled to see the one person who shouldn't have overheard their conversation had been eavesdropping all along.

"We all know that gossip is usually more lies than fact," Sophie said. "How much of the rumor that Lord Monthemer was a pirate is truth?"

The ladies glanced at each other, clearly surprised that Sophie had confronted them.

"Have no fear," Sophie said. "I would appreciate the truth."

They exchanged another look, then the shorter of the two looked around before leaning closer to Sophie. "The news is contributed to a young sailor who said that Lord Monthemer paid his men well to remain silent. The young man said the marquess didn't turn pirate until near the end of his career as a naval officer."

Sophie started to reply, then stiffened when a man brushed against her backside. She snapped her head to the left, but the so-called gentlemen didn't even look back, but continued through the crowd.

"Gentlemen who use a crowded ballroom as an excuse to touch a woman should be shot," she muttered.

"Yes," the shorter of the women agreed.

Sophie returned her attention to the women.

"My brother will happily oblige," the taller woman said. "He loves any excuse for a duel—and hates men who take advantage of women."

Sophie laughed. "Nae, let us not risk your brother's life over something so trivial."

"It's not trivial at all," the woman replied.

"Never mind that for now," Sophie said. "If Lord Monthemer turned pirate, why isn't he in prison?"

"Lord Monthemer's father was very powerful," the shorter woman replied.

"I heard Lord Monthemer paid his father's debts," Sophie said. "A pirate doesn't pay debts."

"Oh yes, everyone knows he paid his father's debts," the taller woman said.

Sophie caught sight of Mr. Gilroy scanning the room, two glasses of lemonade in hand. She thanked the ladies, turned, and headed toward the other side of the room. The orchestra began playing again, and two couples in front of her hurried to the dancefloor. She rounded two men and came face-to-face with a broad chest. Sophie took a quick step back and glanced up. Adam MacAlister stared down at her.

CHAPTER 15

Adam's hackney turned onto the street where Lady Seafield's townhouse was located. Carriages lined the well-lit street. The hackney stopped in front of a carriage parked in front of the townhouse, and Adam opened the door and jumped onto the street. He tossed the driver his fare then rounded the carriage to the sidewalk. Light shone from every visible window of the four-story home and music seeped through the walls into the night. Lady Seafield's ball was always a crush. This year was clearly no exception. He strode up the walkway, then up the three stairs to the front door. The footman standing at the door bowed slightly, then opened the door for him. Adam murmured thanks, then followed another youth up a flight of stairs.

The music grew louder as they ascended, and they reached the next floor to wide open doors that revealed a large ball-room nearly bursting at the seams. The footman bowed, then left Adam in the doorway. Adam surveyed the room. Attaching himself to a woman who lied wasn't worth the money. He would find a way to survive without her father's money. If he could finance another stallion and begin racing this year—and win—that would give him some much-needed funds. His banker John Bateman knew personally that he was debt free. John had handled most of the transfer of funds to Adam's father's larger debtors. Surely, John would extend him a loan?

Was forcing Sophie Shaw to face him and admit she had known all along who he was worth spending even a moment in this hot, stuffy room?

Someone clapped him on the back, and Nicholas and Alistair stepped up alongside him with their wives.

"Adam." Nick grinned.

Adam ignored him and looked at the woman. "Ladies." He bowed.

They both smiled.

"How nice to see you, Adam," Charlotte said.

"And you, ma'am," he said.

"I hope you are saving a dance for each of us," Olivia said.

Adam angled his head. "Of course. A dance with each of you ladies will be the highlight of the evening."

"I should hope not," Nick said.

Adam continued to ignore him.

"Shall we go in?" Olivia said.

"After you." Adam stepped aside.

Nick entered first with Olivia, then Alistair said as he passed with his wife, "I had nothing to do with this."

That, Adam could believe, and he couldn't help a laugh.

After one turn around the ballroom, and many greetings, Adam finally caught sight of Beatrice. Or, more accurately, Sophie Shaw. Her back faced him and she seemed in deep conversation with two women. Adam worked his way through the crowd as quickly as possible, and she turned toward him as he reached her. Her head snapped up and her eyes widened when they met his.

～

Sophie's heart thudded and all she could think of was Adam's warm hand covering her throbbing sex in her dream.

"Good evening," Adam said.

"What are you doing here?" she blurted.

He lifted a brow.

"I mean, I—that is, I hadn't expected to see you here." If her father talked with Adam and learned she had pretended to be Beatrice—

"Come, let's dance." He grasped her hand and tucked it into the crook of his arm.

"I have a dance card, and this dance is promised to"—she didn't know who the dance was promised to—"to someone else."

"I feel certain he will not mind."

They reached the dancefloor, and Adam pulled her too close and stepped into what she realized was a waltz. Her father would throttle her. She had no intention of capitulating to her father's demand that she marry, but to purposefully anger him would not help her cause.

"You look quite lovely tonight," Adam said.

She started at the sound of his voice and missed a step. He yanked her close and executed a sharp turn around another couple. The crush of her breasts against the hard planes of his chest caught her off guard, and she tried to push away. He lifted her feet from the floor for the remaining seconds of the turn, then deftly set her feet back onto the floor in perfect time to the music. Her heart pounded and she feared she would trip again. Adam held her close, and she gave thanks when she stepped into the rhythm.

"You are an excellent dancer," he said.

"What are you doing here?" She winced at the shrill demand in her voice.

He lifted a brow. "You are not happy to see me? You did not meet me the other night, as planned. I was worried."

She forced herself to maintain eye contact. "I am very sorry. My—my mistress was ill."

"Indeed?" he replied.

Sophie nodded. "Yes. I would have sent you a note, but I don't know your direction."

"It was kind of your mistress to allow you to attend the party." He directed them around another couple, then dodged a second couple who came perilously close.

"She is very kind that way."

Sophie caught sight of her father talking to another man. If he turned even a little, he would see them. She told herself not to worry. Her father would take Adam to be one of the many men Lady Seafield had arranged for her to dance with tonight.

Still, she wanted very badly to put distance between Adam and herself. He held her scandalously close, and that would not please her father. Another horrifying thought struck. What if Lord Monthemer saw her dancing with Adam? That would chase him away—which was good—but he would likely tell her father why. That, she realized, she could live with much more easily than her father trying to force her to marry the marquess.

Sophie looked up at Adam through her lashes. "You are an uncommonly fine dancer, sir."

His gaze flicked to her bodice. "As are you."

She blinked. Had that been desire in his voice?

His hand tightened on the small of her back as he side-stepped another couple, and her abdomen pressed against the hard length she instantly recognized as arousal.

He was trying to seduce her.

She flushed warm and broke eye contact before realizing she'd done so. She had to do something. She was willing to do battle with her father and refuse to marry the marquess—and she would have gladly allowed a passionate kiss between Adam and her. But the man was openly trying to seduce her. That would not do.

Sophie caught sight of a short man standing near the dance-floor, his narrowed gaze on them as they passed, and she wondered if he was the dance partner who should have had the dance Adam had taken. Adam steered them to the left, through the crowd and away from the man.

Adam guided her around two other couples, and before Sophie realized his intent, he twirled her in a circle that made her head spin and blazed a path through the crowd and out onto the balcony. They came to a sudden halt near the stone railing. Cool night air brought a rush of gooseflesh across her warm arms. Half a dozen other couples milled about on the balcony. At least her father couldn't fault her for being with a man on the balcony when they were surrounded by other people.

"It is quite warm in the ballroom, is it not?" she asked.

"A stroll in the gardens will cool you off sufficiently," he said. "I hear Lady Seafield's gardens are spectacular."

A stroll? Under almost any other circumstances, she might have said yes, but she half-feared her thoughts would betray her. If Adam had the slightest notion of her dreams... Worse, if word reached her father that she had dallied with a man in Lord Monthemer's employ, her father might try to make good on his threat to marry her to Robert Barrett. Sophie inwardly grimaced. She would run away before she allowed that.

Sophie looked up at Adam. "I really don't think we should."

"Do not think." Adam grasped her arm and nearly pulled her down the steps to the lawn.

"Adam—Mr. MacAlister," she cried. "Really, my father will —" She broke off.

He looked down at her. "Your father will what?"

"Surely, you understand he would not want me to stroll in the garden with a man?"

"Is your mistress here?"

"Yes," she replied tentatively.

A couple passed. Though Sophie couldn't discern their faces in the dim moonlight, she felt certain they were staring as she and Adam passed. They neared a fountain with an angel in the middle. The cold began to work its way through her exposed arms. She shivered.

"Forgive me, Beatrice." Adam shucked his coat and placed it over her shoulders.

The fabric was warm from his body, and she shivered again.

"Are you still cold?" he asked.

"Nae, I-I am fine, thank you." But she wasn't fine. It felt odd to be wearing his coat.

They reached the fountain and sat down on the stone bench that surrounded the fountain. The murmur of voices somewhere deeper in the garden told Sophie they were not completely alone—but they were alone enough. She should return to the ballroom before someone missed her. She had already slighted one gentleman by giving Adam his dance, no doubt the next gentleman on her dance card awaited his turn.

"Is your mistress enjoying herself?" Adam asked.

"What?" Sophie nodded. "Oh, yes, of course."

"What does she think of Lord Monthemer?"

"She thinks no differently of him now than she did when she arrived," Sophie replied.

"Meeting him in person has not altered her opinion?" he asked.

"Why should it? He is only marrying her for her money."

"Ah, yes, I forgot that."

Sophie looked at him and frowned. "Is something amiss?"

"What would be amiss? We are at a lovely party and I'm sitting in the garden with a beautiful woman."

He thought she was beautiful?

He slid an arm around her waist and pulled her closer, so

they sat thigh to thigh. She flushed. This was a dangerous game she played. Everything was fine until her father had arrived. If not for him, she could have continued to see Adam until she left. Now….

Sophie stood. "Perhaps I should return to the ballroom." She took his coat from her shoulders as he stood. Cold air washed over her. "Thank you for the use of your coat." She handed him the coat, then started toward the ballroom.

Strong fingers closed around her wrist and Adam swung her to face him. "Mr. MacAlister," she said in the instant before his mouth covered hers.

He slipped his tongue inside her mouth. He tasted of brandy. She liked brandy, though she'd never tasted it on a man's tongue before. Her stomach did a somersault. He pressed her close and she became aware of the hard length digging into her belly. Her head whirled. It had been too long since she'd experienced a man's desire—though Adam's desire seemed far more insistent than Matthew's ever had.

Sophie broke the kiss. "Sir," she said in a too-breathless voice. "I believe we should return—"

The murmur of voices intruded upon them. Sophie jumped back, heart racing. Embarrassment warmed her cheeks. She was acting like a girl still in the schoolroom instead of a widow. Adam thought her to be Beatrice Frasier, companion to Miss Sophie Shaw. Would a companion be afraid as she was? Yes, Beatrice would be afraid of being considered a loose woman, as *ladies* didn't like having loose women as companions.

A couple emerged from the shadows beyond the fountain, and Sophie realized Adam hadn't put on his coat. She wanted to turn aside in order to hide her face but feared Adam would think her childish. Wasn't she acting childish? She'd protested coming into the garden but had allowed Adam to lead her here. She'd said she should return to the ballroom, yet still stood here with him. The couple passed, and Sophie spun and started toward the mansion. Adam fell into step alongside her as he slipped on his coat.

They reached the ballroom, and she halted. "I am quite thirsty."

"Then I suppose I should get you something to drink," he said.

She nodded, gaze on the floor. "Thank you."

"I shall return in a moment." He started through the crowd.

Sophie immediately scanned the room for signs of her father, Beatrice, or Lady Seafield. She didn't see her father. That meant he was likely with other gentlemen off drinking brandy. She caught sight of Beatrice on the dancefloor with a tall, handsome man who looked down at her as if she were Aphrodite. Beatrice looked as if she wanted to run. It was high time she learned what it was like to have male attention.

Sophie couldn't locate Lady Seafield and decided now was a good time to make an escape. Adam would be angry that she had deserted him, but she couldn't risk that her father might talk to him and learn it was he who had taken her to the oyster cellars. Without doubt, her father would insist the marquess terminate Adam's employment. It would be all her fault for not telling Adam who she really was. He would never have agreed to spend time with her if he'd known. That meant she couldn't see him again.

Sophie grasped the dance card hanging from her left wrist and looked at the second line and gasped at sight of Lord Monthemer's name for the dance Adam had poached. Her father would be furious. Normally, she wouldn't worry overly much about her father's frustrations. He rarely got angry or even upset with her. But on the rare occasions he did get angry or make demands, he seldom relented. Why was he suddenly so insistent that she marry?

She looked around and realized she had better get lost in the crowd. It wouldn't do for Adam to return with drinks. Lord only knew when the marquess might show up, demanding the dance she'd given away.

She glanced again at the dance card and read the name Mr. John Evers on the third line. She didn't know Mr. Evers and didn't want to. Sophie pushed through the crowd to a hallway and turned down the first open door she came. She stopped short and looked around the room. Men occupied nearly a dozen tables playing cards.

Sophie released a breath. Adam would never think to look for her in the cardroom.

CHAPTER 16

ADAM WASN'T SURPRISED TO FIND BEATRICE—MISS SHAW—gone when he arrived with champagne. She might have deduced that he knew her true identity and had gone in search of her father in hopes of finding a way out of the web of deceit she'd woven. He recalled their kiss in the garden and his cock began to rise. A mental picture flashed of the beauty beneath him as he plunged so deep into her that he touched her soul. Adam gritted his teeth. He really was no different than his father. He had terrible taste in women. Adam drank both glasses of champagne and considered going home.

Sadly, Miss Shaw was only half the reason he'd come to the party. He needed to at least let Balfour see him here. He had yet to see the man tonight. Lady Seafield's ball was one of the most important events of the Season. Balfour had to be here.

Adam made one turn around the ballroom in search of Balfour, then was caught by Lady Seafield.

"You are a rogue, sir," she chided in mock sternness. "I did see you on the dancefloor with Miss Shaw." The older lady's eyes twinkled. "She is quite beautiful."

"Indeed, she is, ma'am," he said. "I thank you for arranging the dance."

"You have a second dance with her, you know," she said.

"I am looking forward to it. Until then—"

"Until then, my lord, you will dance with Miss Hawthorne and then Lady Phoebe."

Adam blinked. "I beg your pardon?"

She slipped a hand into the crook of his arm and began slowly walking through the crowd. "You did not think that I could allow a handsome man like you to stand on the sidelines like a wallflower?"

He navigated her around a group of men. "I did not plan on staying late, Lady Seafield."

He patted his arm. "You are young, a few dances will not hurt you."

He snapped his head in her direction. "A few dances?"

She smiled serenely, eyes straight ahead. "Ah, yes, there is Miss Hawthorne."

Nearly two hours later, Adam managed to escape the dancefloor. He hadn't attended a ball in over a year. This would teach him to stay home.

He had seen hide nor hair of Miss Shaw. She had likely gone home. Which is exactly what he planned on doing, once he found Balfour. But where? Then Adam knew.

Five minutes later, Adam found the cardroom where a dozen card tables were set up and games were in progress. He caught sight of an old friend, Sir Henry Waits, at the far table. Of course, Balfour also sat at the same table. Adam headed in that direction. When he neared, Henry's eyes shifted past the players' heads and locked on him. Henry grinned, then threw down his card and rose.

Adam clasped Henry's outstretched hand and shook. "What the devil are you doing in Edinburgh?" Adam asked. "You never leave the north. Is Dorothea with you?"

Henry laughed. "Dorothea is, indeed, with me. In fact, she's the reason I am here. She insisted we visit her cousin, who is expecting."

"And she dragged you here, tonight?"

Henry grimaced. "Aye, the lass can be quite persuasive when she puts her mind to it. Thankfully, she didn't insist I stay with her in the ballroom all night. Why don't you join us for a hand?"

"Against you?" Adam snorted. "I think not."

Henry grinned. "Still have not recovered from the thrashing I gave you last year at Penelope's?"

"You were damned lucky that night," Adam replied. "But then, if I recall, you had Dorothea at your side. She always did bring you good luck."

"She is not here now," Henry said. "Have a seat."

"Yes, do have a seat," Balfour said.

As if only just noticing him, Adam turned slightly toward where Kenrich Balfour sat in the chair to Henry's left. "Not tonight," Adam said.

"If you are afraid of Henry, I am sure we can talk him into sitting out a hand," Balfour said.

Adam gave him a cool smile. "I wouldn't think of asking Henry to sit out. Especially when he is winning." Adam looked at his friend. "You are winning, as usual?"

Henry's gaze sharpened. "I have won a hand or two. Small stakes, though, I assure you. Lady Seafield does not allow anyone to leave her party more than a thousand pounds poorer than when they arrived."

"Surely, even you can afford to lose a hundred pounds," Balfour said to Adam.

"I never gamble with my money," Adam replied.

Balfour's brows shot up. "Not many men learn such valuable lessons from their fathers."

If not for the money Adam would make by catching the

bastard red-handed with the King's money, Adam would ram his fist into Balfour's mouth. Instead, he gave Balfour a cool smile. "I believe it is best you and I stay on good terms, Balfour."

Satisfaction flickered in Balfour's eyes, and Adam knew Balfour believed he had him.

Good.

"Gentlemen." Adam angled his head, then said to Henry, "Perhaps we could meet tomorrow?"

Henry nodded. "I rise early, as you know. You may call at eight."

Adam winced inwardly but nodded, then turned. He got halfway to the door when he caught sight of Beatrice. He mentally cursed. He had to quit thinking of her as Beatrice. She was Sophie Shaw—and she sat at a table, cards in front of her.

What the devil was she doing playing cards? Had she followed him into the room? Nae, that didn't seem likely. She appeared to be well into a game of *Vingt-et-Un*. Adam veered toward the table but stopped five feet away and leaned a shoulder against the wall. If her attention wavered from the game and she looked up, she would see him, but her focus remained locked on her opponent.

Lord Vance Emerson turned over the second of his cards to reveal a jack. With his king, that made twenty. Miss Shaw's two face-up cards were an ace and a four. A hush fell over the onlookers gathered around the table. The dealer asked if she wanted another card. Miss Shaw acknowledged with a gracious nod, and Adam marveled that she gave away nothing of her face-down card. She had seemed far too innocent to be such a good player. But wasn't that how she had deceived him? She grasped the card and turned it face up. A six of spades. Cries of delight from the ladies mingled with the gentlemen's muttered curses.

Emerson angled his head in assent. She reached for the bills piled in the middle of the table—no more than two hundred pounds—but Vance covered her hand with his. She shifted her eyes to his in question.

"One last game?" he asked.

She laughed the same laugh Adam had heard in the oyster cellars, sending a message to his cock that reminded him yet again of their kiss.

She shook her head. "The hour grows late. I am afraid not."

"One more hand." Emerson slid the remainder of his bills in the middle of the table. Another thousand pounds, if Adam didn't miss the mark.

She frowned. "There is only two hundred pounds in the pot. I will not wager another"—she looked at the pot—"eight hundred pounds."

"Closer to a thousand pounds, Miss Shaw." Emerson held her gaze. "I understand you will not be in Town much longer."

A shadow flickered across her face and Adam suspected she was wondering if she would be leaving Edinburgh as the Marchioness of Monthemer.

A murmur rippled through the small crowd, and a man near Adam whispered to another man, "She married at sixteen and poisoned her husband to be rid of him. They call her Belladonna."

"I thought he died of natural causes," the other man replied.

The original man laughed. "Do you believe everything you read in the newspaper? I hear she has half a dozen lovers."

"Perhaps Lord Emerson is counted among that *fortunate* list?" The other man replied with obvious envy in his voice.

"I do plan to return home soon, sir," Miss Shaw said to Lord Emerson.

"The pot against me escorting you home tonight," Emerson said.

"I am to wager the pot against your company on the trip

home?" She frowned. "I think not, my lord." She started to scoop up the bills into her reticule.

"I see," he said.

She paused and looked at him through dark lashes. By God, this woman was far more a vixen than the Beatrice he'd escorted to the oyster cellars.

"Luck may still be on your side," he said.

She laughed. "You are saying that I won by luck?"

"We all get lucky now and then."

She regarded him. "High card wins."

Emerson's brows shot up in surprise. "That is surely a game of luck."

She lifted one shoulder in a shrug. "That will even the odds of you winning."

Laughter drifted through the onlookers.

"You are too kind." Emerson picked up the deck, which sat in front of the man sitting between them, and shuffled. He set the deck in the middle of the table. "Ladies first."

She grasped the deck, then lifted nearly half the cards and turned them face up on the table before her. Jack of spades.

The crowd *oohed*.

She betrayed no emotion. Adam had to admit, she had nerve.

Eyes on Miss Shaw, Emerson cut the deck, then dragged the deck across the table to him and turned it over. If Adam had looked away for the barest of seconds or even blinked, he would have missed the very skilled sleight of hand that slipped a card to the top of the deck. Emerson turned over the card. King of hearts.

Ten minutes after Sophie lost the cut of the cards to Lord Emerson, she stopped alongside him at the front drive and allowed him to help her into his waiting carriage. He vaulted up behind her and pulled the door shut as he dropped onto the seat opposite her.

Despite the note she left her father that she had allowed Lord Emerson to escort her home, he would be angry. Sophie thought of Mr. MacAlister. If her father knew Adam had kissed her, he would insist Lord Monthemer turn him out without a reference. Allowing Lord Emerson to escort her home would show Lord Monthemer that she wasn't the woman for him, and no one would get hurt.

"Miss Shaw," Lord Emerson began, as the carriage lurched into motion, "I—"

The door swung open, and another man leapt inside.

Sophie blinked. "Mr. MacAlister?"

"MacAlister?" Lord Emerson frowned.

"Forgive the intrusion," Adam said. He looked at Lord Emerson. "How are you, Vance?"

Lord Emerson's eyes narrowed. "What sort of game is this?"

Sophie started to ask how they knew one another, but Adam looked at her and said, "I could ask the same thing. Do you know Lord Emerson?"

She liked Adam—perhaps too much—but this was down-right rude. "Our friendship does not entitle you to these personal questions, sir," she said, and wondered if he thought the kiss they'd shared entitled him to intrude upon her business. "What are you doing here?"

"Yes," Lord Emerson said. "What are you doing here?"

"The same thing Lord Emerson is doing," Adam replied.

Lord Emerson gave a small nod. "I am simply seeing Miss—"

"Really, Mr. MacAlister," Sophie cut in before Lord Emerson could say her name, "you are being rude."

He locked eyes with her. "You mean rude, as in when a lady sends a man to fetch her a drink, then she disappears."

She shot him a narrow-eyed look, then turned to Lord Emerson. "Sir, it is one in the morning. Long past my time to retire. You are taking me directly home?"

He hesitated, then nodded.

"Then you won't mind my accompanying you home along with Lord Emerson," Adam said.

It wasn't a question.

"I mind," Lord Emerson muttered. "I wished to speak with the lady alone."

Before Sophie could reply, Adam shook his head. "Why would she want to be alone with a pup like you?"

Lord Emerson scowled. "You are but five years older than my five and twenty."

"Five more years to learn what a woman wants," he replied without rancor.

Sophie's mouth fell open.

Lord Emerson looked at her. "We are old friends, are we not?"

"Old friends?" she repeated. "We have not seen one another since I was sixteen."

"I was a mere boy then," he replied in a low voice.

"What?" she blurted.

Adam laughed. "Is that the best you can do, Vance?"

Lord Emerson's expression darkened, and Sophie half expected him to draw a pistol and shoot Adam.

Lord Emerson moved from the opposite seat to sit beside her. He traced her cheek with a finger." What of me now? Am I a mere boy?"

She swatted his hand away. "You are being ridiculous."

Adam banged on the carriage ceiling. "You are walking home, Vance."

The carriage came to a halt.

Lord Emerson gave a harsh laugh. "This is my hired carriage."

"This is now *my* hired carriage. Get out," Adam said in a voice that seemed to be made of steel.

"The lady promised the ride home to me," Lord Emerson said with equal grit. "Make an appointment with her for another time."

Adam held his gaze. "Perhaps I should play a game of cards with her? As you did?"

Lord Emerson's eyes narrowed. "I don't know what you mean."

Adam threw open the door. "Either get out or I will drag you out."

Lord Emerson leaned back against the cushion. "Let us take the lady home then resolve this problem."

"There is no problem to resolve," Sophie cried. "You are both being ridiculous."

Adam seized Lord Emerson by the lapel and shoved him out the door. Sophie yanked up a slippered foot and shoved Adam's backside as hard as she could. He tumbled out the door nearly on top of Lord Emerson.

"Drive on, Driver! Quickly!" she shouted.

Adam caught himself and stumbled three paces. He spun, and in the dim lamplight, she glimpsed the startled look on his face in the instant before she yanked the door closed. The carriage lurched into motion at a quick pace. A shout went up outside, which she thought came from Lord Emerson.

Sophie yanked back the curtain. Lord Emerson had taken several steps in the direction of the moving carriage. Adam, however, stood just within the small circle of light cast by the streetlight. She couldn't see his expression, but he'd crossed his arms over his chest. Lord Emerson spun to face him and shouted something she couldn't discern. Adam turned and began walking down the sidewalk.

Sophie arrived home and went straight to her room. She was thankful to find her family and Beatrice hadn't yet returned. Sophie stripped off her dress. She had no idea what had gotten into Adam—or Lord Emerson, for that matter. She understood the two men were vying for her attention, but they'd acted like children. She would never have believed Adam capable of being so…so silly. He hadn't been silly when he'd kissed her. She shivered. Oh, she had gotten herself into a mess this time. If only Adam weren't in Lord Monthemer's employ. Her heart sank. Nae, that was not the only problem. She could never use him to force Lord Monthemer to decide against marrying her. She liked Adam, and he seemed to like her. To use him would be cruel.

She added two logs to the low burning fire in the hearth, then crawled beneath the cool sheets. Memory rose of Adam's warm sure hand on the small of her back as he'd expertly guided her around the dancefloor. The warmth of his mouth on hers, the taste of him… How long had it been since a man had touched her with such surety? Never.

CHAPTER 17

SOPHIE AWOKE TO MORNING SUNLIGHT POUNDING ONTO HER face She was certain the blinds had been closed when she'd gone to bed. She blinked and discerned a figure near the window. Sophie turned her head the other way.

"Close the blinds, Bea, please," she begged.

"Up, my girl," her aunt said. "We have much to do today."

Sophie snapped her eyes open and turned her head toward her aunt. She faced Sophie, the sun streaming in through the window behind her.

"Aunt Maddie? What time is it?"

"Eight," Maddie replied.

"Eight?" That was early even for when she was home in Invergarry. "I went to bed late. I need more sleep."

"We are going shopping today."

"Not more dresses?" Sophie groaned.

"Your father has much more than dresses planned for you today," her aunt replied.

Sophie turned onto her back and closed her eyes. "He is angry I left the party. I sent a note telling him Lord Emerson was kind enough to bring me home."

Lord, if her father knew how that ride had gone…

"Indeed, your father was very angry that you left the party —especially in the company of one of the most eligible young men in Edinburgh," her aunt said. "But his mood shifted dramatically when he received the signed marriage agreement from Lord Monthemer this morning."

Signed marriage agreement?

Sophie bolted upright. "What are you talking about?"

Her aunt crossed to the table near the armoire where sat a tray with a silver coffee pot two cups and saucers and a few pastries. Maddie poured coffee in the cups, then added sugar and milk to both and brought one of the cups to Sophie.

Sophie accepted the cup, then set it on the nightstand. "What are you talking about?"

"Where is the confusion?" her aunt asked. "Lord Monthemer has accepted the terms of your marriage."

Sophie stared. "But— How is that possible? You said it was but eight in the morning. When did this happen?"

Her aunt seemed to consider. "I believe it was about three o'clock this morning."

"Three o'clock this morning?" Sophie cried. "That—that is ridiculous. Who decides to sign a marriage agreement at three o'clock in the morning?"

Maddie shrugged. "A man who feels there is no time to waste, I imagine."

"I don't understand. What in heavens name made him do it?"

"When he realized how sought after you were, he"—Maddie shrugged—"he realized someone else might take your father up on the offer to marry you."

"Someone else?" she repeated. "Who?"

"Why Lord Emerson, of course." Maddie sat on the edge of the bed. "Very clever of you to have Lord Emerson drive you home last night." She leaned forward and said in a conspiratorial whisper, "Nothing makes a man want a woman more than when another man wants her."

"You cannot be serious," Sophie whispered.

But her aunt couldn't have been more serious.

Fifteen minutes later, Sophie sat in the chair opposite her father's desk, the signed marriage agreement in hand.

She looked up at him. "How could you do this?"

"Why are you surprised? You knew full well that you came to Edinburgh with the express intent to get the marquess to agree to marry you."

Sophie set the agreement on the desk. "That was your plan. Not mine. I will not marry him."

"There is no good reason not to."

"No good reason not to?" she exploded. "There are half a dozen good reasons not to. He is a pauper."

"I thought you cared nothing for how much money a man had."

She narrowed her eyes. "It is not that he has no money, it is that he is marrying me strictly for my money."

"My money," her father corrected.

"He is a pirate," she snapped.

"I have never known you to listen to gossip."

Sophie rolled her eyes. "This is more than gossip. It is well known he turned from buccaneer to pirate. It would not surprise me to discover the Crown intended to arrest him."

Her father laughed. "Sophie, you are not prone to dramatics. If he was a pirate, where is all the money he stole from the Crown?"

"Exactly!" she cried. "The man cannot manage money."

"Why would a pirate pay off his father's debts?"

"Now who's listening to gossip? You don't know that he paid off a single debt."

"When have you known me to be a fool?" he asked. "Of course I know he paid off his debts."

She shot to her feet. "I will not marry a man just so you can say your son-in-law is a marquess."

Her father's mouth thinned. "I had no idea you thought so little of me. But never mind that," he added before she would reply. "Will you marry a man to ensure your well-being?"

She stiffened. "I do not need a man for that. I am tolerably good with money and will not squander your money when you are gone."

"I see. When do you think this might be?"

"Not for some time, if we are fortunate," she said with more of a bite than intended. "If I had no money, you would have reason to worry. But I am not destitute. I have a brain and will do quite well."

"You will be alone," he said.

She scoffed. "That is better than being with the wrong man."

"I like Monthemer," her father said. "He will give you children and care for you."

"Children are a bother."

"I cannot argue with that," he muttered. "But I do not need to argue. He has signed the marriage agreement. It is settled."

Sophie threw her hands up. "This is Scotland. I do not have to marry him if I choose not to."

He leaned back in his chair. "You will refuse to give me grandchildren?"

Guilt pricked. There had been a time she wanted children. But marriage to Matthew had crushed that desire, and she hadn't been able to resurrect it.

"Perhaps you should remarry and have more children," she said. "You are not yet too old."

He scowled. "I am not so weak-minded as to fall for that line of drivel. I will not have you grow old alone."

"I have Beatrice," she said.

He pinned her with a stare. "Would you have her give up the love of a good man and children just to keep you company?"

Sophie blinked. She hadn't given any real thought to Beatrice's future. How had she grown so selfish? Beatrice deserved happiness. But that didn't mean Sophie had to marry a man who only wanted her father's money. She looked at the marriage contract. The heading read:

Clarke and Osborn Esq.

They would know where to find Lord Monthemer.

SOPHIE RETURNED TO HER ROOM TO FIND BEATRICE STOKING THE fire. Beatrice turned as she entered and clasped her hands in front of her.

"Did you enjoy yourself last night, Bea?" Sophie asked.

"It was very kind of Lady Seafield to include me in the festivities, miss," Beatrice replied.

Sophie might have been able to argue her father's logic that Beatrice wanted a young man, if not for the heightened color in her cheek. She had clearly enjoyed the male attention she'd received last night. In truth, Sophie didn't need Beatrice to confirm that fact. Sophie had seen her on the dance floor last night. Beatrice had tried to hide her feelings then, as she was now, but she had glowed.

Sophie sat on the chair near the window. "Lady Seafield is very kind to have included you in the festivities."

"Your aunt said she is taking you shopping today." Beatrice went to the armoire and began looking through Sophie's clothes.

Sophie had been a fool to see a future with just Beatrice and her. Her father was right, of course—at least on that score. How did she feel about being alone for the rest of her life? She didn't know. She was still young. Might she meet someone who made her want to remarry? Adam rose in memory, tall, ridiculously handsome—and childish. Perhaps not childish. Lord Emerson had been forward. Any more forward than

Adam had been in the garden? Her insides gelled with the memory of his warm mouth on hers—and his hard body pressed so intimately against hers. What a shame Adam wasn't in the market for a wife. Or was he?

Heaven help her. She'd lost her mind. She had to stay on track.

The way she saw things, she had three problems. How to convince Lord Monthemer that he didn't want to marry her. Find Beatrice a nice young man. Then Sophie would deal with her father once she convinced Lord Monthemer he didn't want to marry her. But Lord Monthemer had decided he did want to marry her—sight unseen. She found that strange, but everything about the man seemed strange.

Instead of convincing Lord Monthemer that he didn't want to marry her, she had to show her father that the marquess was not the honest, upstanding man her father thought him to be.

THE DAY DRAGGED ON. THEY WERE TO ATTEND A DINNER THAT night with a group of Aunt Maddie's friends. No doubt, Sophie's father and aunt would announce Sophie's engagement to Lord Monthemer and by morning the news would be all over Edinburgh. There was only one way to put a stop to her father's schemes. She had to marry. If she was going to be forced into marriage, it wouldn't be with some old man who wanted her only for her father's money and whose touch was probably even colder than Matthew's had been.

She had given the matter thought. She couldn't hurt Adam by using him to make Lord Monthemer think she was a loose woman, but she could marry him. Adam was being let go, and he seemed to have no other prospects. At least she knew she could tolerate him. Tolerate him? She still hadn't been able to push from her mind the memory of their kiss. It had been one kiss for goodness' sake. Adam certainly wasn't the first man she'd kissed. Though Matthew hadn't once kissed her with such passion. How was that possible? Matthew had kissed her… She thought back. Before they had married, Matthew had wooed her in what she had—at sixteen—thought to be the most romantic way a man could woo a woman. He'd read her poetry, sent her glances filled with longing and had stolen a handful of quick kisses that left her certain they would share endless nights of passion.

On their wedding night, he'd treated her as if she was made of porcelain. She'd thought that meant he was initiating her into the intimacies between a man and a woman with tenderness and consideration. As it turned out, he simply knew little about women and didn't care to learn. The promised passion never materialized, and their kisses quickly became less frequent. It had taken a little while, but Sophie had come to understand that her husband chose her not because of any particular affection or even because she was beautiful. He had chosen her because her father was wealthy, and she was too inexperienced to know Matthew was a fortune hunter.

Was she making the same mistake with Adam? Was he skilled at making women believe he knew how to touch them? Or was she so desperate for the touch of a man she would so easily be fooled again? Nae, the latter definitely wasn't true. After Matthew's death, she had given men little thought. Why, then, did the memory of Adam's kiss make her heart beat faster and the juncture between her legs throb?

Adam was nothing like Matthew. At least that much she could be sure of. She and Adam didn't love each other. Sophie was startled at the small prick to her heart the thought elicited. She liked Adam much better than she had ever liked Matthew —and she was certain she liked him more than she ever would the fortune hunting Lord Monthemer.

Now all she had to do was find Adam and propose. He would understand her deception, surely? After all, how many women pretended *not* to have money? If he agreed to her proposal, they would marry immediately and consummate the marriage before her father knew she had eloped. A mental picture flashed of Adam, his long, lean body over hers, as he drove into her. Her heart thumped. God help her, she was still that sixteen-year-old girl who believed in passion.

CHAPTER 18

ADAM SIPPED DEEP OF HIS BRANDY, THEN BALANCED THE GLASS on his abdomen and dropped his head back onto the bed pillow. The liquor reached his belly, and warmth began to spread through him. He was glad he had decided to accept Mrs. Eldridge's offer of staying at her home for the weekend house party. He was growing tired of the boarding house.

A short rest would refresh his mind, for this evening he faced Sophie Shaw, his future wife. He almost felt sorry for her. *Almost*. Her ridiculous plotting had gotten her into this mess—and had made him realize she had some grit. She hadn't tried to play him against Emerson last night, but had called Adam rude and Emerson ridiculous, then left them standing on the street. With that swift kick to Adam's arse, she had gained his respect. Many a marriage had been built on far less.

He finished his brandy, then rose and crossed to the tray where sat the decanter. Adam refilled his glass and by the time he'd returned to his bed, he'd drank half. Miss Shaw also hadn't allowed him to take too much advantage of her in Lady Seafield's garden. He grimaced. He'd half expected her to cut off his bollocks. Damn, but the kiss had been worth the risk.

Adam finished the remainder of his brandy and considered getting up for another. He glanced at the clock on the mantle. Five forty-five. He didn't have to be down to dinner for another hour. One more brandy wouldn't hurt. He closed his eyes and contemplated getting up.

A KNOCK SOUNDED ON THE DOOR. ADAM JARRED AND REALIZED he'd dozed off. The knock became more insistent.

"Sir," came the voice of Kirk, the footman who manned the front door.

Something was wrong.

Adam leapt to his feet and called, "Enter."

The door opened, and Kirk stepped inside. "Forgive the intrusion, my lord, but a Mr. Daily asked to see you. He says it's important."

Tate Daily, Balfour's man of affairs? What was he doing here?

"Where is he?" Adam asked.

"In the front parlor, sir," Kirk replied. "If you will follow me, I can show you."

Adam nodded and gabbed his coat from the chair as he followed the lad from the room.

They reached a small drawing room on the second floor and Tate Daily stood from the couch where he sat as Adam entered.

"What is it?" Adam demanded as he stopped in front of the man.

Daily glanced at the footman.

"Kirk, leave us," Adam ordered.

The young man bowed and hurried away.

When he disappeared from sight, Daily said, "Mr. Balfour sent me to tell you that he has acquired a shipment of gold."

Adam started. "The shipment has not yet arrived. How is that possible?

"This is not *that* shipment, sir."

Adam blinked, uncertain he'd heard correctly. "What the bloody hell does that mean?"

"Mr. Balfour asks that you come immediately," Daily said.

Adam silently cursed, but nodded agreement and wished mightily that he had a pistol.

AFTER A DAY OF SHOPPING WITH HER AUNT, SOPHIE ARRIVED AT Mrs. Eldridge's home with her father, Beatrice, and Aunt Maddie at seven that night. Sophie had no idea what the chances were that Adam would be present, but she prayed he would be there. If he wasn't, how would she find him? He had given her no direction as to where he lived, and the most she'd learned from her father was that Lord Monthemer had an estate in Inverness. Her father didn't know where he lived in Edinburgh. If Adam wasn't present tonight, she would have to contact the attorneys who drafted the marriage contract. Once she found Lord Monthemer, she would find Adam.

Sophie pushed up the strap of her reticule from where it had slid to her wrist as a footman showed them into a large drawing room on the third floor. Sophie's pulse picked up speed as she scanned the guests in the room. Adam was nowhere in sight, but she did notice a tall, handsome man who stood in conversation with another man. Was he Lord Monthemer?

"Elsie." Sophie's aunt addressed a short stout woman about her age who hurried toward them.

The two women kissed one another on the cheek, then her aunt said, "This is my sister's husband Liam Shaw."

Sophie's father bowed over the woman's hand.

"And, of course, this is Sophie." Her aunt put an arm around Sophie.

"Very pleased to meet you, ma'am," Sophie said. "This is my friend Miss Frasier." Sophie nodded toward Beatrice.

"Ma'am," Beatrice said.

"You are the last guests to arrive," Mrs. Eldridge said. "I believe dinner will be served directly."

Sophie wanted to ask which one of the gentlemen was Lord Monthemer but knew she couldn't. Would they seat him beside her? Her spirits fell. Adam was nowhere to be seen. Perhaps Lord Monthemer hadn't brought him. That was likely the case. After all, it was one thing for Lord Monthemer to bring a man like Adam to a party, quite another to bring him along to a house party.

Mrs. Eldridge made introductions to some of the quests. Sophie's nerves further frayed when the older woman introduced two more gentlemen, but neither were Lord Monthemer. Twenty minutes later, when dinner was ready, Sophie walked down the hall alongside Beatrice behind Sophie's father and aunt, who followed the other guests toward the dining room. She suddenly longed for home where she could ride Ophelia and forget her troubles. Her father had accompanied her on one ride two days after he'd arrived. Perhaps she could talk him into a morning ride tomorrow.

The hallway opened up and Sophie looked over the banister at the second floor and caught sight of two men going out the front door. Her heart jumped. She would recognize Adam's broad shoulders anywhere. Was he leaving?

Her knees weakened, and she gripped the banister. In her room, the plan had seemed perfectly logical. Now that she was about to face Adam and Lord Monthemer, she wasn't so sure. What if Adam didn't understand why she'd lied about who she was? After all, a man in his social position might feel a woman of her wealth had intended to make a fool of him. No, Adam was too level-headed to think so irrationally. Wasn't he? Only last night, he had dragged Lord Emerson out of Lord Emerson's carriage. That wasn't rational. She and Beatrice neared the stairs leading down to the foyer. Sophie slowed, with Beatrice beside her.

"Keep going," Sophie whispered.

Beatrice frowned.

"Keep walking," Sophie whispered. "I will return soon."

Sophie veered to the right and started down the stairs. She looked over her shoulder to find that Beatrice had halted. Sophie waved for her to keep going. Beatrice's frown deepened. Sophie gave her a pleading look, then turned her attention forward and hurried down the rest of the stairs.

Sophie burst through the front door and out onto the steps in time to see a carriage headed down the drive. Her heart fell. Adam was leaving. She looked wildly about—for what she didn't know—and found no help.

Sophie yanked up her skirts and hurried around the side of the house. The stables came into view. She had to hurry. The carriage wasn't as fast as a single rider, but she could still lose Adam on the country road if he had too much of a lead.

The young stable hand balked at giving a young woman a horse when night was quickly falling, but Sophie threatened to have him discharged if he didn't comply. He had a horse saddled in ten minutes, and Sophie was off.

Her father would be furious, but if things went as planned, that wouldn't matter, for she and Adam would be married. Her father said he didn't want her to be alone. She wouldn't be alone.

Sophie rode to the end of the long road without catching up to the carriage and reached a fork in the road. She didn't know where the left road went, but the road to the right led back into town. That was probably the direction Adam had taken. She urged her mare into a gallop for one mile, then slowed to a canter. Night was fast approaching. She was suddenly glad of her muff pistol in her reticule. The small weapon wasn't powerful enough to be fatal, unless fired at near point-blank, but she would frighten any assailant. Thankfully, a three-quarters moon hung among sparse clouds, and she could see well on the road. The night was unseasonably warm for autumn, and she was only slightly chilled.

Panic tightened her stomach. If she didn't find Adam, her father would likely get Lord Monthemer to procure a special license and force her to marry right away. There was no way to avoid her father learning that she had left Mrs. Eldridge's estate. She fought tears and wondered if she shouldn't return to her aunt's home and hire a carriage to take her back to Invergarry—but that would only end with her married to Robert Barrett. Surely, her father wouldn't really be that cruel?

The creak of a carriage wheel caught her attention, and she dug her heels into her horse's ribs. A moment later, she discerned a carriage up ahead on the road. Sophie started to urge her horse to go faster, then realized the carriage might not be Adam's. Even with the moonlight, she couldn't be certain. There was no turning back, but that didn't mean she wanted to make a scandal by stopping a stranger's carriage on the road.

She resisted the urge to glance back, for the estate was long out of sight. She had made her bed, and now had better hope she didn't have to lay in it with Lord Monthemer—or Robert Barrett.

The carriage turned up a long drive, and she followed at a safe distance. Tall hedges lined the drive on each side. A large well-lit mansion came into view up ahead. Was this Lord Monthemer's estate? She knew this place. The hedges hadn't been here eight years ago, and it was nighttime. But she was sure this was Imogen's home. Had Imogen's family sold the house to Lord Monthemer?

Sophie maintained her distance from the carriage in readiness to gallop away should it turn out that Adam wasn't inside.

She slowed. If she got any closer to the front entrance, she might be seen. Wonderful. She had nowhere to hide once the carriage stopped—if, that is, someone didn't spot her first. Sophie urged her mare through the hedge and off the drive toward a large tree. She reached the tree, dismounted, and tied the horse to a low branch.

Sophie lifted her skirts and hurried as fast as she dared alongside the hedge until she neared the house. She peered through the hedges just in time to see the carriage stop. She pushed through the foliage and winced when her feet crunched on gravel and slowed in her creep forward. She reached the rear of the carriage as the carriage door opened and a man stepped out.

Adam.

Sophie thought she might cry. He started toward the mansion. Fear froze her in place.

Move!

She stepped out from behind the carriage. "Adam."

He spun. With the light behind him, his face remained in shadow, and she couldn't discern his expression. The carriage started forward.

"What the devil?" Adam strode to her and seized her arm. "What the bloody hell are you doing here?"

Her heart thundered. "I wanted to speak with you." She hated the tremble in her voice.

"Speak with me? Have you any idea of the danger you're in by being here?"

"I-I have a proposition for you."

He glanced back at the departing carriage, then faced her. "What are you doing here?"

"Marry me," she blurted. A heartbeat of silence passed, and

she plunged into an explanation. "I know this is sudden. I hadn't planned on telling you this way."

"You are mad," he growled.

"I had thought you might be at the house party," she babbled. "But you left before I could talk to you."

He shook her arm. "How did you get here?" Before she could reply, he said, "You followed me? By God, you followed me from Mrs. Eldridge's home. It's bad enough you galivant about Edinburgh with men in carriages, now you are following them at night? Have you no shame?"

"I beg your pardon." She really did fear she would cry. "I only wanted to—"

"What is going on?" a man called.

Adam snapped his head in the direction of the mansion, then he turned back to her. "Have you any idea what you've done?" His grip on her arm tightened.

"Release me," Sophie ordered.

"Hush," he hissed.

Boots crunched on gravel, and she glimpsed a man approaching.

"Do as I say, and you might live through this night," Adam hissed. "Don't, and he will kill us both."

Sophie blinked, then Adam yanked her against him and crushed his mouth against hers.

CHAPTER 19

ADAM RAVAGED HER MOUTH WHILE HIS MIND RACED. BALFOUR would kill him and Miss Shaw. Bloody hell, but he wished that Daily hadn't taken the carriage.

"What the hell is going on?" Balfour demanded.

Adam broke the kiss. Sophie blinked up at him.

With his gaze on her, Adam said, "You will have to forgive me, Balfour. My betrothed couldn't wait to see me and followed me here."

"Is that so?" Balfour drawled.

"Allow me to see her safely home then I will return," Adam said.

"Nae, I think she will join us."

Adam mentally cursed. He'd been right. He should have brought a pistol.

"Shall we?" Balfour stepped aside in invitation—more an order—for them to proceed him inside.

Adam started to shove Sophie behind him and charge Balfour, then stilled when a hulking man emerged from the mansion.

"Let me send her home, Balfour," Adam said.

Balfour shook his head. "I am intrigued by a woman who would follow a man in a carriage. Where is your horse, my dear?"

"I tied her to a tree in the lawn." Miss Shaw pointed to their right where large hedges lined the drive.

Balfour chuckled. "A resourceful woman. Let us go inside." He began walking, and Adam pulled Sophie close, then followed. Thankfully, she had the good sense to remain quiet.

Once inside, Adam caught sight of another large man waiting outside the open door of the study where light spilled out into the hallway. They followed Balfour into the study, and Adam urged her to sit on a sofa near the hearth. He read fear in her eyes. She should be afraid.

Balfour crossed to a sideboard near the bookshelves. "Would you like a brandy?"

His tone was amiable, but Adam knew better. One wrong move, and the man would shoot them both, then have the bodies buried where no one would find them. For the first time in his adult life, Adam was at a complete loss. How should he proceed?

"Nothing for me." Adam kept his gaze locked on Sophie.

Her eyes flashed, and he suddenly realized how beautiful she really was. Dread abruptly tightened his insides. Balfour had a penchant for beautiful women.

"I can see I will have to teach you yet another lesson," Adam told her.

Balfour faced them, a glass of brandy in hand. "Another lesson?" he asked in a conversational tone.

Adam kept his gaze fixed on Sophie. "Aye. This time, I will make my point."

"Has—" Balfour cleared his throat. "You haven't introduced us."

"Forgive me. Miss Shaw, meet Kenrich Balfour." Adam

tensed in readiness for a reaction when she realized he knew her identity.

"Kenrich Balfour?" she blurted, and he could have kissed her.

"You have heard of me?" Balfour asked.

She glanced at Adam, then said, "Forgive me, sir, but at Lady Seafield's ball there was…talk of how you have debauched certain ladies."

Adam tensed.

Balfour stared for two heartbeats, then laughed. "Surely, you do not believe everything you hear?"

"I try to remain objective," Sophie replied.

"Excellent." Balfour sipped his drink. "Tell me, Miss Shaw, do you make a habit of following men at night?"

Color tingled her cheeks, and Adam suspected she was remembering the carriage ride with him and Emerson. Adam really did want to teach her a lesson.

"Tonight was my first time following a gentleman," she said.

"Has anyone ever told you that you are a little mad?" Balfour asked.

Her eyes shifted to Adam. "So I was told tonight."

Adam gave a slow nod. "You and I definitely need to come to an understanding."

He'd never meant anything more in his life.

"When are you two to wed?" Balfour asked.

Adam looked at him. "Her father and I have not yet set a date, but I imagine three days hence."

Balfour sipped his whisky. "Tonight would be even better."

Sophie gasped in unison with Adam's, "I beg your pardon?"

"A gentleman can depend upon a wife to stand by his side at all times," Balfour said.

There was no mistaking his meaning. Balfour didn't like the fact that Sophie was witness to their association. As Adam's wife, she couldn't be forced to make any statements against Adam.

"Balfour, I need a moment with my intended," Adam said.

Hesitation flickered in his eyes. "I will have a minister fetched while you two discuss…your wedding."

Sophie looked at Adam in confusion.

"You seem distressed, Miss Shaw," Balfour said in a smooth voice.

"I-I simply planned to marry surrounded by family."

Balfour laughed. "I imagine you should have thought of that before you followed a man at night."

She thinned her lips, and Adam feared she would lose her temper.

"How can we marry tonight?" she asked in a calm voice. "We have no license."

Balfour gave a slow nod. "Never fear. I can take care of that. You will excuse me." He started toward the door.

When the door clicked shut, Sophie shot to her feet. "I knew it!"

Adam frowned. "Knew what?"

"That Lord Monthemer is involved in criminal activities."

"Indeed?" he asked in a half-strangled voice. "Exactly *what* do you know?"

"I have heard that Mr. Balfour is also a pirate—just like Lord Monthemer. Perhaps I do not have to marry at all. Once I tell my father what I have learned, he will not force me to marry the marquess."

"Have you any idea what just happened?" Adam asked.

"Indeed, I do. I have found the proof I need to put a stop to my father's ridiculous matchmaking. You will have to forgive me, Adam, but I am withdrawing my offer of marriage. You understand, do you not? After all—" Her eyes widened. "You— you introduced me as Miss Shaw. You know who I am?"

"Just now figuring that out, eh?" he said.

"What is going on?" she demanded.

"What's going on, Miss Shaw, is that you have gotten yourself into trouble that I cannot get you out of."

Her brow knit. "I do not need you to get me out of trouble."

"Look around you. You are in trouble. You are correct on one point. Balfour is a pirate—and a nasty one at that. The smallest slip on our part and he will kill us."

She glanced toward the door, then returned her gaze to him. "Why would he kill us?"

"As I said, he is a nasty pirate. There is no way out of this, Miss Shaw. You are about to be married to me."

Panic widened her eyes. "There is no need."

"That was before you left the safety of Mrs. Eldridge's house party and followed me here. Christ, what possessed you? Have you no sense at all?" he muttered.

"What possessed me was the fear that my father was marrying me to—to someone like *him*." She pointed at the door Balfour had disappeared through.

"Even if your fears were founded—" Adam broke off and raked a hand through his hair. "To say your actions were foolish does not begin to say how serious this is."

"I know I offered you marriage, but I have changed my mind," she said. "I will not marry you. He cannot make me. Neither can you."

Adam snorted. "Balfour will force laudanum down your throat, if necessary. If that doesn't work, he will shoot you—though he will likely shoot me first, as he will not risk that I will kill him first."

"Not if I shoot *him* first," she said.

Adam stared. "Madam, you are, *indeed,* mad."

She rolled her eyes. "I have a pistol, you fool."

"A pistol." He narrowed his eyes. "Where on your person could you possibly have a pistol?"

She hesitated.

"Miss Shaw," he growled.

"In my reticule, of course."

"A muff pistol?" When she nodded, he extended a hand. "If you please."

She gave a dark laugh. "I would advise you not attempt to take it from me. You can overcome him." Her gaze sharpened. "I believe you are afraid of him. I had no idea you were a coward."

"It is easy for you to speak of courage when you are not the one doing the fighting. Make no mistake, the odds will not be one to one, or even two to one. They will be ten to one." When she frowned, Adam sighed. "Balfour always has men nearby to protect him. You saw those two large brutes in the hallway. They will not hesitate to kill you—after they have done things to you that you cannot imagine."

"What part do you have in this?" she demanded.

He glanced at the door, then stepped close and whispered, "I am working with the Crown to recoup stolen gold."

She drew a sharp breath.

Adam nodded. "And you very well may have brought the operation to a premature end. We have little time. Listen carefully. We will say the vows, then we will deal with our *marriage* later."

She sat back onto the chair. "I cannot think. This is…too much."

Adam dropped to one knee beside her. "My first priority is your safety. Once you are safely away from here, I must finish what I have started."

He considered wresting the pistol from her, but she may well need some measure of protection, and even a tiny muff pistol might save her life. He stood and extended a hand. She took a deep breath, released it, then placed her smaller hand in his and stood. He gave her hand a reassuring squeeze as the door opened.

Balfour entered. "I hope I am not interrupting."

"Not at all," Adam said. "Miss Shaw and I were just discussing where we will go on our honeymoon."

Balfour lifted a brow in polite inquiry.

"France," Adam said. "Once our business here is finished."

"A fine choice." Balfour smiled at her. "Will this be your first visit to France, Miss Shaw?"

"Nae, but I was very young, and remember little of the trip," she said, without giving away any of the anxiety she'd revealed to Adam only moments ago.

Balfour turned toward him and pulled a sheath of folded paper from his inside jacket pocket. "You are to take this note and fetch the special license from the bishop." He handed the paper to Adam.

Adam checked the surprise that flashed through him. "If it is all the same to you, Balfour, you may send one of your men for the license."

Balfour smiled congenially. "Rest assured, Miss Shaw will be safe in my keeping until you return."

Fury swept through Adam. What was the man up to? Why force him to get the license himself. He looked at Sophie.

"I will be fine. Mr. Balfour will keep me company." She turned a charming smile on him.

Balfour looked at Adam. "A horse awaits you out front."

Adam gave a slight bow to Sophie. "Miss Shaw." He turned to Balfour. "Balfour, a word before I go."

They went into the hallway. Adam wasn't surprised to see half a dozen men now standing guard outside the room. No doubt, another half dozen lurked in the shadows somewhere.

When they'd taken three steps, Adam halted. "Harm a hair on her head, and I will kill you."

"Now why would I harm her?"

"Do not toy with me, Balfour. If anything happens to her, I will lose a fortune."

"Ah, she is an heiress."

"Don't be a fool, of course she is an heiress," he snapped. "I have invested a great deal in her and have no intention of letting her fortune slip through my fingers."

"Given the circumstances, you should thank me for ensuring your marriage tonight. We will see you in about half an hour?" Balfour said.

"Twenty minutes," Adam said, and strode away.

CHAPTER 20

THE CLOCK STRUCK ELEVEN WHEN MR. BALFOUR WALKED through the door of the study. Another man accompanied him, a minister, Sophie realized, along with a woman she assumed was the housekeeper. Sophie didn't fully understand what was happening, other than she was marrying Adam MacAlister this very night.

The minister smiled and greeted her as if being roused late at night to perform a wedding was the most natural thing in the world. He had a large book tucked beneath his arm. The registry, she would wager.

Mr. Balfour had barely made the introductions when Adam returned. Sophie had to admit she'd never been so glad to see anyone. He produced the marriage license, then took her hand and held it as the minister conducted the service.

Her head whirled and, despite the fact marrying Adam posthaste had been her plan, when the minister said the words "Do you, Sophie Shaw, take this man to be your husband?" they echoed in her head like a cannon boom.

When he finished, she had to force her reply. "I do."

He faced Adam. "Do you, Adam Scott, take this woman to be your wife?"

Adam *Scott?* Sophie snapped her head up to meet Adam's gaze.

He looked at her without expression. "I do."

To Sophie's shock, Adam produced a sapphire ring from his jacket pocket, then he repeated the vows after the minister and slipped the ring on her finger.

The minister then glanced around the room. "Will you who have witnessed these promises do all in your power to uphold these two persons in their marriage?"

Mr. Balfour and his housekeeper replied in unison, "We will."

The minister said in a loud voice, "Those whom God has joined together let no man put asunder."

"You must seal the pact with a kiss," Mr. Balfour said.

Pact? Sophie fisted her hands. The man was a brute.

Adam pulled her close and his mouth descended on hers. Their lips touched and, unlike the other night in the garden, this kiss was gentle. She almost wondered if he was apologizing. He broke the embrace, and Mr. Balfour and Mrs. Childers signed the registry as witnesses. Sophie's hand shook as she signed her name. A headache began to pound behind her eyes. All she wanted to do was return to her room, close the door, and sleep for a week. Adam stepped up and signed his name Adam Scott. She stared at his signature, and fear began a slow crawl through her belly.

Mr. Balfour clapped him on the back. "How does it feel to be a married man, Monthemer?"

"Monthemer?" Sophie blurted.

"The title sounds strange at first, do you not agree, Lady Monthemer?" Mr. Balfour asked.

Sophie's heart pounded. Monthemer? The room spun.

"I will call for champagne," Mr. Balfour said.

Adam shook his head and slipped an arm around her waist. She started to break free, but his hold tightened.

"Nae," Adam said. "I believe my bride and I should go. You understand."

A strange light appeared in Mr. Balfour's eyes. "Indeed, I do. Which is why I have made arrangements for you to stay here tonight."

"Stay here, tonight?" Sophie glared up at Adam.

"Thank you, but there is no need for you to put yourself out," Adam said. "Let me send her home, then you and I can conclude our business."

Business? So, Adam, the Marquess of Monthemer, was involved in criminal activities.

Mr. Balfour shook his head. "This is your wedding night. You cannot send your bride home alone. I already have a room prepared for you."

Anger tightened her insides. She wanted to punch Adam in the stomach as hard as she could. "Surely, you understand that I would rather be home," she said through gritted teeth.

"It is late," Mr. Balfour replied. "I really must insist."

"Mr. Balfour, Sophie and I are married," Adam said. "My wife is now under my protection. She will not do anything to fall out of grace with me."

Fall out of grace with him?

He looked at her. "In fact, I believe I will send her to the country. She does not care for city life."

Sophie stared.

"Is that true, my lady?" Mr. Balfour asked.

She wanted to scream that Adam knew nothing about what she cared for, but she nodded and said, "I do prefer a quiet life."

"How very interesting," he said. "Will you go right away?"

"Tomorrow, I imagine," Adam said before she could reply. "I see no reason to delay."

"Surely you will want to throw at least one party in celebration of your marriage?" Mr. Balfour asked.

"A *party*?" Sophie could barely believe the man.

He laughed. "I thought all women loved parties."

"There is no need for a party," she said stiffly.

How she wanted to break free of Adam's iron grip around her waist.

Mr. Balfour gave a slow nod. "I must insist. A party here at my home two days hence. That will give your husband time to get the announcement of your marriage into the papers."

"You want to have a party…here?" Sophie said. "That is too much."

Mr. Balfour smiled. "Not at all. I feel certain your husband would do the same for me. Now, Phillip will show you to your room."

Sophie looked at Adam. "Sir, really, I prefer to be home. After all, it is our wedding night."

To her shock, he thinned his mouth in disapproval. "Mr. Balfour has been kind enough to prepare a room for us. It would be rude to refuse." He released her and winged his arm, but she knew the gesture wasn't a request.

Sophie slipped her hand into the crook of his arm, and they followed the large man named Phillip from the room. They climbed one flight of stairs and twisted through the hallways until they reached the room Phillip said was theirs. They entered the bedchambers to find two maids waiting in front of a four-poster canopy bed with dark gold silk curtains.

The maids curtsied. "My lady," the dark-haired girl said. "Mr. Balfour instructed us to help you with your toilet."

"I assume that door leads to a sitting room?" Adam angled his head toward a door to their left.

"Aye, sir," the maid replied." A fire burns in the hearth and there is French brandy waiting for you."

He gave a slight bow. "Then I will leave you ladies to your business."

Sophie shot him a narrow-eyed glare as he passed, but he made no comment. When the door clicked shut behind him the maids started toward her.

ADAM ENTERED THE SITTING ROOM TO FIND A LAD WAITING beside the chair located before the hearth. As the maid had said, a decanter sat on the table beside the chair alongside a full brandy glass.

A gentleman's robe lay across the back of the chair, and a basin, pitcher, and cloth sat on the table near the window. Balfour was taking no chances that the marriage might be declared invalid. He no doubt intended for everyone in the household to testify that Adam and Sophie had consummated the marriage.

"If you sit down, sir, I will remove your boots," the lad said.

Adam gave a slight nod and sat in the chair. He sipped brandy while the boy removed his boots. When finished, the boy placed the boots outside the door, then returned and stood at attention before Adam.

"They will be cleaned and ready for you by tomorrow morning, sir. Along with your clothes." He waited.

Adam shook his head. "That will not be necessary."

"Oh, but it is, my lord. Mr. Balfour instructed me not to leave without your clothes."

"I wager he did," Adam muttered.

"I beg your pardon, my lord?"

"Never mind." Adam finished the brandy, then stood.

He removed his clothes, then put on the robe the boy held out for him. Once he dismissed the lad, Adam resumed his seat before the fire and sipped brandy as he contemplated the situation. He wouldn't be surprised if their clothes weren't returned until well after lunch. Sophie would be livid. It would serve the wench right. He still couldn't believe she had followed him here. The little fool. She was fortunate Balfour hadn't just killed her.

Adam lost himself in thoughts of what gold Balfour had stolen.

A knock on the door connecting the bedchamber snapped Adam from his thoughts.

"Enter," he called.

The door opened, and one of the young maids entered. "Your wife is ready to receive you, my lord."

Receive him? He would wager she was ready to throw him off the tallest building she could find.

He stood and strode past the maid, and she followed him into the bedchamber. Sophie sat on a chair near the hearth, a sheet wrapped around her shoulders like a shawl. The maid hurried to the door, where the other maid stood, and they left him and Sophie alone.

"Were you divested of your clothes as I was?" she asked.

"I am as naked as the day I was born," he said. "Beneath my robe, of course."

She stood and faced him. Adam immediately understood the reason for wrapping herself in the sheet. The hem of her nightgown was so sheer he discerned supple calves beneath the thin fabric. A shame she was so modest. He wouldn't have minded the view. His cock pulsed in agreement.

She met his gaze square. "So, tell me, *Lord Monthemer*, did you enjoy trapping me into marriage?"

He had planned on asking her a similar question, but her shock when Balfour had called him by his title had been genuine. She hadn't known his identity. Still…

"Why did you pretend to be a maid?" he asked.

"Because I grew tired of men trying to trap me into marriage for my money."

Adam blinked. Then he laughed. Hard.

"You think this is funny?" she demanded.

He nodded, still laughing. "Forgive me, but I do."

She took two steps toward him then halted. "What is going on here with Mr. Balfour?"

He grasped her arm and pulled her to the bed. She balked, but he shot her a warning look, then scooped her up and tossed her onto the mattress. She started to crawl off the other side, but he seized her arm.

"Hold fast, Miss Shaw," he whispered.

Adam pulled the curtains down around the bed until they were enclosed. In the gloom, he couldn't see her features but discerned the tremble in the arm he still gripped.

He leaned close and she drew back. Adam grasped the back of her neck and brought his mouth to her ear then whispered, "We cannot be certain who might be listening."

"No doubt, your criminal partner," she hissed. "Rest assured that I will not stay married to a criminal. I will have this marriage annulled. I told my father you were not to be trusted. Little did I know how right I was."

He said in a low voice, "Criminal or not, after tonight there will be no annulment."

"We are not truly married until the marriage is consummated—which you may depend upon not happening."

"Why do you think Balfour insisted we stay here tonight?" he asked.

"How would I know? The man is clearly mad."

"You may be right on that score," he said. "However, there is a method to his madness. He forced us to stay here in order to have witnesses that the marriage was, indeed, consummated."

"That is ridiculous. With no one here to watch us, they cannot know."

"Come, Miss Shaw, we are closeted alone in a bedroom without our clothes. No one will believe otherwise. That was his plan."

She let out a very unladylike growl. "I will not stay here another instant with you." She started to crawl off the bed.

Adam grabbed her arm and yanked her back.

"Forgive me," he said. "You will stay, even if I have to sleep on top of you."

She stilled.

"Sophie"—the devil possessed him, and he amended—"my lady"—which elicited another growl from her—"Balfour will think nothing of killing us both should he feel threatened."

"You are saying that to frighten me," she said, but he detected fear in her voice.

"Only because it is true," he replied.

Thankfully, she acquiesced, but he insisted she sleep on the side of the bed farthest from the door. He slept not a wink, and by her tossing and turning, he knew she didn't either.

CHAPTER 21

Sophie came awake with a heavy body on top of her. She snapped open her eyes and looked straight into Adam's eyes. She drew a breath to scream.

He clamped a hand over her mouth, pressed his mouth to her ear, and whispered, "Someone is in our room."

She stilled. He removed his hand from her mouth, and she was suddenly aware of the hard length that dug into her abdomen and—

"You are not wearing any clothes," she hissed.

He clamped his hand over her mouth again. "That is what married people do, if you recall," he whispered.

She did remember, though she didn't remember a man's naked body being so heavy or so hard, and his...desire was more persistent than had been Matthew's.

Sophie caught sight of a figure through the curtains around the bed. She yanked her gaze back to Adam. He nodded. Then he kissed her. Her head spun. This kiss wasn't soft as had been the one when the minister pronounced them man and wife. His weight pressed her into the mattress in a way that made her want to wrap her legs around his waist and rub her mons against his erection.

Over the thud of her heart pounding in her ears, she discerned the light rattle of teacups and realized the maid who'd entered their room had set a tray on the table. She wanted to tell Adam he could stop—should stop—kissing her, but she didn't want him to stop. Sophie broke the kiss and turned her head aside. He nuzzled her neck, and the juncture between her legs tightened. The maid had halted and was staring at them. Heat suffused Sophie's cheeks. Not because she was embarrassed.

"It is impolite to stare," Sophie said.

The maid gasped and fled the room.

Sophie pushed at Adam, and he slid off her onto the mattress. She caught sight of his erection, thick, straight, and far more masculine than anything she'd ever seen.

She yanked her gaze away to his face. He arched a brow. Sophie shoved at him. He chuckled, then his expression sobered. He drew back the curtain and jumped from the bed. Sophie got a wonderful view of his rounded backside. Matthew had been a nice-looking man, but Adam was a sculpted god.

"We have coffee and pastries," Adam said.

Sophie started to get up, then remembered the thin nightgown she wore. She fished the sheet from the tangled bedcovers and wrapped it around her like a towel. She stepped from the bed, and Adam looked up from the coffee he was pouring into one of the cups. He had put on the robe he'd worn last night.

He ran his gaze down her body, then straightened. He regarded her, expression serious, and she forced herself not to squirm under his scrutiny. He set the coffee pot down, then crossed to her. Sophie drew back when he reached for her. He lifted a brow in clear challenge, and she lifted her chin in response. Amusement sparked in his eyes, and she was surprised when he threaded his fingers in her hair. She braced for him to pull her against him. Instead, he mussed her hair, then pulled his fingers free.

He gave a slow nod. "Now you look like a woman who made love all night."

She flushed. He returned to the table and filled the second cup with coffee.

He picked up one of the pastries and took a big bite. "These are delicious. How do you take your coffee?"

"Cream and one sugar," she said. "I want answers."

He took another bite and nodded. "After we leave."

Sophie opened her mouth to argue, but he shoved the last of his pastry into his mouth and shook his head. It wasn't his refusal that stopped her, but the look in his eyes that told her danger was close.

"Please sit." He indicated a chair at the table. "You will feel better after you have eaten."

She acquiesced and had to admit that after coffee and a pastry she did feel refreshed. The clock on the mantle chimed the nine o'clock hour, and Sophie had just begun to wonder how long they would have to wait for their clothes when a knock sounded on the door, and a maid entered with their clothes washed and pressed. She placed them on the bed, then curtsied and left.

Sophie sipped her coffee, then set the cup on its saucer. "I know this house."

Adam's head snapped in her direction.

"When I was young, my father used to bring me and my mother to Edinburgh every year," she said. "I had a friend who lived in this house. Her stepfather sent her away to school in France. I haven't heard from her in years."

"What was her name?" Adam asked in a low voice that gave her pause.

"Imogen Rose."

"Balfour's sister," he said.

"His sister? That horrid man is her brother?"

"Stepbrother. I've never met the girl, but I hear he keeps a close watch on her."

"She's here?" Sophie demanded.

"Aye."

"I had no idea." It hadn't even occurred to her to see if Imogen was in Edinburgh.

"We used to play on the estate," Sophie said. "When she went away to France, I assumed she simply became too busy to write." Sophie met his gaze. "She told me her stepfather sent her away to school."

"That would have been Balfour's father," Adam replied.

"I should see if she is here. I can ask Mr. Balfour—"

"Nae," he interrupted. "I ask you to leave the matter to me." Before she could reply, he instructed her to dress, then excused himself to the anteroom.

Fifteen minutes later, a maid showed them to the breakfast room where Mr. Balfour was sat at the breakfast table.

He looked up as they entered. "Please, have a seat. I made sure to have plenty for breakfast this morning."

"I can stay," Adam said. "You and I have business, I believe. Sophie will go home."

"Our business will have to wait," Mr. Balfour said. "I am leaving in ten minutes."

"I can ride with you," Adam said.

He shook his head. "We can meet this evening, say seven?"

Adam angled his head in acknowledgement. "Of course."

"I have begun preparations for your wedding celebration," Mr. Balfour said.

"There is no need, sir," Sophie said.

He shook his head. "It's no trouble." He took a sip of coffee then stood. "I have a carriage waiting outside to take you home.

You really should have some breakfast first, though. Cook outdid herself." He looked at Adam. "I will see you tonight, Monthemer."

Adam nodded and Balfour left.

"Would you like some breakfast?" Adam asked.

"I do not want to spend another minute in this house," she said, though she did wish she could ask after Imogen.

Adam gave a slight bow. "I do not blame you."

The footman waiting outside the room escorted them to the front door. Adam grasped her hand and helped her inside the waiting carriage, then vaulted in after her and too the seat opposite her.

The vehicle lurched into motion, and Sophie suddenly felt certain she was walking in a dream. No, a nightmare. Adam—the Marquess of Monthemer—sat across from her in the carriage as casual as could be. She would again accuse him of trapping her into marriage—if the situation weren't so outlandish. It simply was beyond comprehension that anyone could have planned this…situation. Of course, he had no idea she would be so foolhardy as to follow him from Mrs. Eldridge's home. Lord, she could scarce believe she'd done it.

What would her father say? He wanted her to marry—that part would please him. He wouldn't, however, be pleased at how she accomplished the matter. She would like to think that because she was now married that her father would have nothing to say. She knew better. Not to mention, she had no intention of staying married.

"What is going on?" she demanded.

He met her gaze. "What happened is that you expedited our marriage."

Sophie narrowed her eyes. "You and Mr. Balfour are engaged in illegal activities."

Poor Imogen.

Adam hesitated, and her heart fell. She'd had some small hope there was a good explanation for his actions.

"As I told you last night, I am working for the Crown," he said.

That was too on the nose. "I am not so gullible as to believe that."

He shrugged. "It is the truth. But you are to keep that to yourself. If word reaches Balfour, we are both dead."

"A fine way to keep me from asking questions," she retorted. "I shall begin annulment proceedings immediately."

"That will get us both killed."

She rolled her eyes.

"Besides, your father will never allow it."

She tossed her head. "He cannot stop me."

"I feel certain he can."

"You just want my money."

"Your father's money. Yes, there is that," he said in a thoughtful voice. "But please keep in mind it was you who followed me to Balfour's, which is what facilitated the current circumstances."

She stomped her foot. "You lied to me."

"Just as you lied to me."

"Yes, but I did that to protect myself. You lied to use me."

"Not at first," he said.

Sophie frowned. "You are talking in circles."

"You may recall I met you while you were riding—and wearing breeches. That was enough to tell me what a hoyden you are."

She scoffed. "You care little for any of that. You only care for my money."

"Your father's money," he said, again.

"I will come into my money in two years—which, by the by, you may not have."

He angled his head in assent. "I wouldn't dream of touching *your* money."

They rode in silence and when they neared her aunt's town-house, Sophie wished mightily she were anywhere else but here. It was too much to hope that her father would be away. The carriage halted, and Adam opened the door as her aunt's front door burst open, and Aunt Maddie hurried down the four front steps, Sophie's father close behind.

Adam took Sophie's hand and helped her from the carriage as Aunt Maddie arrived. She pulled Sophie into a hug Sophie thought would strangle her.

"Oh, we were so worried," her aunt said. "If you and marquess decided to elope, why did you not at least send a note?" Sophie opened her mouth to reply, but Maddie cut her off. "It is not as if your father would have tried to stop you."

"We—"

"Do not ever do that again," Maddie scolded.

This time, Sophie waited to see if her aunt intended to continue her scolding.

"I assume you have a good reason for whisking my daughter away without so much as a by your leave?" Sophie's father asked Adam.

"I do, sir. Though the reason may not be quite what you expect."

"Sophie!" her aunt exclaimed. "Never say you let him ravish you without getting married."

Sophie flushed.

"Oh Lord." Maddie shook her head. She whirled on Adam. "Do not think that because she isn't a virgin that you will get away with not marrying her."

Adam threw up his hands, palms out. "Never fear, ma'am. We are married."

"But not for long," Sophie said.

CHAPTER 22

aunt.

"You are damned lucky he didn't kill you," her father muttered.

He was angry, but Sophie read the fear in his eyes. "I am sorry," she said.

He gave her a curt nod and instructed Adam to follow him into the study. Sophie and her aunt were to wait here for them. Sophie resisted the urge to argue.

Beatrice entered the parlor five minutes later. Sophie glimpsed the moisture in her eyes and jumped to her feet and raced to her.

They threw their arms around each other, and Beatrice said, "I was terribly worried, miss."

"I know." Sophie drew back. "I was beastly to run off like that."

"And now you are married," Beatrice said.

Sophie sighed. "For the moment."

She grasped Beatrice's hand and pulled her to the sofa. They sat, and Sophie poured Beatrice some tea from the pot sitting on the coffee table. Beatrice drank and they sat in silence for half an hour before Sophie told her aunt, "I have no intention of remaining married to the marquess."

Maddie regarded her for a long moment. "You were perfectly willing to marry him when you didn't know he was the marquess. We both know that man is not a criminal, Sophie."

"You would not say that if you would've heard him speaking with Mr. Balfour."

Her aunt nodded. "There are, indeed, rumors about Mr. Balfour. But the marquess explained that he is working for the Crown."

"How can we possibly believe such an outlandish story? Matthew had many outlandish stories. I will never again be foolish enough to believe such a ridiculous tale."

Aunt Maddie's expression softened. "Does Lord Monthemer seem anything like your dead husband?"

Sophie gave a mirthless laugh. "Nae, but that does not mean he isn't just as bad. Think, Aunt Maddie, how many men truly work for the Crown?"

"Not many, I am sure. You needn't worry, though. Your father will get to the bottom of this." A sparkle lit her eyes. "And I am not without my own connections."

"I am certain your father will make sure Lord Monthemer is honest," Beatrice said.

Sophie started to reply, then didn't when bootfalls approached down the hallway. The men had finished their business and were now on their way to inform the women— her in particular—of their decisions. Sophie jumped up and hurried to the bookshelves. She pulled a book from the shelf, then raced back to the sofa and dropped onto the cushion. She yanked the book open two seconds before they entered. Then she looked up with what she hoped was the most placid expression in existence.

Adam's eyes caught on Beatrice and narrowed. Sophie remembered when she'd heard his voice in Lady Ella's garden maze. Oh Lord, he had met Beatrice when she had been pretending to be Sophie. Lord Blair had been there, as well. Her father had done some business with Lord Blair. Hadn't she been introduced to him at some party? Why hadn't he said something when Beatrice introduced herself as Sophie? Oh! The odious men. Lord Blair hadn't said anything because they already knew Sophie wasn't Beatrice. He and Adam had both known!

When she and Adam had danced at Lady Seafield's party, and when she'd been in the carriage with Lord Emerson, Adam had known who she was. That explained why *Lord Monthemer* had signed the marriage agreement in the wee hours of the morning.

Sophie locked gazes with Adam and tensed in readiness for him to tell her father that she had pretended to be Beatrice— and that Beatrice had pretended to be her. Perhaps Adam had already told her father. Fear welled up in her. Her father would immediately dismiss Beatrice. Determination shot through Sophie. She would take Beatrice with her to Adam's household. But she didn't plan on staying married to him. If her father dismissed Beatrice, Sophie would leave with her.

Adam crossed the room and seated himself on the couch to Sophie's left while her father paced. Sophie's heart pounded, but she kept her attention on her father.

"I have sent notices to the papers with the announcement of your marriage to Lord Monthemer," he said.

Sophie gasped.

He halted and looked at her. "Did you expect otherwise?"

"I was very clear that I intend to annul the marriage," she replied stiffly.

"Sophie, you left Mrs. Eldridge's party unescorted and followed a man to another man's home at night. There was never any question that your marriage to Lord Monthemer would remain intact."

"I am no virgin, Father. I am a widow and am allowed my dalliances."

"Then you should never have agreed to the annulment from Matthew."

"Agreed?" she whispered. "You insisted on the annulment. You—you did that on purpose. This was your plan all along."

"You give me too much credit," he replied. "My plan was to protect you from Matthew's family."

"Lot of good that did," she muttered, though she knew she was being melodramatic. The annulment had curtailed their demands for money and attention.

"Society understands that you have no connection with Matthew's family," her father said.

"Invergarry's society."

"Not just Invergarry," he said.

"I care nothing for Society," she said.

"That much is clear," he replied in a harsh voice. "You ran off last night with the intention of marrying Lord Monthemer."

"I ran off with the intention of marrying Mr. Adam MacAlister!"

"They are the same man," he said. "You cannot suddenly decide you do not like what you got."

Sophie shifted her gaze to Adam. "Lord Monthemer is involved in criminal activities."

"Lord Monthemer is working for the Crown," her father said.

Sophie frowned. "You are not so naïve as to believe that?"

"I have no reason to believe otherwise, but we will soon have confirmation."

"I am agog to learn the truth," she said with mock sweetness. "Until then, I will remain here at Aunt Maddie's."

"I wouldn't think of forcing you to leave the safety of your aunt's home," Adam replied.

She scowled. "This is a trick."

"A trick?" he repeated. "You do not wish to stay at my lodgings here in Edinburgh, and I am obliging."

"Lodgings?" She nodded slowly. "You do not own a home in Edinburgh."

"Not anymore," he said.

Sophie looked at her father. "How can you allow a man who doesn't even own a home to marry your daughter?"

"Lord Monthemer owns a home, just not in Edinburgh," he said.

"Where?" she asked warily.

"Inverness," Adam replied.

"Is this "home" a summer cottage?"

"Nae."

"A townhouse?"

"Nae."

"An estate?" she asked.

Adam regarded her. "Forgive me, my lady"—she winced at the address—"what difference does it make? I thought you cared nothing for money."

"I do not care if a man has money—but when a man marries me for money, I want to know if he plans to leave me in squalor while he lives in luxury."

Adam gave her a smile she felt certain had dazzled many a lady. "Rest easy, my dear. I have no intention of doing either."

"What does that mean?"

"You will find out soon enough."

"I shall have your belongings moved into the Blue bedchambers, Sophie," Aunt Maddie said.

"Whatever for?" Sophie demanded.

"We cannot have you and Lord Monthemer sharing that small bedchamber."

"What?" Sophie blurted. "I have no intention of sharing my bedchambers with him."

"He is your husband, Sophie," her father said. "We cannot have his lordship staying in a boarding house now that you two are married."

"Surely Sophie does not have to move," Adam said. "I can stay in another room."

To Sophie's surprise, her aunt shook her head. "Do you want the servants telling everyone that you are not sharing a room?"

Adam rubbed the back of his neck. "I take your point, but we needn't move Sophie. I can sleep in a chair in her room."

"No husband sleeps in a chair in his own bedchambers," her father growled.

"These are *my* bedchambers," Sophie said. "Do you truly plan on leaving me with this man?"

"I do," her father replied. "You two will live as husband and wife."

"Then I wish for my finances to remain my own," she said.

"That is acceptable," Adam said. "As I said earlier, I have no desire to spend your money."

"Even once you have squandered my dowry?" she demanded.

"That will take some time to do, so you need not concern yourself."

She scoffed. "I have found that it is easy to spend money."

"Then perhaps I should inform you that once you have squandered *your* money, I will give you an allowance of fifty pounds a year."

"Me, squander my money?" She stared at him. "It is you who will squander my money."

"Your father's money," he corrected.

"Did you hear that, Father? I shall be responsible for all my personal expenditures, and when my money is gone, I will be given a generous sum of fifty pounds a year."

"Then I suppose you had best be careful how you spend your money," her father replied.

"Oh, I will. In fact, I have already spoken with my man of affairs about investments." This was a lie—she didn't even have a man of affairs—but she would hire one before they knew otherwise.

"What kind of investments?" Adam asked.

She smiled sweetly. "None that need concerning you, sir."

"If those investments include gaming hells that does concern me."

"Gaming hells?" She grimaced. "Good God, no. Who in their right mind would invest in a gaming hall?"

"No one," he murmured.

CHAPTER 23

SOPHIE SAID A QUIET THANKS WHEN ADAM HAD BUSINESS THAT took him away directly after their meeting. Congratulations on their marriage poured in, so by teatime, Sophie hid away in her room until her father commanded her to come down to dinner. The family ate in silence, and afterward, Sophie adjourned to the parlor not wanting to be in her bedchambers when Adam returned.

The clock struck nine, and Sophie still sat in the parlor pretending to read a book when the front door opened. Adam had returned. She remained seated and listened to his footsteps as he strode down the hallway. He had to be headed for the small study where her father had taken up residence.

She wanted very badly to eavesdrop but didn't know this house like she did her own. Plus, if a maid happened upon her while she was listening in on the men's conversation, she couldn't guarantee the maid would remain quiet.

AN HOUR TICKED BY WHEN THE STUDY DOOR OPENED AND bootfalls approached the parlor. Sophie looked up when Adam entered the room. When he closed the doors behind him, her heart began to pound.

He crossed the room and sat on the couch beside her. "You are looking well."

She closed the book of which she hadn't read a single line. "There is no need to make small talk, sir."

"Sir?" He lifted a brow. "What happened to Adam?"

"Adam is the man who accompanied me when I sneaked out to go to the oyster cellars."

"I am that same man," he said. "Did you like me at all?"

"I liked you a great deal. I simply had no idea you were lying to me."

"You were lying to me, as well, Sophie."

"I lied to protect myself—and I had no idea who you were. If I had known—" She took a deep breath to calm herself.

"If you had known, would you have told me?" he asked gently.

"Indeed, I would have," she cried. "I meant to avoid you."

He laughed. "If it helps, that night at the oyster cellars, I didn't know your identity."

She didn't want to admit that the knowledge did help. "But when you found out, you made a fool of me," she said.

"That was not my intention."

She pinned him with a stare.

"All right," he said. "I did want to teach you a lesson. But you must own that I had no way of knowing that you *didn't* know who I was. I thought you were trying to trick me."

She wanted to argue just to be contrary, but he had a valid point.

"You knew I didn't want to marry you," she said. "So why marry me?"

He shrugged. "I believed you and I would get along well enough."

"Well enough," she repeated. "That is a fine reason to marry."

"Would you rather marry for love?"

She grunted. "I married for love the first time. There was no need to repeat that mistake."

"There you have it. We enjoy one another's company." He grasped her hand. "I do intend to live up to my vows. I will protect you with my life, if necessary. I will provide for you. If you are agreeable, with children, as well."

He would expect an heir.

Adam stretched out a hand on the back of the sofa. "Balfour will host a party in our honor tomorrow evening."

She shook her head. "There is no need. He accomplished his goal. You saved me by pretending to marry me."

"I did not pretend to marry you. We are married."

Sophie inclined her head. "As you wish. You saved my life by marrying me."

"I likely save my own life, as well," he murmured.

"We had no intention of marrying one another," she said.

He lifted a brow. "I had every intention of marrying you."

"You did not—and you know it."

"I signed the marriage contract," he said with far too much nonchalance.

"You did that to bother me."

He laughed. "Forgive me, my dear, but a man does not sign a marriage contract to 'bother' a woman. Your father would have ruined me in court. I admit, I wanted to teach you a lesson —but not at my expense."

"You told me that Lord Monthemer didn't want to marry Sophie Shaw," she insisted.

"What did you expect?" he asked. "I saw your companion Beatrice when she descended from your carriage, and she looked very displeased. Now that I know the story, I cannot say I blame her. How often did you have her pretend to be you?"

"I deduced that you knew she wasn't me in Lady Ella's garden." Sophie regarded him. "Did you tell my father I was pretending to be Beatrice?"

"Of course not."

She had thought not. Her father hadn't said anything to her.

"Why?" she asked.

"Because a husband doesn't tattle to his wife's father."

"He doesn't?" she asked. Matthew hadn't been above complaining to her father for some perceived wrongdoing. A strange nervousness rippled through her stomach. Oh, she recognized that feeling and she wasn't falling for that again. Adam was no different than Matthew.

"It's stupid to marry for money," she blurted.

He chuckled. "Spoken like a woman who has always had money."

Sophie pinned him with a glare. "Pray, do not play the pauper. You have been rich most of your life."

"And now I am not."

"There are plenty of rich heiresses. Why not marry one of them?"

"I got to know and like you," he replied.

She blew out a frustrated breath. "You did not 'get to know me.' You danced with me once at Lady Seafield's soiree."

"I also danced with you at the oyster cellars and accompanied you when you bought oranges and medicine for you aunt. And lest you forget, I rode with you in the carriage with Lord Emerson," he said.

"You didn't really think he intended to offer for me?" she asked.

Adam shrugged. "Why not? You are a beautiful woman."

"And rich," she said.

"And rich."

"If you are concerned about the money after I annul the marriage, you need not fret," she said.

A corner of his mouth twitched in amusement. "Indeed?"

Sophie shook her head. "Nae. I will make sure my father compensates you."

"Compensates me?" he repeated, and she had the feeling he was enjoying himself at her expense. "But that would deprive me of the pleasure of your company," he said.

She reigned in her temper. "You will be compensated, then can find another heiress and get even more money."

"As I said, you and I will deal well together." He stood. "You will not attend Balfour's ball." She opened her mouth to reply, but he shook his head. "It is too dangerous. Your father has put the announcement in the papers. That will satisfy Balfour. I will tell him that you simply were not comfortable returning to his home. It's the truth."

Sophie considered arguing, but really, she didn't want to attend the party. She wanted to return home and forget she had met any of these people.

"As you wish," she said. "I will stay home."

"You will be off to my estate in Inverness, actually."

"What?"

"In the morning," he said. "That way, you will be out of harm's way until I finish with him. Of course, you may take Beatrice with you if you wish, and she is amenable."

"So, you *are* sending me to the country," she cried.

"Inverness is hardly 'the country.'" His expression hardened. "Never fear, you will be able to attend as many parties and be a part of Inverness's society.

She didn't want to be a part of society. She had wanted to marry a simple man like Adam MacAlister who at least liked her for who she was and might even come to care for her. Instead, she'd gotten another man who wanted a rich wife.

CHAPTER 24

ADAM HAD ADJOURNED TO THE STUDY WITH LIAM AND GAVE Sophie an hour's head start before finally climbing the stairs to their room. The third door on the right where he now stood before the closed door. Adam knocked. No one replied. He eased the door open and stepped inside. A low fired burned in the hearth on the wall directly ahead, illuminating the form buried beneath the covers of a four-poster bed that sat to the right. That must be his bride. He closed the door, then crossed to the fireplace. He removed his coat and waistcoat, then laid them over the bench at the foot of the bed. He sat in the large leather chair in front of the fireplace and removed his boots.

He'd had two large glasses of brandy and should have no trouble sleeping even in a chair. He stretched his legs out in front of him and contemplated the fire. Balfour had stolen gold owned by an Englishman, the Duke of Bransbury. The theft wasn't massive like the one Balfour intended to steal from the king, but it would add nicely to Balfour's coffers. What he needed from Adam was a way to cut and sell the diamond necklace that had been in the chest with the gold. The necklace had been a nice addition to the theft, and the diamonds would bring an extra ten thousand pounds.

By now, Adam figured the duke had already taken the case of his being robbed before the king. The loss of gold and the necklace was likely a hard blow. The Crown could now convict Balfour of theft and threatening a nobleman with a gun. The fool had waylaid the coach like a common highwayman. The threat alone was enough to send Balfour to the gallows. But Adam suspected the Crown cared nothing for an English duke's losses and wanted only the gold that Balfour had filched while in His Majesty's employ in the navy. Adam hoped to get a clue to the whereabouts of the hidden gold tomorrow night at the party Balfour was hosting.

Sophie would be safely away by then, and he could deal with Balfour as he deserved. Sophie sighed in her sleep, and Adam twisted and looked past the chair at her. He'd wondered if she truly were asleep, but she seemed to be, at least now. What would she do if he climbed into bed with her? His cock began to rise in anticipation. He grimaced and faced the fire. His wife had a long day of travel ahead of her tomorrow.

His wife.

After Lena, he hadn't anticipated having a wife. His chest tightened. He liked the way the words sounded. Would Sophie be willing to work alongside him while he built a life for them? He chuckled. That question would begin to be answered tomorrow. Sophie's father had agreed to allow them the use of his carriage for her trip to Brewhold. Adam didn't envy her that ride.

Adam recalled that first day when she'd been wearing men's breeches and had ridden her mare like the wind. He frowned. He would have to have a talk with her about that. There would be no more wearing breeches and riding without an escort. She was sure to balk, but he would make sure someone was always at her disposal to ride with her. He would go himself, sometimes. Perhaps he might be able to talk her into allowing her mare to breed with Merlyn. They would produce magnificent offspring. Just as he and Sophie would produce beautiful children.

He recalled how she had left him and Emerson standing on the road while she made off with Emerson's carriage. That was when he realized he wanted her to be the mother of his children. Money or no.

SOPHIE AWOKE THE FOLLOWING MORNING AND TENTATIVELY scanned the room. She was alone. A sliver of disappointment dampened her spirits. She had half expected Adam to demand his husbandly rights. Maybe all men were like Matthew. They doled out passionate kisses to entice a woman, then ignored her once they had her.

She relaxed back against her pillow. Today, she and Beatrice were being sent to Inverness. Maybe that was for the best. She had no idea how long Adam might remain in Edinburgh. Perhaps she would return to Invergarry, instead. She might be happier spending time at home before being forced to take up residence in Inverness.

Sophie rose and had washed her face when Beatrice arrived with coffee and pastries. She wondered if she would see Adam before she left. She and Beatrice spent the morning packing then had an early lunch with her aunt. Maddie informed Sophie that Adam was in the study with her father, but the men likely wouldn't join them for lunch. Sophie simply couldn't stand not knowing what they were talking about. She excused herself from the table with the pretext that she wanted to take a last look at the packed trunks but went, instead, to the study. To her relief, the hallway was empty. She pressed her ear to the door and distinguished her father's voice.

"I don't like it one bit," he said. "I suggest you forget the matter."

"I cannot do that," Adam replied.

"You do not need the money the king is offering," her father said. "You have ample funds from Sophie's dowry. Plenty more will follow when you have children."

Sophie started. Adam would receive *more* money when she gave him children? How much more? Her heart twisted. She really was nothing but one big fat chest of money to her new husband.

"If you need more, I can always extend you a loan," her father said.

A heartbeat of silence passed, and Sophie envisioned Adam calculating how much money he could bilk her father for.

"It may interest you to know, Liam, that I did not marry your daughter for your money," Adam said.

Sophie's mind froze. Had she heard correctly?

"That is good to hear," replied her father. "She is a fine girl and deserves to be valued."

"You may rest assured she is," Adam said.

"That being the case, perhaps it really is best you forget Balfour," her father said. "Let someone else risk their life."

Risk their life?

"I can handle Balfour," Adam said, and Sophie recalled that she had called him a coward.

Guilt washed over her. She had tried to egg him into fighting Mr. Balfour.

"I will be there tonight," her father said. "It is not unusual for me to carry a pistol."

Adam laughed. "That will not be necessary, Liam. I would prefer to know that everyone is safe. That way, I can deal with Balfour as I need to without worry."

"I am a navy man myself, you know," her father said. "I know how to take care of myself."

"You fought in the Peninsular War, if I recall."

"That's right," he replied, and Sophie detected a note of pride in her father's voice. "As Sophie will not be there tonight, Balfour will expect her aunt and me."

"Madeline?" Adam said.

"You needn't worry about her. I will watch after her. We will make an appearance, then I will take Madeline home."

"Just an appearance?" Adam said.

"It would be too suspicious if we didn't come at all," her father replied.

Seconds of silence passed, then Adam said, "Agreed. I had better see Sophie off."

Sophie jerked away from the door, then spun and raced down the hallway. She hurried up the stairs and reached her room to find Beatrice directing two footmen to carry out the last of their trunks. Beatrice frowned in question as Sophie hurried across the room and flopped down on the chair in front of the window. Sophie shook her head in warning, and Beatrice remained silent.

Two minutes later, bootfalls approached. Beatrice swung her gaze to Sophie. Sophie gave a slight nod, jumped to her feet, then hurried to the table where a teapot and cups sat on a tray. She poured tea into two cups and looked up when Adam and her father entered the room.

"Are you ready?" her father asked.

"The footmen have taken down the last of the trunks," Sophie said. "We were just having a final cup of tea."

Her father crossed to her. She set down the teapot and turned.

He grasped her shoulders. "This is best, lass."

She nodded, and he surprised her by pulling her into a hug. She leaned into the embrace and hugged him back.

He drew back and looked down at her. "Be good."

Sophie sighed. "Of course."

He faced Beatrice. "You stay safe, Beatrice."

She angled her head. "Thank you, sir."

"Why don't you come with me to the kitchen?" he said to her. "I will have Cook make you something to take with you and Sophie. That will give Sophie and her husband a moment to talk."

Beatrice looked at Sophie. Sophie gave a tiny shake of her head that Beatrice should stay, but Beatrice said, "Of course, sir."

They left, and Sophie's father pulled the door closed behind them. Adam locked his gaze onto her, and her stomach did a somersault. Was that gentleness she read in his eyes?

"I intended to ask you to marry me in a more gentlemanly manner than what happened at Balfour's home," he said.

She arched a brow. "You did not intend to ask me at all. You signed the marriage contract in the wee hours of the morning."

His mouth twitched in amusement. "You are right, of course. But be honest, Sophie. You deserved the lesson."

She stiffened. "I deserved to be sold like a prized horse?"

His expression sobered. "Nae. You do not." Adam crossed the room, and she stood frozen when he halted in front of her. "I believe you will like Brewhold," he said. "The land has been in my family for nine generations. You asked if my home was an estate. Will a castle do?"

"A castle? I can make do with a castle."

He laughed. "Good. I will do my best not to dally here in Edinburgh."

He stared down at her, and she was piqued when her knees weakened.

"I will ask you to behave yourself." He winked. "At least until I arrive at Brewhold."

Sophie turned away, for his stare discomfited her too much. Far too much. The man truly was a rogue.

"I suppose I have gotten into all the trouble I can possibly get into for now," she said.

"Somehow, I doubt that."

She easily detected the amusement in his voice and was glad he couldn't see the smile that touched her mouth.

"Sophie," he said in a serious voice.

She faced him.

"Guards will meet you two hours outside of Edinburgh," he said. "They will ensure that you reach home safely. Someone will return with word that you've arrived, but I will likely already be on my way by then."

But she wouldn't be there.

CHAPTER 25

A DAM ARRIVED WITH S HAW AND M ADELINE FASHIONABLY LATE TO find Balfour's party in full swing. A large orchestra had set up near the right wall, and the dancefloor overflowed. Guests even milled about the balcony that ran the length of the room and overlooked the ballroom. Rumors circulated that Balfour operated outside the law, yet everyone wanted to be at this party. Society loved drama.

"Monthemer."

Adam turned to face Mr. Hancock as he entered the ballroom behind them. The man extended a hand, which Adam accepted.

"Congratulations." Hancock pumped Adam's hand. "Where's the lucky lady?" he said loudly to be heard over the din.

"Henry," Madeline said. "I haven't seen you in an age."

"Maddie." Hancock beamed, and Adam had the distinct impression they had a romantic history.

"I hope you will save me a dance," Hancock said to her.

"Of course. First, shall we have some champagne?"

He grinned and leaned close. "If I recall, you like champagne very much."

Madeline gave a throaty laugh. "You remember correctly." She slipped a hand into the crook of his arm, then winked at Adam as they descended the stairs.

"The woman always did enjoy male company," Liam said.

"Why not? She's a beautiful woman," Adam replied. Liam lifted his brows, and Adam grinned. "Simply an observation." He began to scan the room. "I wonder where Balfour is."

"Probably playing cards," his father-in-law said. "The man cannot seem to resist a game."

Adam looked at Liam. "Speaking of cards, where did Sophie learn to play?"

"From her cousins. They taught her to play from a young age. She is a tolerable player, though I forbade her from playing with anyone save family." He narrowed his eyes. "Did she play with you?"

Adam laughed. "Nae."

Liam regarded him but didn't pursue the subject. They descended the stairs, then meandered through the crowd and were stopped every few minutes by well-wishers.

"Lord Monthemer," a woman called.

Adam recognized that voice and grimaced. Mrs. Walker. She stepped in front of him, her young daughter at her side.

"Congratulations on your marriage," Mrs. Walker said.

Adam bowed. "Thank you."

"I do hope you will be as happy with the widow as you would have been with our innocent Lucy," she said in a loud voice.

"Mrs. Walker, may I introduce my father-in-law, Liam Shaw," Adam said.

The woman paled. "Um, so nice to meet you, sir. This is my daughter Lucy."

Lucy smiled shyly. "Very nice to meet you, sir."

A gleam appeared in Mrs. Walker's eyes, and she pinned Liam with a stare. "Lucy's dance card has room for one more gentleman, sir. She is a superb dancer."

"Very kind of you, ma'am," he replied. "But I am otherwise engaged." Liam looked at the girl. "I'm sure Miss Walker will enjoy herself by dancing with the young men who are sure to fight for the honor of a dance with her."

Lucy dropped her gaze to the floor.

"Nonsense," Mrs. Walker said. "Older gentlemen are far more skilled and know how to treat a lady. She would be honored to dance with you."

Liam leveled a hard look on the harpy. "As I said, madam, I am otherwise engaged." He gave a slight bow, then pushed past them.

Adam angled his head at the two women, then started after him. Adam sidestepped two women and caught up to him.

"A hopeful mama?" Liam asked.

"Aye."

His father-in-law looked at him. "The girl is stunning."

"And barely out of the schoolroom."

"No money?" he asked.

"Not as much is you," Adam replied. "But I do not rob the cradle."

Liam gave a small nod. "You could have married her and waited."

He pushed past a group of women who openly watched them. "If you're asking why I married Sophie, the answer is simple. I like her. The night in the carriage, she left Emerson and me on the street and made off with his carriage."

"You were there?" Liam asked in surprise.

They halted, and Adam scanned the room before he turned back to Shaw. "Emerson cheated at cards and won the right to escort Sophie home."

"She was playing cards?"

"That is no concern of yours," Adam said. "She is my wife."

"You dealt with the situation by marrying her."

"Aye. Where the devil is Balfour?" he muttered.

"I still say he is at the card table," Liam said.

"Probably. The man is a fool. I shall find him on my own. That way, we can be done with his business."

Liam nodded. "I will find Madeline and keep an eye on her. The women on her side of the family can be troublesome."

Adam looked at him. "Like Sophie?"

Shaw shrugged. "What is life without a little trouble?"

WHEN SOPHIE'S CARRIAGE PULLED UP IN FRONT OF MR. Balfour's home, music filtered from the large home out onto the drive. Carriages crowded the drive all the way to the road. Her heart thudded. Her father and Adam would be furious with her, but she simply couldn't let Adam face Mr. Balfour alone. If Adam wanted to appear the heartless criminal he was pretending to be, then Mr. Balfour couldn't know that Adam was concerned for her safety.

The driver jumped from his seat on the carriage and opened the door. She laid her hand in his as he assisted her to the ground. She paid him and added a generous tip. He dipped his hat in thanks, then leapt back up onto his perch and drove away. Sophie stared at the large home for half a dozen heartbeats, then went to the front door where a footman bowed then opened the door for her. Another footman inside led her up one flight of stairs to a large ballroom overflowing with guests. She winced at the loud music and din of voices. Her vantage point on the top of the balcony gave her a view of the entire room. Sophie didn't see Adam or her father, but how could she possibly see anyone in this massive crowd?

She caught sight of a woman to her right and recognized

her as the woman who had captured Adam's attention the night he escorted her to the oyster cellars. She was even more beautiful here. Tall, dark, and willowy. Her creamy, flawless skin reminded Sophie of a goddess. The woman caught her staring, and Sophie yanked her gaze away. She glimpsed movement from the corner of her eye and resisted the urge to race down the stairs when the woman approached.

"Lady Monthemer," the woman said in a throaty voice that made Sophie wonder how many hours she spent practicing just the right tone.

Sophie faced her. "Do we know one another?"

"We have not been properly introduced," the woman said. "We saw each other at the oyster cellars recently. You were there with Adam, if I recall."

Sophie arched a brow. "His lordship, you mean? Yes, I do believe we were there together."

"I am Lady Fleming, my lady." She dipped into a perfect curtsey, and Sophie was glad, for her mouth dropped open.

Lady Fleming? The woman who had stolen Adam's fortune and contributed to his father's suicide? The woman Adam had intended to marry? The woman he had loved? No wonder Adam had been so discomfited after seeing her that night.

Lady Fleming straightened and frowned. "Is something wrong, my lady?"

Sophie lifted her chin. "Nothing that cannot be remedied by you leaving."

She blinked. "I beg your pardon?"

"This party is a wedding celebration for Lord Monthemer and me. The woman who betrayed him by stealing his father's fortune is not welcome."

Surprise flickered across her face, then she narrowed her eyes. "I was invited by Mr. Balfour."

Sophie motioned to the footman standing near the doorway. He hurried over.

"Please escort this woman from the party," Sophie ordered.

The footman's eyes widened, and he glanced from Lady Fleming back to her. "I beg your pardon, my lady?"

"You heard me," Sophie said. "See her out." She shifted her gaze onto Lady Fleming. "And feel free to use any means necessary to ensure she leaves."

Lady Fleming's eyes flashed.

The footman stepped up to her and said, "If you will, my lady."

She didn't move, and he grasped her arm. She yanked free.

"I would advise against making a scene," Sophie said. "I will not be the one everyone is talking about tomorrow, if you do."

Lady Fleming shot her a dagger-filled look, then spun and walked at a leisurely pace from the room.

Three women suddenly surrounded Sophie.

"Well done, Sophie," cried Lady Ella.

Sophie jerked her gaze to the right as Lady Ella clutched her arm.

"I wanted forever to tell that woman off," Ella said with a laugh.

Sophie realized her heart pounded, and she suddenly wished she could sit down.

Ella grasped Sophie's shoulders and kissed her cheek. "Why didn't you tell us you were to marry Adam?" she demanded.

"What?" Sophie's mind still spun, then she recognized Ella's question. "Oh, it was all rather sudden."

Lady Ella's eyes sparkled. "So we heard."

"Have you seen Adam?" Sophie asked. At Ella's sharpened gaze, Sophie waved her hand. "We lost one another in the crush. I came up here for a better view of the ballroom."

Ella nodded. "I haven't seen him. But I'm sure we can find him. Oh, where are my manners? Sophie—Lady Monthemer—may I introduce Lady Ann and Mrs. Perkins?" Ella indicated the two women with her.

The women curtsied.

Sophie grimaced. "That is not necessary."

"But it is necessary," Lady Ella said. "Remember, Lady Monthemer, this is not a private house party." She lifted her brows.

Sophie nodded, then shifted her gaze to the two women. "It is a pleasure to meet you both."

They beamed.

Sophie returned her attention to Lady Ella. "It is wonderful to see you again, Lady Ella, but you must excuse me. I would like to find Adam."

"I'm sure we can help," she said.

Sophie shook her head. "That won't be necessary. I am sure I shall find him."

She feared he was off in some room alone with Mr. Balfour and had already told Mr. Balfour that she hadn't accompanied Adam to the party. On the far side of the room, French doors stood open to a balcony. Sophie glimpsed a man slightly taller than those around him as he went out the door.

Adam. She was sure of it.

She looked at Lady Ella and the ladies. "Please excuse me. I believe I just saw Adam." She smiled, then hurried away before they could reply.

She feared she would be stopped by well-wishers, but she reached the balcony doors without anyone speaking to her. Of course not. No one really knew her. She hurried outside onto the balcony where at least two dozen people milled about. She scanned the balcony but found no sign of Adam. Had he gone onto the lawn? She brushed past a small group and reached the stairs, where she scanned the lawn. Small lamps had been placed on benches and around a large fountain. Sophie glimpsed a tall figure walking near the fountain and hurried after him. He headed toward a small grove of trees to the left.

Sophie yanked up her skirts and hurried as fast as she dared in the scant light.

"Adam," she called.

He kept going.

Was he not Adam?

"Adam," she called more loudly.

He halted and turned, then started toward her. In half a dozen paces, he met her and gripped her arm. "Sophie, what the bloody hell are you doing here? You should be forty miles away from Edinburgh by now."

"I am sorry, Adam, but I simply couldn't allow you to face Mr. Balfour alone. He believes you to be a mercenary fortune hunter, does he not?"

"What the devil are you talking about?" he demanded.

"Mr. Balfour believes you to be a mercenary fortune hunter who married me for my money."

"How would you know what Balfour thinks?" Adam demanded.

"A simple deduction. A man who marries a woman only for her money would not protect her from a man like Mr. Balfour. He would bring his wife to prove he was the heartless criminal he appeared to be. You have not already told Mr. Balfour that I was on my way to Inverness, have you?"

"By all that is holy, Sophie, I swear, I shall take you over my knee the moment we return home tonight. You are to return to your aunt's house—immediately."

She shook her head. "Nae. I will stay, but I will return to the party. Tell Mr. Balfour that I am here." She tried to pull free of his arm, but he held tight.

"I am taking you home, and this time, I shall tie you to the bed." He pulled her alongside him, then the murmur of men's voices reached them. He halted. "Bloody hell." He backed her against the nearest tree and pressed his body against hers. He mussed her hair.

"Adam? What are you doing?"

"Hush," he ordered.

He pulled one sleeve of her dress down her shoulder. The voices drew closer.

"Remember, you followed me—yet again," he whispered before he plundered her mouth with his.

Sophie threw her arms around him and pressed closer. He groaned and thrust his tongue inside her mouth as he rotated his hips against her abdomen. His hard length dug into her belly, and she suddenly wanted his skin against hers. She lifted one leg over his hip, and he thrust again. This time his cock slid along her mons.

Sophie broke the kiss and dropped her head onto his shoulder. He dragged a wet kiss down her neck to the front of her dress and to her nipple, then closed his warm mouth over her stiff bud through the material of her dress and sucked. Desire surged through her. In just moments, he had made her want him more than she ever wanted any other man. Sophie thrust her hips against him. Adam abruptly drew back. She grabbed his shoulders and tried to pull him to her again, but he swung around, so his back faced her.

"Forgive the intrusion."

Sophie recognized Mr. Balfour's voice and remained hidden behind Adam. Someone laughed. Another man, she realized.

"It seems my wife and I should have stayed home tonight," Adam said.

Mr. Balfour laughed. "It is hard to resist a beautiful woman. We will leave you to your privacy. When you are finished, perhaps we can talk?"

Adam shifted in the darkness. "My wife and I will have plenty of time to conduct our…business. I came here to finish my business with you, Balfour. Perhaps we should get to it."

"As you wish," Mr. Balfour said. "Charles and I were on the

way to the groundskeeper's cottage. It's just a little farther down this path. Why don't you join us once you escort your wife back to the party?"

"I will only be a few moments," Adam said.

The two men continued walking down the path. Adam faced Sophie, grasped her arm, and began walking back toward the house.

"That certainly made an impression," Sophie said. "Wouldn't you agree?"

"Can I trust you to do a single thing I ask?" he demanded.

Sophie yanked free of his grasp and halted. "Not when I know your life is at risk." She didn't wait for an answer but continued toward the mansion.

When they entered the crowded ballroom, Sophie faced Adam. "Be gone with you, sir. I can find my father and aunt."

He glared at her, and if he intended to reply, he was interrupted by Lord Blair. "There you are, Adam." His eyes shifted to Sophie. "And Lady Monthemer is with you." Lord Blair bowed. "My lady, may I introduce my wife, Lady Blair?"

The petite woman at his side curtsied. "We have met before, my lady," she said. "You may remember in Invergarry."

Sophie smiled. She didn't remember which party, but she had met Lady Blair not long after her husband died.

"And this is Lord Cassilis and his wife, Lady Charlotte," Lord Blair said.

Lord Cassilis bowed over Sophie's hand, and Lady Charlotte curtsied.

"A pleasure to meet you all," Sophie said.

Lady Blair met her gaze. "Perhaps you would like to go with Charlotte and me to the ladies' retiring room, my lady?"

"The ladies' retiring room?" Sophie repeated.

Lady Blair glanced meaningfully at her hair and Sophie recalled that Adam had mussed her hair.

"Oh, yes, I would." She looked at Adam. "Please continue with your business, sir. I shall be fine."

Adam blinked and Sophie resisted the urge to grin. She had him on the run.

His eyes narrowed. Well, perhaps not "on the run."

"Sophie—"

She laid a hand on his arm. "Please, Adam, I will be fine." She looked at the two men. "Will I not, sirs?"

They nodded. "You will, my lady," Lord Blair said.

"Sophie," she corrected, then turned to the women. "Shall we, ladies?"

The two women glanced at their husbands, then linked arms with Sophie and started through the crowd.

"Like I said, an intelligent woman gets a man into trouble every time," Lord Cassilis said behind them.

Lady Blair leaned close to Sophie and said, "Very nicely done."

Sophie snapped her head in the woman's direction. "I beg your pardon?"

"The way you handled your husband. I knew you and Adam would deal well together."

"You knew Adam and I would deal well together? You don't mean that it was you who—"

"Well, Charlotte and me," Lady Blair said.

"Oh, Adam, there you are," Lady Ella said behind them. Sophie started to turn, but when Lady Ella said, "You will not believe what your wife did to Lady Fleming," Sophie kept walking.

CHAPTER 26

ADAM SCOOPED UP THE SMALL LANTERN ON A BENCH IN THE lawn as he strode toward the groundskeeper's cottage. His wife had ejected Lena from their wedding celebration.

According to Ella, Sophie had told Lena she wasn't welcome. Sophie was an innocent. He wouldn't have thought she had the nerve to face an experienced woman like Lena. Though Sophie *had* defied him and come to the party because she thought his life was at risk. Pride washed over him. Sophie was a loyal woman—everything Lena wasn't. He was, indeed, a fortunate man.

He continued on the path, past the tree where Balfour had caught him with Sophie, and, five minutes later, a cottage came into view. Light spilled out of a window into the darkness. Adam reached the cottage, knocked, then entered. Balfour sat at a table with one other man.

"Glad to see you could make it," Balfour said. "I had begun to wonder if your wife was too much to resist again."

"She is a distraction." Adam crossed to the table and sat down. "Shall we get down to business?"

Balfour nodded. "I believe we should." He lifted the hand

hidden by the table and pointed a pistol at Adam. "I would like to have a talk about you and Lord Wilmingly."

Sophie leaned against the chair back in the ladies' retiring room as Lady Blair and Lady Cassilis continued to chat. Her head whirled. It was they who suggested to their husbands that she and Adam would make a good match. She wasn't yet certain whether to curse them or thank them. The look in Adam's eyes when he'd gotten her back to the ballroom had startled her. She'd known he would be angry, but she'd seen fear as well as frustration in his eyes. He'd been worried about her.

"I suppose we should return to the ballroom if we don't want our husbands to storm the ladies' retiring room," Lady Blair said.

Sophie pictured Adam charging into the room and couldn't help a smile.

"I do believe our newly married Sophie is thinking about her husband," Lady Cassilis said.

Sophie's cheeks warmed. "I was picturing him invading the ladies' retiring room looking for me. I fear I have given him the impression that I am going to be trouble."

Lady Blair laughed. "Good. It's only proper you set precedence early on. You wouldn't want him being surprised later." She stood. "Come, our husbands owe us at least one dance."

Lady Cassilis rose, and Sophie followed suit. They brushed past three ladies, who smiled at Sophie. She didn't know them, but they seemed to know her. She and Lady Blair and Lady Cassilis filed out the door into the small hallway leading to the ballroom. The orchestra strings and flutes echoed in a lively waltz. They reached the ballroom and halted.

"We might not find them at all," Lady Blair said. "Let us take a turn around the ballroom."

"Please, go without me," Sophie said. "I believe I will have a bite to eat in the refreshments room." She hadn't eaten since breakfast, and her stomach was making it known she had ignored it too long.

Lady Cassilis frowned. "Perhaps we should go together?"

Sophie shook her head. "Nae. My father and aunt are here. I will look for them. If you do not unearth your husband, you will find me in the refreshments room—unless I locate my family." They hesitated, and Sophie laughed. "Surely, you are not going to act like my husband?"

Butterflies skittered across the inside of the stomach.

Husband.

She was well and truly married. Her heart fell. Nae. In the eyes of the world, she was married, but she wasn't truly married. She wouldn't be until they consummated the marriage in the marriage bed. When would that be?

"You are sure you will be all right?" Lady Blair asked.

Sophie smiled and hoped none of her thoughts shone on her face. "Quite sure."

"All right, then," Lady Cassilis said. "We will check in the refreshments room in a bit."

"I hope you find your husbands," Sophie said.

They smiled, then quickly disappeared into the throng. Sophie spotted a waiter with a tray of champagne and started toward him.

"Sophie, is that you?" a woman called.

Sophie turned and cried out at sight of Imogen. Sophie sidestepped two gentlemen to where Imogen stood and threw her arms about her old friend. Imogen hugged her back, and they separated.

"I had no idea you were here," Sophie said.

"I'm not supposed to be here," Imogen replied.

Sophie frowned. "What do you mean?"

Imogen glanced around, then motioned for Sophie to follow her. They hugged the wall until they reached a hallway. Imogen picked up the pace, and Sophie hurried to keep up with her. They reached a room, and Imogen went inside, then closed the door after Sophie entered.

Imogen spun to face her. "I had no idea you were in town until the day after you were here."

"You knew I was here?" Sophie asked in surprise. "Why did you not visit me?"

"I only heard from the servants the next morning. By then, you were gone."

"But it's so wonderful to see you," Sophie said. "I'm supposed to leave for Inverness." She assumed Adam—and her father—would insist she leave tomorrow. "But now that I know you are here, I will insist on staying a few more days."

Imogen shook her head. "That is what I am here to tell you. You must leave as soon as possible. You are in danger."

"From your brother?"

"Stepbrother," Imogen shot back. "He is no brother of mine. But, yes, from him. I believe he intends to kill you."

Sophie gasped. "Kill me?"

Her mind catapulted back to the night Mr. Balfour insisted she and Adam marry. He had forced her marriage to Adam in order to ensure she would be under Adam's control and wouldn't be able to report Adam to the authorities for his criminal activities, and by extension, protect Mr. Balfour.

"He has no reason to want to kill me," she said.

"He knows your husband is trying to trap him into revealing where he hid the gold he stole from the king," Imogen said.

How could Mr. Balfour possibly know Adam was working for the Crown?

"If he knows, why didn't he kill Adam and me when he found us in the garden?" she asked.

"He learned the truth only fifteen minutes ago."

Sophie pinned Imogen with a stare. Though she had fond memories of Imogen, Sophie had to admit that she didn't really know her anymore.

"How do you know all this?" Sophie asked.

Imogen's expression clouded. "I learned long ago to pay attention to Kenrich's business. When I discovered that you had been here and he had forced you to marry Lord Monthemer, I paid close attention to Kenrich. He is a very suspicious man." She gave a dark laugh. "He believes everyone is dishonest because he is dishonest. He has many connections. I do not know which of his connections told him about Lord Monthemer, but I do know someone did."

"Good God." Sophie remembered Mr. Balfour telling Adam to meet him at the groundskeeper's cottage. Sophie took two steps to Imogen and grasped her hands. "Where is the groundskeeper's cottage?"

Imogen frowned. "What? Why?"

"Your stepbrother instructed Adam to meet him there."

Sophie's mind raced. Mr. Balfour and his companion had been on the way to the groundskeeper's cottage when they had come upon her and Adam. He had said the cottage was on the path.

"I must go." Sophie pulled the door open and hurried from the room.

Imogen caught up with her. "Where are you going?"

"The groundkeeper's cottage."

"But why? Oh, Sophie, you must leave. This is too dangerous."

"No more dangerous than it is for you," she replied.

Imogen shook her head. "I am perfectly safe—at least until

my twenty-fifth birthday. That is when I am to receive my trust. Then Kenrich will not need me anymore."

They neared the ballroom. Sophie halted and grasped Imogen's hands. "I am so sorry I knew nothing of your troubles all these years. I thought you were off living a grand life in France. Once this is over, we shall make up for lost time. For now, I need you to find my father or aunt and tell them what you have told me." She took a breath. "Then tell them I have gone to the groundskeeper's cottage to help Adam."

"I do not know your aunt, and it has been so long. Will I know your father?" Imogen asked.

Sophie laughed. "Ask anyone who Madeline Forsyth is. Everyone knows her. Can you do that?"

Imogen nodded. "I will find them right away."

Sophie hugged her, then they hurried to the ballroom and parted ways.

ADAM GLANCED AT THE OTHER MAN SITTING TO BALFOUR'S LEFT, then returned his attention to Balfour. "Lord Wilmingly? What about him?"

"How he engaged you to find the gold I am accused of stealing from the king," Balfour replied.

"You did steal gold from the king." There was no use in pretending they didn't know why they were here. "As for Wilmingly," Adam continued. "I have nothing to do with him."

Balfour shook his head. "I am deeply disappointed. We would have made excellent partners. It's my fault, I suppose. I should have known a man who paid his father's debts was simply too honest."

"You're a fool if you believe that." Adam had known the fact he'd paid his father's debts would be his undoing.

"Brigands do not pay their father's debts." Balfour said.

"Not that." Adam paused for effect, then said, "I didn't pay my father's debts. Well, at least not most of them."

Balfour lifted a brow. "Everyone knows you paid his debts and made yourself a pauper in the bargain."

"Everyone thinks that because I paid just enough to set the rumor into motion."

"Why would you do that?" Balfour demanded.

"Because I wanted to obtain a sizeable loan from the bank, and I knew they wouldn't extend the loan if they thought creditors were waiting in the wings to seize the funds once I had them in hand."

Balfour's eyes narrowed. "If you hadn't paid those creditors, they would be shouting their demands from the rooftop."

Adam met his gaze squarely. "They are keeping quiet for the very reason you approached me: I am a skilled businessman. I negotiated with them for their silence. As things are now, they stand to gain nothing by making demands. My father lost all our property, except the entailed estate, which cannot be sold. I told them I was in the middle of a business deal, and if they remained quiet about my father's debts, I would pay them once I received funds. Of course, I expected to obtain a loan—of which they would have received nothing. Then fortune smiled on me, and I married Miss Shaw.

"Granted, my marriage has pulled me from the brink of ruin, but my wife's dowry will ensure I keep the creditors quiet until I have obtained the loan. Then..." He shrugged. "They are welcome to take me to court."

"That would be a clever trick, indeed."

Adam shrugged again. "The creditors have nothing to lose by remaining silent for a short time."

"I think he's too slick," the other man said.

"Oh, Lord Monthemer is, indeed, slick," Balfour said. "Sadly, I believe our king has made him an offer he couldn't refuse."

Adam laughed. "There is no offer the king could possibly

make that would benefit me more than the agreement I made with you." He pinned Balfour with a hard look. "Unless, that is, you do not know when our king is transporting his gold."

"Oh, I do, indeed, know," Balfour said. "But I want to be certain you aren't telling him what I have told you."

"I have not spoken with Wilmingly or the king or anyone else associated with him."

That much was true. He had yet to report anything Balfour had told him. Though Adam hadn't detected anyone following him, he knew Balfour for the suspicious sort he was, and Adam felt certain Balfour had people watching him. If the king knew Adam hadn't reported that Balfour intended to rob the king's shipment, they would likely toss him into prison—which was why Adam counted on finding the gold Balfour had stolen.

Balfour sighed. "A pity. You would have made a good partner." He lifted the gun.

Adam tensed in readiness to shove the table up and at the two men. A knock sounded on the door. Balfour jerked his head in that direction. Adam shoved the table onto the men as he dived for the door. The pistol roared. The door flew open, and Adam rolled and came up in a squat. He glimpsed Sophie, muff pistol gripped in one hand as she leveled the weapon on something beyond him and fired.

Movement in the corner of his eye yanked Adam's attention to the left, and he leapt forward as the unidentified man charged Sophie. Adam rammed his shoulder into the man's gut and forced him backward into the wall. He glimpsed Balfour pushing to his feet from behind the overturned table.

Another weapon roared. Adam rammed his fist into the man's jaw, then whirled and took two steps before his mind registered Balfour on the floor, and Sophie, still standing just inside the doorway, pointing a revolver with a whisp of smoke rising from the hammer. A large stain grew on the front of Balfour's waistcoat. Sophie swung her gaze to Adam. He reached her in three paces and grasped the hand holding the revolver.

"You can release the revolver, Sophie," he said gently.

She looked at him. "He meant to kill you."

Adam nodded. "Aye, but I am well."

She released the weapon, and he took it. Adam caught sight of three figures racing the last few feet to the cottage. Liam Shaw, his sister, and another young woman Adam didn't recognize.

"What in bloody hell is going on?" Liam demanded as he rushed past the two women into the cottage.

"It would seem my wife saved my life," Adam said.

"Is he dead?" Madeline demanded.

"I suspect Balfour is," Adam said. "The other man is only unconscious."

The young woman crossed to Balfour and knelt beside him. She pressed a finger to his neck, then stood. "Yes," she said without taking her eyes off him. "He is dead."

"Then this business is finished," Liam said. "We will send for a constable." He looked at Adam. "Did you get the information you needed?"

Adam slipped an arm around Sophie. "Nae. Our king will have to do without his stolen gold."

"Oh, I know where the gold is hidden," the girl said.

CHAPTER 27

A NOISE OUTSIDE THE WINDOW CAUGHT SOPHIE'S ATTENTION. She paused in writing the first letter she would send to Imogen from Brewhold, and she looked out the parlor window. Adam, coat off, sleeves rolled up his forearms, stood alongside young Calum as they fitted a wheel to the rear of a wagon. Her pulse quickened when Adam's shirt went taut across his back. God help her. What was it about the mere sight of the man that sent butterflies skittering across the insides of her stomach?

A month had passed since she'd shot Kenrich Balfour. No charges had been filed against her for his death. She had, after all, been protecting her husband. Imogen had led them to the gold, which was beneath the very floorboards where they stood in the groundskeeper's cottage. The necklace stolen from the Duke of Bransbury was nowhere to be found. King George, however, was satisfied, and Adam had received a handsome reward.

Adam had been a paragon of a husband—kind, patient, solicitous. But not a real husband. They had yet to consummate their marriage. Maybe all men really were alike. Much promise of passion before marriage, then…nothing. Or maybe he simply didn't see her that way.

The two men got the wheel fitted to the wagon, and Adam clapped Calum on the back, then turned. As if aware she was watching, Adam looked up. He lifted his brows in question, and her cheeks heated. He started toward the castle, and she told herself to look away but watched until he was out of view. Her spirits sagged, but she forced her attention back to her letter to Imogen.

Sophie had promised Imogen she could visit soon, and she saw no reason to delay. She, Imogen, and Beatrice could find plenty to do in Inverness. Sophie paused in writing. She hadn't seen Beatrice since after breakfast. Where was the girl? Sophie would go in search of her once she finished her letter.

Sophie had just signed her name when bootfalls sounded outside in the hall. She looked up as Adam entered. He still wore no jacket, and he still had his sleeves rolled up to his fore-arms, revealing tanned arms.

He halted inside the room and regarded her. "Do I overstep my bounds when I say I have never seen a more beautiful woman?" he asked.

Sophie's pulse quickened, but she kept a neutral expression and arched a brow. "I would say you live up to your reputation as a rogue, sir."

He crossed the room, and she remained motionless when he stopped in front of her, grasped her hand, and lifted it to his lips. "On the contrary. I have never said that to another woman."

He brushed his mouth against her fingers, and a shiver slid down her shoulders. The man's reputation was well-deserved. He was desire incarnate. Adam released her—though she had the feeling he was reluctant.

"I have invited Imogen to visit next month," she said. "I hope you do not mind."

He nodded slowly. "As you wish."

Though he sounded cordial, she had the distinct impression he wasn't pleased.

She regarded him. "If you prefer she not come here, I could go to Edinburgh."

"I think not," he replied with such alacrity that she blinked.

"I beg your pardon? Why not?"

"Forgive me, my dear, but the last time you went to Edinburgh, you kept following a certain gentleman all over kingdom come and back."

Her mouth fell open. "I-I beg your pardon. That gentleman was you—though you did not act like a gentleman."

"Then we are even," he said. "For you did not act like a lady."

She stiffened. "You are no gentleman to keep reminding a lady of that, sir.

A devilish light gleamed in his eyes. "A lady—"

"Would not have followed a gentleman." She rolled her eyes. "Aye, so you have said a dozen times."

"I do not think I have said it quite a dozen times."

He sounded genuinely affronted.

"So, I shall go to Edinburgh to visit Imogen," Sophie said, more out of the sudden desire to bother him than anything else.

He threw himself onto the small couch to her left and shook his head. "I believe I said I prefer you not go to Edinburgh."

Sophie leveled her gaze onto him. "You cannot honestly believe I will follow any other gentleman around. After all, the only reason I followed you was to keep from marrying you, and look where that got me."

"Married?" he said.

She dropped her gaze to the letter before her. "In name only."

"Whose fault is that?" he murmured.

Sophie yanked her head in his direction. "I-I… That is, it is *your* fault."

"Contrary to what you believe, my dear, I *am* a gentleman, and a gentleman does not force his way into a woman's bed. Even if that woman is his wife."

Sophie stared. "Do you mean to say that— I mean, you have not consummated our marriage because you believe I do not *want* to consummate our marriage?"

"You did tell me on our wedding night that our marriage would not be consummated."

"But that is ridiculous," she cried. "You could not expect to agree to consummate a marriage you tricked me into."

He shrugged. "As I said, a gentleman does not force a lady."

Sophie shook her head. "Nae, you misunderstand. You could not have expected me to agree to consummate the marriage *that night*."

"True," he replied. "But you have no indication you had changed your mind."

She stared. "I shot a man to save you."

"For which I have thanked you."

Sophie jumped to her feet. "I would not do that for just anyone."

"Nae?" he asked in a too-casual voice.

"That is, I would help someone in need, but I specifically set out to save you because…"

"Because…"

"Oh," she said on the rush of a frustrated breath. "You are odious."

He regarded her. "I did not marry you for your money, Sophie."

She threw her hands into the air. "But you did."

"You were not the only heiress thrown in my path. In fact, there was one young heiress who would have been much less trouble than you."

Sophie narrowed her eyes. "Then why did you not marry her?"

He pushed to his feet and took two steps, then stopped so close she could feel his warmth. "Because she did not shove me out of a carriage—nor did she defy my instructions and save my life." He smiled. "Though, if I recall, you did that after I married you."

Her heart fell. "Then you feel obligated to me."

He laughed. "God help me, no."

The man was a bundle of contradictions.

He grasped her arms, and she stared up at him. "Are you inviting me into your bed, Sophie?"

The timbre of his voice made her stomach do a somersault. Part of her wanted to run away and hide under the bed, but she nodded. He wrapped his arms around her and pulled her so close he crushed her breasts against his hard chest.

"We do not have to have children right away," he said.

Sophie blinked. "I-I beg your pardon?"

"I do not want you to think that I am after the money your father promised for each child you give me."

"Oh, that is right," she said in a small voice.

"I care nothing for the money, Sophie." He released her and stepped back.

Sophie grasped his arm. "You do not want me?"

His eyes darkened. "I want you more than life itself."

"Oh," she said again. "But why? I am nothing like Lady Fleming."

"Good God, no." He paused. "I told your father I will not accept the money for the births of our children."

"You did?" She frowned. "You need not have done that."

"It is done."

Sophie looked at the carpet. "Imogen will not visit until next month."

"Is that so?"

"I would not want to lie to her."

"Lie to her about what?" he asked softly.

"About being a married woman."

"Then you are saying you now want to consummate our marriage?"

"It is the right thing to do."

"Do you want me?" he asked.

"A lady does not admit to such things," she said.

"My dear, a gentleman does not want a lady in his bed."

Sophie snapped her head up and met his gaze. Desire burned in his eyes. Sophie cried out and threw her arms around his neck. He swept her into his arms and fell with her onto the sofa. His body crushed her into the cushion, and she was enveloped by his musky scent. His hard length dug into her belly like a hungry beast, and she longed to feel his maleness slide in and out of her.

He covered her mouth with his, and before she realized her own intent, Sophie sucked his tongue inside her mouth. He groaned and covered her breast with one large, warm palm. Her nipple tightened in pleasurable discomfort as he kneaded her breast. The juncture between her legs throbbed, and she was reminded of the dream she'd had of him the night after they'd gone to the oyster cellars. Sophie arched her hips and rubbed against his erection. Adam abruptly broke the kiss, and she seized his shoulders and tried to drag his mouth back to hers.

He laughed low. "Easy, my sweet."

Adam pushed up into a sitting position and pulled her onto his thighs, so she straddled him. He made quick work of the ties on his breeches, and Sophie drew a sharp breath when his cock sprang free, hard and oddly beautiful. Adam pulled her close and yanked down one sleeve of her dress to reveal her breasts. He bent his head and took one nipple into his mouth.

Matthew had never done this! When Adam sucked, a bead of desire stretched from her breast to her sex.

"Adam…"

He reached beneath her dress and cupped her buttocks. Sophie wanted to touch him. She fumbled with the buttons on his shirt and yanked the shirt so several buttons flew into the air.

Adam lifted his head and grinned. "Cannot wait to ride me, love?"

No, she could not!

Gaze locked with hers, Adam lifted her up and onto his erection. She braced her hands on his shoulders, and as she settled slowly onto him, the muscles in his shoulders tensed.

"You intend to tease me, sweet?" he asked in a hoarse voice.

Sophie wasn't sure what that meant, but she liked the way the question made her feel. Adam's fingers tightened on her buttocks as he gently lifted her, then brought her back down again. He lifted then lowered her several more times, then Sophie braced her knees on each side of him and lifted herself up then down.

"By God," he muttered.

She lifted again, and when she lowered, he drove into her. Sophie cried out.

He stilled. "Did I hurt you?"

She gasped. "Lord, no. Please do that again."

He did. Then again and again.

Sophie had a sudden, horrifying thought. "Oh no."

Adam drove into her. "Is something amiss?"

She looked over her shoulder, and as she had remembered, Adam had left the parlor door open.

She faced him. "The door, we left it open."

He flashed a wicked smile. "Beatrice already streaked past. Never fear. She will tell everyone we are occupied, and we will not be disturbed."

Sophie gasped. "My lord, we must go upstairs."

He drove into her again.

"Sophie, I couldn't walk if the devil were on my heels."

She started to lift off him, but he slammed her hilt deep onto his erection, then reached between her legs and slipped a finger between the folds that hid her sex.

"Adam," she squeaked.

"Ride me," he ordered.

She hesitated, then began a rhythm he copied with the long digit that massaged her. This was far beyond anything she'd dreamed of. Need coursed through her, and the pleasure point between her legs abruptly burst with pleasure. Sophie cried out and allowed her head to fall forward on Adam's shoulder. He hugged her close as pleasure rolled over her in waves. With each thrust, the pleasure seemed to reach deeper and deeper. He drove so deep that she felt he must have touched her soul.

"I didn't quite know it then, but I believe I fell in love with you that night," he said in a strangled whisper.

Sophie tried to shake herself from the murk of pleasure. He gave a final thrust and groaned. He hugged her so tight all the air seemed to leave her lungs.

She realized what he'd said and lifted her head to look at his face. "Fell in love with me?" Her heart skipped a beat. "What night?"

His chest lifted with the deep breath he took. "The night you kicked Emerson and me out of his carriage."

Sophie shook her head. "I do not understand."

He smoothed back from her face locks of hair that had come loose from her chignon. "You are an honest woman, Sophie."

"But I lied to you and pretended to be someone else."

He smiled. "You lied about your name, but you never pretended to be anyone but who you are."

She frowned. "But that's silly. A person cannot be anyone but who they truly are."

"Well, you cannot, at any rate." His expression turned speculative. "Perhaps one day you will find you love me, as well."

"Oh, I already love you."

He blinked. "When did that happen?"

She lifted herself off him. He righted himself and closed his britches as she got to her feet and smoothed her dress.

"When did you know?" he asked.

Sophie looked up. "Know what?"

"Know that you love me."

"Oh, well, that is my secret, is it not?"

His gaze sharpened. "Indeed?"

She nodded, then rose and started for the door. "I suppose you will have to find a way to get me to tell you."

Sophie threw him a glance over her shoulder, then squealed and broke into a run when he leapt to his feet and started after her.

SNEAK PEEK AT BALLAD OF DISCORD

BALLAD OF DISCORD

If the man you love won't trust you with the truth, how can you ever again trust him?

The pieces of Elizbeth McKinley's world scatter when her father, in an act of pure madness, joins forces with a mysterious Frenchman in an attempt to claim the Scottish crown. Now, pawns in a game far vaster than they can imagine, Elizbeth and her sister must flee or be shipped off to France to wed strangers. To make matters worse, the one man who should most wish to help her, the man Elizbeth loves, refuses to believe she's in danger. His betrayal will cut deeper than any sword.

CHAPTER 1

Giggles and rapid footfalls sounded in the corridor outside the sunny parlor. Elizbeth smoothed a stitch in her needlework while she waited for the bittersweet prick of tears to subside. It had been two years since their mother died. Laughter and joy were long overdue in their household.

"You know we ought to chide her for running," Aunt Davina said.

Elizbeth glanced at Davina, who sat across the parlor.

"She's nineteen," Davina went on. "A child no longer. When the two of you come out this autumn, we can hardly have her running about in company."

Elizbeth nodded as her strawberry-haired little sister charged into the room. Elizbeth wouldn't reprimand Margarette, and she doubted their aunt would, either. Only four years Elizbeth's senior, Aunt Davina was more an older sister than a matronly aunt and was as apt to join in their schemes as curtail them.

"The mail came," Margarette cried. She slid to a halt in the center of the Kidderminster carpet and waved a handful of letters.

Aunt Davina smiled down at her book, her bowlike lips pressed closed, her only censure to ignore the display.

"Oh?" Elizbeth looked up with feigned disinterest even as she tried to discern familiar handwriting on the flapping envelopes.

Her dear friend, Mister Robert McFarlan, was away on business for their father. Their three-week separation was the longest they'd been apart since...she fought down a blush... since he'd kissed her a month past. Although writing her was inappropriate—they weren't officially engaged—she considered a letter far less scandalous than his single, decidedly unchaste, embrace. So, she'd wheedled from him a promise to write. Though he was due to return that evening and she'd searched the mail for such a letter every day, he had been remiss thus far.

Smile wide, Margarette twirled on her toes, letters held aloft. Somehow, she'd noticed Elizbeth's recent interest in the mail and was determined to tease.

"Margarette, dear, shouldn't you be at your lessons?" Aunt Davina asked sweetly.

With a final spin, Margarette twirled over to the settee and plunked down beside their aunt. "After I see who's written." She began shuffling the envelopes. "Father," she said, and tossed two in a pile. "Father again." Another followed. "And again."

Elizbeth returned to her stitching. Attempts to contain her sister would only fuel her teasing. Perhaps Aunt Davina was correct and they should try to instill more decorum in Margarette. What man wanted a wife who ran giggling up and down the corridors of his home?

An intelligent one, she decided, who wanted a home full of joy. Not the same sort of man who would marry their aunt, but similar. She suppressed a grin. Little did Aunt Davina know, but as Elizbeth had already settled on a suitor, she planned to use her delayed season to find a man for Davina. It wasn't right that one disastrous romance, undertaken nearly a decade ago when Davina was just seventeen, should prejudice her against all gentlemen.

Margarette's sudden silence caused Elizbeth to look up. Her sister's blue eyes sparkled, her grin full of mischief. She'd finished her sorting and held two letters back from the pile for their father. Seeing she had captured Elizbeth's attention, Margarette pried one open and unfolded the pages within.

"Now, this one is interesting," Margarette drawled. "Great Aunt Saundra writes that she's returned from Italy for another visit."

"Has she?" Aunt Davina raised one delicate brow. "What is she now, eighty? I am surprised she made the journey."

"She says she wishes to see us, when we can." Some of the joy left Margarette. "She's of the opinion this will be her final visit to Scotland." Margarette blinked rapidly. "She means then to return, to die in Italy and be laid to rest there."

Aunt Davina plucked the letter from Margarette and scanned the page. "I know she's pious, but I will never understand how a good Scottish noblewoman grew so enamored of Italy."

"She is not even our real great aunt," Margarette said with a sniff. "It's not as if we will lose a real family member." Margarette's unspoken words echoed through the room: *as we did when mother died.*

"True enough, but our families were close, and she has never forgotten that." Aunt Davina folded the letter. "She's been Great Aunt Saundra since before I was born, and we shall visit her as she asks."

"Yes, of course, we shall," Elizbeth said. "What is the final letter, Margarette?"

As hoped, her sister's frown disappeared and mischief lit her eyes. "This?" Margarette held up the envelope, careful not to reveal the handwriting. "This letter must be an error. I shall have it returned. After all, only an engaged miss would receive a letter such as this one."

Elizbeth smiled before she could stop herself. Robert had written? Her soon-to-be betrothed cared more for her than for propriety, and more than he feared her father's wrath. Not that Father had ever indicated displeasure in their courtship… assuming he'd noticed.

Margarette popped to her feet. The pile of letters for their father toppled in her wake and spilled across the settee toward Davina. "In fact, such a letter as this is so scandalous, could do such harm to a lady's reputation, that I say we must burn it." Margarette whirled toward the tall fireplace at the far end of the room.

"Margarette," Elizbeth cried before she could help herself.

Her sister turned back with a victorious grin. She thrust the letter behind her back and took two steps backward toward the hearth. Elizbeth didn't know if she should laugh or shriek. She felt caught between the girl she was at twelve, tormented by her little sister, and the woman she'd become at twenty-two.

"For Heaven's sake." Aunt Davina laughed, her chocolate-colored curls a jumble as she shook her head. "Give me that letter and take yourself off to your lessons, Miss. I believe 'tis Italian today."

"French," Margarette said, then clamped her lips closed with a grimace. She crossed to their aunt and proffered the envelope, which Davina accepted with a smile.

Although she still didn't have her letter, Elizbeth couldn't contain a smirk. Margarette hated French.

"Well, off you go to the library." Aunt Davina made a shooing gesture. "I will quiz you later."

"Yes, Aunt Davina." Margarette made a great show of becoming somber before she smiled and skipped from the room.

Aunt Davina gathered the scattered letters, placed Elizbeth's on top, and held out the stack. "Will you take these to your father? He likely wishes to have his mail."

Elizbeth set aside her needlepoint and stood. Eyes on the top envelope, she took the pile and hurried from the parlor. She reached her father's office to find the door closed. The thick wood panel shutting him away meant he didn't wish to be disturbed, so Elizbeth deposited his mail on the small table outside his office door. She couldn't help but recall a time when their golden-haired mother had been alive and his door was always open. Elizbeth sighed. Mother was not alive, and their father's office door was nearly always closed.

She turned from the door to find Mary hurrying toward her. The maid took in the closed office and proffered a card. "There is a Frenchman here to see your father, Miss. Claims he's a lord of some sort, or I wouldn't have let him in."

Elizbeth took the card. Etched on the surface was simply *Seigneur Faucon.*

Lord Hawk, she thought, her French considerably better than Margarette's.

She looked at the maid. "Do you think he truly is a French lord?" A lord would be worth disturbing her father.

"Well, Miss, he seems quite fancy, to be sure, and very French." This last, Mary delivered with a wrinkle of her nose.

"Show him to my office," came her father's clipped voice behind the closed door.

Elizbeth winced. She'd forgotten about her father's keen hearing. She offered the card back to Mary. "Bring him to Father."

"Yes, Miss." Mary took the card and scuttled away.

Elizbeth stood for a moment, gaze on the door. Should she ask her father if he needed anything? He had a bell pull, and servants to fetch for him, but since their mother's death, he'd taken to skipping breakfast. Now, they rarely saw him outside the dinner table, if then. She shook her head. He knew she was there. If he wanted to see her, he would ask her in. Besides, she had Robert's letter to read.

Elizbeth turned on her heels. Though guilt assailed her, she went to the little room that had been her mother's office. She withdrew the key from her bodice—a key none knew she possessed—opened the door, and slipped inside.

Stuffy heat warmed her arms. Her mother had kept the window open nearly year-round. Elizbeth preferred the fresh air, as well. Today, however, she dared open the curtains and beveled panes just enough for a sliver of light and a flicker of breeze. She couldn't risk being caught. Her father, who thought he had the only key, would be livid.

Elizbeth understood his feelings. He wished this room, where Mother was once so often found, to remain undisturbed, in some fruitless hope to preserve a glimmer of her spirit. But it didn't. When mother was alive, light poured in through the open window. Her household notes and correspondences lay scattered about the desk and the second table, which overcrowded the little room. Father had pressed her to take one of the parlors for her office, but Mother liked her cramped little space with its lavender walls and flowery upholsteries.

Now, desk and table were bare, their papers long since sorted by Aunt Davina. After Mother's death, Aunt Davina arrived with their wayward, unpredictable Uncle Graham, and she'd taken over running the household. While Elizbeth appreciated Aunt Davina and was daily grateful for her competence, she had no real notion why Uncle Graham was there. All he did was soak up Father's whisky—when he could pry himself away from his harlots long enough to come home.

Shrugging off her now-grim mood, Elizbeth settled into the armchair by the window. She ran a finger along Robert's concise handwriting then, carefully, she opened the envelope.

This was her first letter from Robert and she wished to cherish every word.

ELIZBETH:

As promised, I am writing. I comply only because I abhor breaking a promise. However, I must remind you how inappropriate it was for you to ask me to write. Your father would be displeased not only that you asked me, but that I allowed you to extract my promise to write. Be warned, in the future, I will not give in to your pleading.

ELIZBETH ROLLED HER EYES. IF THERE WAS ONE LITTLE FLAW IN Robert, it was that he was too serious, but that was also what she cherished about him. His seriousness drew her in. To call forth his laughter made her heart sing, and she knew, when Robert spoke, he meant each word. Still, he could stand to be a touch less severe.

Her eyes went to the final line.

With the very greatest affection, yours always, Robert.

Elizbeth pressed the letter to her chest. Those words made the rest of the letter worthwhile. Her gaze caught on the quill sitting on the desk. The quill had been her mother's favorite. Tears unexpectedly pricked. It was terribly unfair that she had died without seeing Elizbeth fall in love. Elizbeth recalled the delight in her father's eyes whenever her mother walked into the room. Elizbeth wanted a love like that. She'd found a love like that.

"You would have loved him as much as I do, Mother," she whispered.

Elizbeth held the page back in the line of sunlight to reread the short missive.

"This request to speak in the garden is ridiculous," her

father's voice, speaking French, emanated from somewhere outside, near the window.

Elizbeth snapped her head up.

"Not ridiculous, but necessary," a man replied in the same tongue. "The manor has ears."

"I assure you, none of my staff speak your language," her father snapped back. "Half of them barely speak English."

Movements slow, least the chair creak, Elizbeth grasped the window and drew it back toward the sill. Father would not appreciate being made a liar of.

"Humor me, *Seigneur*, for my news is life shaking," the Frenchman said. "Any who hear it will face mortal danger."

The window clicked quietly closed, muting her father's reply into unintelligibility.

Face mortal danger? Elizbeth would have laughed had *Seigneur* Faucon's tone not been deadly serious. What news could possibly be of such importance? Her fingers tightened on the latch. She hesitated a heartbeat, then drew her hand back.

Eavesdropping was unacceptable. Doubly so when the two men were going to great lengths not to be overheard, and especially if the information they shared was truly somehow dangerous. If the Frenchman's words were for Father's ears alone, Father alone should hear them.

A thought struck. The library windows also opened onto the garden. Margarette!

Elizbeth surged to her feet. She folded and tucked Robert's letter into her skirt pocket as she crossed the room. She poked her head into the corridor—empty, as hoped. She slipped from the room and hurried down the hall.

Halfway to the library, she came up short. Lord, she'd forgotten to lock the door. Elizbeth hurried back and secured her mother's office, then again headed toward the library. She pushed the door open, stepped in, and nearly collided with Margarette. Elizbeth stumbled back.

Her sister recoiled. "Elizbeth," she cried. "You cannot believe what I heard."

Elizbeth contained a sigh. She leveled a frown on her sister. "You listened in on Father's private conversation."

Margarette gaped. "How do you know?"

"I heard them talking and came to stop you." Elizbeth grasped her sister's arm and pulled her into the center of the large room, away from windows or door, then realized the Frenchman's words had truly rattled her. "It is wrong to eavesdrop."

Margarette yanked free. "I do not care. 'Tis a good thing I heard. I don't want to go." Margarette's voice broke off in anguished tears.

Elizbeth stared. "Go where?"

"To France," Margarette cried.

"Why would you be going to France?" Elizbeth asked, unable to follow Margarette's tearful declarations.

"The Frenchman said we must." Margarette rubbed at her eyes. "He said we are to marry Frenchmen so Father can have an army."

"What under Heaven are you talking about?" Elizbeth demanded. "What do you mean, 'we'?"

"You, me and Aunt Davina," Margarette said. "Father is going to send us to France so they will send back an army to help him become king of Scotland."

"Margarette," Elizbeth hissed. "Do not say such things. That is treason. Stop making up stories."

Margarette lifted her chin. "It is not a story. The Frenchman said Father is the secret descendent of the Jacobite kings, and so we are princesses—which would be great fun—except that France sent him with a ship to take us away."

Elizbeth planted her hands on her hips. "Did you fall asleep over your lessons?"

Margarette grimaced. "Aye, because French is so boring, but that is *not* the point."

"It is exactly the point," Elizbeth corrected. "That is what you get for eavesdropping—and for not studying properly. Your French is terrible, which is why you so badly misunderstood their conversation."

Despite her admonition, a thread of unease wound through Elizbeth. Margarette might not speak French well, but Elizbeth did, and she hadn't misunderstood the Frenchman's warning about mortal danger.

Margarette's gaze sharpened. "You heard something, too."

Elizbeth groaned inwardly. Margarette eschewed books, but she was too intelligent for her own good.

"If I am wrong, why were they talking in the garden rather than Father's office?" Margarette demanded.

"There could be many reasons," Elizbeth said, but doubt persisted. While Margarette's story was obviously a mad mixture of dream and miscomprehension, the meeting was odd. Why was a French lord speaking with their father to begin with?

"My French may be atrocious, but I comprehend much more than I speak," Margarette said. "I know what I heard. We cannot let Father send us away to France. Especially you. What about Robert?"

"Mister McFarlan," Elizbeth corrected absently as she sought to make sense of Margarette's story.

"We must warn Aunt Davina," her sister urged. "The Frenchman said they want her, too." Elizbeth shook her head and started to tell Margarette to return to her French lesson, but Margarette grasped her hand. "Please, we must tell Aunt Davina."

The fear in Margarette's eyes stopped the refusal that leapt to Elizbeth's lips. Margarette feared nothing.

Elizbeth gave her hand a gentle squeeze. "You must try to see that you dreamed up this silly story."

Margarette stubbornly shook her head. "Aunt Davina can decide."

Elizbeth bit her lip. Their aunt was forgiving, but eavesdropping on Father's private conversation was a graver transgression than running down a hallway.

Margarette's hand clutched harder. "Elizbeth, I am afraid."

"We may have to tell Aunt Davina," Elizbeth allowed. "Or we may be able to keep your misbehavior between us. Tell me everything you think you heard, as near the original as you can, in French, and I will decide."

Margarette hesitated, then nodded and launched into her tale.

Davina closed Debrett's *The New Peerage*. She weighed the etiquette book in her hands. Debrett's, and all of Britain, agreed that a proper chaperone must be wedded or widowed.

Due to Bhradain's betrayal, Davina was neither.

Mister Haywood, she corrected. He never should have been Bhradain to her. After nine years, some other woman must have the honor of addressing Mister Haywood by his Christian name.

She rubbed eyes tired of reading Debrett's dry, restrictive words. Across the room, the mantle clock ticked off slow minutes. The dinner hour approached, and Elizbeth hadn't returned. Margarette wouldn't. She would hide from a French exam for as long as possible. If the girl devoted as much effort to learning the language as she did to avoiding her lessons, she would be fluent.

Elizbeth, though, should have returned to her sewing. The envelope from Mister McFarlan had been thin. How many words could the page contain, and how many times could Elizbeth possibly read them? Davina considered fetching her niece.

A smile flittered across her lips. Elizbeth, as conscientious a young woman as Davina had ever met, thought no one knew where she hid when she wished to be alone. Sweet Elizbeth had no idea Davina—who had never been very well behaved—routinely followed, snooped, and spied on her nieces. In their best interests, of course.

She drummed her fingers on the book in her lap. Nae, Debrett would never condone her as a chaperone. But she was all her nieces had, and she was determined to safeguard their wellbeing.

Which brought her to Mister McFarlan. A kind man. Intelligent. An attorney. Not a true gentleman, though from a genteel family. Born the same year as Davina, so not too old for Elizbeth, nor so young as to be foolish. In truth, she felt him a good match for her niece. There would be no trouble there, except that Davina had no idea how her eldest brother felt about the notion of his daughter wedding one of his attorneys.

One might assume, as James permitted the courtship to continue, he was pleased. That would be, if one didn't know James. Or rather, the man he'd become since Maryanne's death. With his wife's passing, James had lost all attachment to the world. Like as not, he hadn't noticed the glaringly obvious affection between his daughter and the attorney.

Hurried footfalls, growing in volume, sounded in the hall without. Davina stilled her fingers. The footsteps were too heavy to be Elizbeth or Margarette. Her brother James burst into the parlor. His gaze darted about the small room, minnow-like. A strange pallor had leached all color from his face and his normally neat brown hair was wind tossed, as if he'd been outdoors. Of late, James never went outdoors.

"Whatever is the matter?" She set the book aside and rose. "James?"

"Where are my daughters?" he barked.

"Not here, as you can see. Is something amiss?" In view of his distress, she tried to keep a check on her temper, a thing more easily accomplished were it not the case that James was continually brusque these days. "James?" she repeated.

"What? Nae. Nothing is amiss." He raked long fingers through his dark hair.

At forty, James was still a handsome man. Only a hint of gray touched his temples and his broad shoulders and arms were well muscled. Unlike many other men his age, he had no paunch. She saw the way women looked at him, even young women. He could find happiness again. If only he would try.

He looked about the room again. "Where did you say they are?"

"Margarette is most likely in the library." She would not betray Elizbeth's secret. He would be furious should he learn his daughter possessed a key to her mother's office. "I have no notion where Elizbeth is."

James's mouth thinned. "Is not your one purpose in this household to know where my daughters are?"

She tamped down harder on her anger. "Indeed. Shall I launch a search, or would you rather wait an hour and see if they join us for dinner?"

His frown deepened into a scowl. "A husband would have curbed your tongue years ago. But I suppose it's better this way." He turned on his heel and stomped from the room.

Davina stared at the empty doorway. "That was rude even for James," she murmured.

Should she go after him? Was something truly amiss, aside from his self-absorbed sorrow over Maryanne? Before she could decide, new footsteps filled the corridor. Recognizing both sets, Davina retook her place on the settee. Perhaps the answers were on their way to her.

"Aunt Davina." Much as her father had, Margarette hurtled into the room.

Behind her, Elizbeth entered, her lovely face marred by worry and her steps considerably more graceful. Instead of sitting, they stopped before Davina. She looked up at them, expectant.

"Aunt Davina, Margarette has overheard something that concerns us," Elizbeth's voice was grave.

"Overheard?" Davina cocked a brow. "How did you manage that, dear?" Davina understood all too well how one *overheard* things.

Margarette had the grace to blush. "I did not do it on purpose. I was in the library, studying French. I truly was."

Davina nodded.

"The window was open, and Father and that Frenchman started talking in the garden."

"Frenchman?" Davina asked.

"Yes," Elizbeth said. "He arrived shortly after we left you, and asked to speak with Father. He gave the name Seigneur Faucon."

"Lord Hawk?" Davina didn't like the sound of that. The name was obviously false. She turned back to Margarette. "What did this Lord Hawk have to say to your father, and how does it concern you both?"

"It concerns you as well." Margarette popped up on her toes as she spoke, hands clasped before her. She shot Elizbeth a look.

"Tell her," Elizbeth ordered. "Only, do try to make sense."

"He said it all in French." Margarette scrunched her nose. "Elizbeth says I must repeat it as nearly as I heard, so you may interpret the words for yourself, since my French is abominable." This last, she accompanied with a supplicative glance upward.

Davina didn't know if she should be amused or alarmed. James's harried visage came to the forefront of her thoughts. "Let's have it, then."

Margarette embarked on a monologue. She used two voices, one apparently her idea of her father and the other the Frenchman. Some of the syllables that left her mouth resembled no language.

As Davina took in the half-intelligible babble, her pulse quickened with each word. Lord Hawk had told James he was the descendent of Henry Benedict Stuart, Cardinal-Duke of York, and the last of the Jacobite kings? Davina clenched her hands in her lap, for the tale grew even stranger. Seigneur Faucon had asked, and James agreed, to be given custody of her, Elizbeth and Margarette. He planned to take them and their considerable dowries to France and marry them to men of power. Their new husbands would raise an army, and return with it to Scotland, to fight for James, the Jacobite king. Davina stared up at her nieces. Tall, lovely young women whose hands would be a prize for any man but…princesses?

"And then they went deeper into the garden," Margarette concluded.

Davina looked at Elizbeth. "You heard none of this?"

She shook her head. "Nae, but I did hear the Frenchman say they must discuss something very secret and dangerous."

Margarette stared, her blue eyes filled with uncharacteristic worry. "Aunt Davina, what are we going to do?"

Davina shook her head, dazed. She had no idea. "You are sure that is what they said? You weren't dreaming? I know how French puts you to sleep."

Margarette blew out a frustrated breath. "I repeated the words to you—badly, I might add. How could I have dreamt all that? I don't even know some of those words. Please, I do not want to go off to marry some horrible French lord."

Davina scrubbed at her forehead. It couldn't be true. They were not royalty, not even gentry, though possessed of considerable wealth. Even if Margarette had heard correctly, it simply couldn't be true. The most shocking part was that James might believe any of the tale. His frantic eyes, his pallor, rose in her memory.

"Let me think on this. Please," she murmured.

"Yes, of course," Elizbeth said.

"But, what if Father tries to send us away?" Margarette demanded.

"He will hardly have us abducted," Davina soothed. "Go ready for dinner. We will see how your father is then. Like as not, he'll tell us the tale of this strange Frenchman and his bizarre ideas, and we will all laugh together. Tomorrow, Seigneur Faucon will be but a memory."

Elizbeth smiled. "You are quite correct, of course." Margarette looked mutinous, but Elizbeth caught her arm and tugged her toward the door. "We'll see you at dinner, Aunt Davina."

"Yes," Davina murmured absently as they stepped from the room into the hall.

She hadn't wanted to further alarm her nieces by speaking of their father's odd behavior, but there was someone to whom she could report the entire series of events. Her brother, Graham. Davina rose and went in search of him.

Davina found her brother sprawled face down and shirtless atop his bed. Beside him, curled to one side and, blessedly, fully clothed, though grass clippings decorated slippers and hem, lay a blonde woman Davina had never before seen. Nor, if she knew Graham, would she ever see the woman again.

Nose wrinkled at the stale sweat that permeated the chamber, Davinia crossed the room to the window. She yanked back the curtains and unlatched the windows. As fading daylight and fresh air spilled in, a groan sounded behind her.

"Davinia, what the devil are you doing?"

She turned to find Graham seated on the edge of his bed.

The blonde, snoring softly, didn't stir. Graham blinked rapidly, eyes bloodshot in a face still striking, despite his lack of sleep and what had undoubtedly been an abundance of whisky. Bare chested as he was, Davinia was reminded why her brother remained a favorite of the ladies. She would have thrown a shirt at him, but the one discarded on the floor looked too sweat-infused to touch.

"What am I doing?" she repeated. "I am here to tell you to ready for dinner. You have avoided consciousness long enough for today."

He pushed a hand through tangled brown locks, then cast a look over his shoulder. When he turned back, he wore a perplexed frown, as if he didn't quite know what to make of the unconscious blonde.

"Consider me told, sister dearest."

"That is not all," she said in clipped tones. "I must also, though Heaven knows why I bother, ask your opinion on a matter that may be significant."

Graham groaned and fell backward onto the bed. He fumbled for a pillow, found one, and pulled it over his face.

Davinia hurried back to the bed and kicked him in the shin. "Graham, this is important."

He lifted one half of the pillow. "I'm listening." He dropped the down-stuffed fabric back into place.

"I cannot very well discuss this in front of her." Davinia waved at the woman on the bed.

Graham lifted the pillow and craned his neck. Again, that perplexed look crossed his face.

"You *do* know her?" Davinia's voice dripped sarcasm.

"I suppose I must." He stretched out an arm and poked the slumbering woman in the shoulder.

Thick lashes fluttered open. Blue eyes focused on Davinia. "Hello."

With one word, the woman revealed her English

origins. Davinia grimaced. Leave it to Graham to bring home an Englishwoman. Offering Davinia a shrug, he tucked the pillow under his head. The Englishwoman sat up and looked about, appearing just as perplexed as Graham.

"Hello, Miss…" Davinia let her voice trail off in question.

"Ingram." She offered a bright smile. "Anastacia Ingram. And you are?"

Davinia bit back a sharp retort. "Miss McKinley. If you could excuse my brother and me, Miss Ingram, I should like to speak with Graham alone."

Miss Ingram's head snapped toward Graham. "*You* are Graham McKinley?" She frowned. "I was told to stay away from you. You're a terrible rake."

"Posh." Graham smiled his most charming smile and tucked his clasped hands behind his head. "If I am such a rake, why are we clothed?"

Miss Ingram looked about again. "If you aren't a rake, why am I in this bed?"

"I haven't the foggiest." Graham shrugged. "But if you would care to remain, I can think of several ways to test my fortitude. We must put this rake business to rest."

"Graham," Davinia snapped. Between James's half-madness since losing Maryanne and Graham's devotion to sin, Davinia sometimes felt as if she were responsible for the entirety of their family's wellbeing—and sanity.

Graham pointed toward the door across from the bed, leading to an antechamber. "Go in there, sweetheart, and ring for a servant to ready you a bath. I will come to you shortly."

Miss Ingram stood. She tugged her skirt straight and squared her shoulders. She was tall for a woman, her build slender. "I will give you your privacy, but you will not find me waiting for you in the bath." Her blue eyes snapped. "Just because we ended up in this bed, does not mean I am here for your frivolous pleasure, sir." She cocked her chin in the air and marched from the room.

Graham watched. A slow smile stretched across his face.

"You have no idea who she is or how you both ended up here?" Davinia asked once the door clicked shut behind the woman.

"You heard her. She's Miss Anastacia Ingram."

Davina had a few choice things to say about that, on the heels of which, she launched into the details of both their nieces' story and her encounter with James. Halfway through, Graham's brow furrowed. By the time she finished, he sat upright on the edge of the bed, his features hard with thought.

"I suppose it is possible," he murmured.

"That we are decedents of the Stuart family and James is a Jacobite king?" Davinia snorted. "Hardly. My only fear is James might believe the mad tale and turn our nieces over to some strange Frenchman. Likely, this is some sort of ransom plot to get at his wealth."

Graham regarded her with worried eyes. "And you."

"Me what?"

"If he really believes the Frenchman's tale, he could turn you over as well."

"I am six and twenty. I am no more subject to James's will than I am to that of a random passerby." *Unlike Elizbeth and Margarette.*

Graham shook his head. He levered himself to his feet, towering over her. "I cannot imagine James being taken in by some Frenchman's tale. Besides, Margarette likely dreamt the whole thing."

Davinia nodded. For all his debauchery, Graham was dependable when it came to family, and he, if anyone, knew their older brother well. "Of course, you are correct. I am going to prepare for dinner." She glanced toward the door through which Miss Ingram had departed. "Do not let your English harlot keep you."

"She is not a harlot. She is Miss Anastacia Ingram."

Davinia raised her brows. "Graham, I found her asleep in your bed. She is a harlot." Without another word, she left the room.

www.ingramcontent.com/pod-product-compliance
Lightning Source LLC
Chambersburg PA
CBHW060929190726
48286CB00002B/695